Greig Beck grew up across  Sydney, Australia. His early d ing, and reading science fiction on the sand. He then went on to study computer science, immerse himself in the financial software industry, and later received an MBA. Today, Greig spends his days writing, but still finds time to surf at his beloved Bondi Beach. He lives in Sydney, with his wife, son, and an enormous German shepherd.

If you would like to contact Greig, his email address is greig@greigbeck.com and you can find him on the web at www.greigbeck.com.

Also by Greig Beck

The Alex Hunter Series
Arcadian Genesis
Beneath the Dark Ice
Dark Rising
This Green Hell
Black Mountain
Gorgon
Hammer of God
Kraken Rising
From Hell

The Matt Kearns Series
The First Bird
Book of the Dead
The Immortality Curse

The Fathomless Series
Fathomless I
Fathomless II - Abyss

The Valkeryn Chronicles
Return of the Ancients
The Dark Lands

EXTINCTION PLAGUE

GREIG BECK

First published 2020 in Momentum by Pan Macmillan Australia Pty Ltd
1 Market Street, Sydney, New South Wales, Australia, 2000

A CIP record for this book is available at the National Library of Australia

Extinction Plague: Matt Kearns 4

EPUB format: 9781760982409
Print on Demand format: 9781760982393

Original cover design: Danielle Hurps

Cover images: stock.adobe.com

Macmillan Digital Australia: www.macmillandigital.com.au

To report a typographical error, please visit www.panmacmillan.com.au/contact-us/

Visit www.panmacmillan.com.au/ to read more about all our books and to buy books
online. You will also find features, author interviews and news of any author events.

More than ninety percent of all organisms that have ever lived on Earth are extinct. Some species can take millennia to die out and some vanish in the blink of an eye. In Earth's history there have been many mass extinctions, and in a handful of times in the last half billion years nearly all of the species on Earth have been wiped out. Asteroid impact, volcanoes, ocean acidification, and catastrophic climate change are all given as reasons. But some extinction events could never be explained. Until now.

The next great plague will be the last.

– Greig Beck

PROLOGUE

Guchengzi amber mines, Liaoning province, China – 1984

Liu Chen splashed water onto the rock face and then rubbed it with the heel of his hand. He held up his lantern and then grinned. The seam of golden fossilized resin shone like a ribbon of sunshine. And it was big.

He rubbed at it again. The Guchengzi mines had been in operation for one hundred and twenty years, and were one of the richest amber producers in existence. The amber mined here was of varying quality and all derived from woody plants dating back from tens of millions to hundreds of millions of years ago.

The miners worked in backbreaking eight-hour shifts, right around the clock. Whoever discovered a good find received a bonus.

Liu turned and called for the mine boss, Huang. The other miners moved aside as the stocky man shuffled closer in the confines of the narrow tunnel.

Liu held up his light again. "It's big, very big." He wiped it again with his hand. Just from what was exposed it looked to be a single block three feet in length.

Huang slapped his shoulder. "Well done." He turned, snapped his fingers and called for more of the men to help remove the block from its age-old resting place.

Liu supervised them, trying to ensure no one damaged the huge block. Amber was highly prized in China. In the Middle Ages it was burned with incense as a sexual stimulant, and also ingested for rheumatism and dozens of other maladies. But these days, unmarked resin was made into attractive jewelry, and if the resin contained fossilized creatures it was either sent to the laboratories for study, or sold onto the global fossil market.

In another forty-five minutes, the men managed to loosen and then haul the block out. It was heavy and Liu and his three helpers groaned as they strained to lay it carefully on the mineshaft floor.

The now fully exposed block was just on four feet long, two feet wide, and that much again in thickness. Huang splashed water from his canteen onto it and rubbed it with his hand. Together the men all brought their flashlights and lanterns in closer.

It was then they could see what was inside. Huang crouched and then knelt, his nose almost touching the ancient resin.

"What is it? What has been caught by the amber?" He splashed more water and used the front of his sweat-stained t-shirt to rub the surface to create a clearer window into its interior.

Liu stared. The thing inside looked to be as thick as a human arm. But it was a glossy black like oil, and was covered in vicious spikes and bristled hairs.

Huang frowned. "Looks like a bug. A giant bug."

Liu straightened. The bug would have been as big, or bigger, than a man.

Huang looked up at him. "Praise your ancestors this thing doesn't live today." He held out an arm to be assisted to his feet. "Bring it out."

CHAPTER 01

Milford Sound, New Zealand west coast – June 1944

Captain Wolfgang Krause drew in a deep breath through his nose, inhaling the smells of oil, metal, hot electronics, and body odor.

His submarine, *UX-511*, was one of Nazi Germany's elite Kriegsmarine, a stealthy craft known as one of "the wolves of the sea".

The Type IXC U-boat was slightly larger than the normal U-boats of the time, and, due to her two supercharged four-stroke, nine-cylinder diesel engines, produced a total of 4340 horsepower, giving her a maximum surface speed of 18.3 knots and a submerged speed of 7.3 knots, meaning she could outmaneuver, outrun, or chase down any vessel she chose.

Normally the *UX-511* had a full complement of forty-eight sailors and officers, and was fitted with twenty-two torpedoes, a heavy SK C/32 naval gun, as well as a C/30 anti-aircraft gun. But on this mission Captain Krause had just six men, and no weaponry. Everything had been ripped out and stripped down. He carried nothing but spare fuel and an object he'd been ordered to retrieve from one of the most remote places on Earth and bring back to the Führer, personally.

Krause had been handpicked for the dangerous and crucially important job, as he was fearless, smart, and had never failed on any mission he had been tasked with.

He placed a hand against one of the railings, feeling the chill of the frigid steel. Outside, it was a murderous cold with the water a mere thirty-four degrees, and inside, the men could feel the cold permeating the steel skin of their craft. There was no excess fuel to continually run the heating units so the men had donned woolen clothing and gloves, and many looked like over-padded bears.

The U-boat hugged the New Zealand coastline to avoid shipping lanes, but the crew knew that soon they'd need to pull away and head up through the warmer Asia Pacific waters. It would be more bearable, but much higher risk.

It was their sonar operator who picked up the vibrations first. Then they all felt the shuddering through the iron-plated hull as the tremor shook the seabed below as well as the water around them.

"All stop."

Krause breathed in and out slowly, ignoring the bite of freezing air in his nostrils as he fought to keep his impatience in check. In his submarine's hold he might have the key to a German victory in the war – potentially a weapon of destruction or a savior. His sole job now was to get it home, at any cost.

Krause let the steel ship hang in the water as he waited and listened. They were close to the shoreline so if a tsunami followed, there might be a problem.

He decided he needed to be in deeper water; shipping lanes be damned.

"Hard to starboard, full speed ahead."

The horns sounded throughout the steel corridors, and the muscular twin engines turned over with the sound of heavy machinery cranking up to speed. The familiar smells of salt water, diesel oil and perspiration swirled in the control room with the burst of activity, as the roar of engines became near deafening. Captain Krause ignored it all and stared unblinking at the instrument panels.

The outside vibrations passing through the U-boat reached a crescendo. Then came a new tearing and grinding sound that froze everyone in the command room.

"Landslide?" Krause asked his sonar operator.

"Bigger." The sonar man frowned deeply as he concentrated on the sounds. "And seems to be coming from ... everywhere."

Then their boat was hit, or they hit something, and the crew was thrown to the panels and decking.

"We're running aground!" Krause yelled. "Blow all tanks, *all rise, all rise!*"

Men yelled and hands flew over instruments. Krause couldn't work out what was happening as just seconds ago they were at least twenty feet up from the seabed, had clear running, and there was nothing on the near and far sonar.

Then came the words every submariner dreaded: "We have a hull breach – nose heavy – *shallow water, shallow water.*"

"Surface, surface, surface!" Krause roared above the confusion and leaped forward to grab the console and read over his man's shoulder.

It was true, suddenly they found themselves in only thirty feet of water, where mere seconds ago they had been in around seventy feet. Somehow the sea bottom had shifted.

"It's not responding." The engineer turned to face him as around them the machines hissed and strained, and the mighty vessel groaned like a wounded cetacean. "We're flooding."

Krause straightened; the water was shallow enough to abandon ship and maybe make it to shore. But then they would be alerting the enemy to their position, and possibly to what they carried. It could then fall into their hands.

Krause stiffened his spine. It could not be allowed; the enemy could never obtain what they carried.

"We need to close the bulkhead doors," his man yelled over the din.

Krause looked back at their sweat-soaked and reddening faces. "Leave them open."

Krause's words were soft, but every man heard them. And every man understood them. Some came to their feet and saluted, while others sat back in the seats, hands slowly coming off their equipment.

There would be no rescue attempt as there was no record of their voyage. They all knew this might have been one of the outcomes of their mission. They all had chosen death before dishonor. And that meant death before letting enemies get their hands on the secret.

The next instant the U-boat's engine room flooded and the mighty propellers stopped. The generators soon followed. The lights dulled and then they also went out. The iron craft settled on the bottom.

"Sorry, mein Führer," Krause whispered in the ink black darkness. He heard men praying and perhaps someone softly sobbing. But over the top of it all he heard the roar of the bone-numbing water rushing up toward them.

"Seig heil!" He yelled as the freezing water exploded into the room to take them all.

CHAPTER 02

Milford Sound, New Zealand west coast – one year ago

Manawa Kawheina was thrown to the ground. At seventy-five years old, he was still a stout and strong man but his balance wasn't what it used to be.

Earthquake. The tribal chief knew what to expect so he stayed down. He was up on the cliffs and thankfully wasn't close to the edge. Huge chunks of rock were known to calve away from the cliff face and, if he fell with them, it was two hundred feet down to the water.

His jaws clenched as the earth shook even harder and with it came a noise like the grinding of a titan's millstones. Underneath him the earth jumped. Then came the sound of cascading water but he didn't fear a tidal wave as he was up too high. The small pristine bay down below was probably getting stirred up and would be muddy for days – and there'd be no fish for weeks.

A shimmer and shake and a sound like a deep sob, and then it was over. Manawa stayed down a moment more, and then finally sat up. Around him there were rips and wrinkles in the earth like a rumpled rug, but everything else was as it should be.

He quickly gave thanks to his gods and forefathers and then turned to his beloved ocean. Manawa could only stare.

The bay was gone. Really gone. The land had risen from the ocean and completely taken his beautiful bay. Where there was once sparkling blue water with a few shadows of reef just showing closer in, now there were rocks, weed, and patches of sand for hundreds of feet out to the headlands.

Stranded fish, some huge, flopped and danced on the rocks; crustaceans and shimmering blobs of large jellyfish were also left high and dry. But that wasn't what made Manawa's mouth gape – there, lying like a beached whale on the raised sea bottom, was a ship. An iron ship, heavily crusted with barnacles and weed, and lying on its side.

Manawa quickly edged down and along the cliff face, and carefully made his way out to the exposed vessel. Large fish were trapped in pools, and lobsters tried to take cover in mounds of exposed weed – it was a free feast that would soon rot in the heat and sunshine.

Up close he saw the riveted iron, the upturned bow and also the sealed deck. He was old enough to recognize the remnants of the flag and its insignia showing through the crusted sea life – red flag, black cross and at its center the swastika with iron cross in the top right corner.

"A German U-boat, eh?" He whispered. "What you doing here?"

Maybe the boat might have been hiding, or lost, or had come into the bay for repairs, and that was why it was so close to the shoreline.

Manawa stepped across more rock pools, and reached the hull of the boat. It was lying on its side with its nose slightly buried and already its exterior was drying in the sun. He leaned forward and rapped on it with his knuckles.

The returned sound was dull and solid, telling him the interior was flooded with either water or sand. He stood looking down at it for a moment. If he reported it the government would contact Germany and then the boat and all its contents would be taken away.

But this was Maori land, and Manawa claimed right of salvage. He'd do his duty and report the wreck, but first he wanted to find out why this ship was in this part of the world while a war was raging so far away to the north.

*

"*Phew*, stinks," Rawiri said as he crowded in close.

"No worse than your place." Manawa turned to his son and grinned. "Hurry up."

The chief slowly moved his light around in the cramped space. The air inside the sub smelt of brine, rusting steel, and something else unpleasant, like a whale carcass that had washed up on the tide.

The pair had to crawl along the angled central corridor. It was darker than a moonless night inside and the algae-blackened steel was slick and slippery.

The next room they entered was crowded with dials, handles, pipes, and all manner of electronic devices stuck to the walls and ceiling. There was a periscope tower in the center.

"The control room." The chief shone his light around. "And the crew."

They'd finally found them. The black and slimy skeletal remains were piled up in the corner as if a tidal surge had crushed them all together.

"Feking gross," Rawiri whispered.

"You wait until the sun heats them up a bit." Manawa turned his light away from the grisly sight. "Come on, one last room."

They crawled to the metal door that was open only a few inches, and it took all their strength to drag the rusted steel wide enough for them to enter.

"This is more like it." Rawiri smiled broadly as he rushed to crouch beside a huge metal chest. There was an ancient padlock still hanging on the front, but a few stout cracks with the butt of his flashlight and the mechanism fell to corroded pieces.

Rawiri lifted the lid with a squeal of protesting hinges. The stout chest looked to have been sealed with wax and inside was still dry after all these years.

"Something in here ... wrapped." Manawa crowded in closer and saw an object around four feet long tightly bundled in an oilcloth.

Rawiri threw the cloth aside and shone his light down on the thing. "What the hell, man?" He looked up. "It's just a big green stone." Rawiri slapped the steel chest with his hand. "Why would they seal an old stone in a strongbox?"

"Maybe because of what it says." Manawa edged out of the way. "Bring it out. Just the stone."

"Aw, man, it's gotta weigh a hundred fifty pounds." Rawiri scowled up at his father.

"Yeah, and I know you can bench-press more than twice that. I want to see it in the light." Manawa headed back down along the slimy corridor, sick of the stench of rust, slime, and death.

CHAPTER 03

Boston, Massachusetts – today

Matt Kearns flopped into his favorite leather chair, picked up the TV remote while also sipping his beer. He let out a long sigh of satisfaction followed by an open-mouth burp that he was sure must have been a record breaker somewhere in the world.

He sipped again as he channel surfed, looking for something interesting. He stopped at a station showing a large triangular-headed insect capture another bug. It immediately started eating it alive, the rapidly moving mouthparts munching through its prey's head like it was a large biscuit.

Matt felt his gorge rise. He quickly changed channels.

Matt was a professor of paleo-linguistics at Harvard University but didn't look it. At thirty-six, he was a long-haired surfer, and still with boyish good looks. But he also had an amazing brain for facts, pattern recognition, and logical intuition. He was one of the few language specialists in the world who could read and understand some of the most obscure and ancient languages on the planet.

He was currently on his spring break – and that meant no classes, no rules, and no administrators trying to get him to apply for more grant money. For now, all he wanted to do was eat tacos, drink beer, sleep, and maybe travel to the coast to find some waves ... starting this very weekend.

His phone rang and he grabbed it up, about to send whoever it was to message bank until he saw the name – *Mom*. He answered it.

"Hi, Mom."

"Happy birthday, my handsome son."

Matt grinned. "That was last Sunday, you know that."

It was a running joke between them that Matt seemed to make his birthday celebrations run for at least a week.

"Did you open my card?"

"Yes, thank you, and thank you for the money." He turned to look at the card sitting on his side table. It was of a dog wearing a paper party cap and blowing a horn. There was a fifty-dollar bill resting beside it. "You don't need to do that anymore. I have plenty of money of my own now."

"Buy yourself some socks or something. But not beer," she said with mock stern in her voice.

"Oops." He chuckled. "Okay, but only if you promise not to let Belle sleep on your bed. She takes up all the room."

"It's only on special occasions, or when she's scared of something," Karen replied.

"Mom, that dog of yours is as big as a timber wolf. The only thing she's scared of is missing her dinner." He grinned.

"Oh Matt." Karen laughed. "Don't forget that Megan is arriving tomorrow sometime. Do you know when exactly?"

"Tomorrow afternoon, I think." He inwardly groaned. His cousin was okay, but had a personality as big as Texas, and had steamrolled him ever since they were kids.

"Good, and no fighting, okay? You're her favorite cousin."

Yeah, right, he thought. Megan was going to be in town for some sort of pointy-head mathematics convention and, as it coincided with Matt's birthday, she had browbeaten him into letting her crash at his place. "I'm looking forward to it," he lied.

"And ...?"

"And what?" *Here it comes*, he thought.

"Have you met any nice girls lately?" Karen asked.

His phone pinged with a message.

"One second, Mom." He pulled the phone from his ear to read – it was from his dating app, and he smiled as he read the handle: LanaPHD.

Matt had grown tired of hunting the bars or waiting to meet interesting women at parties, so had taken advice from one of his colleagues and set himself up as Matthew267, a profile on WASSUP, the newest site for meeting people.

His reticence had dissolved after a few weeks, and once he got the hang of swiping one way or the other, and weeding out the grifters, sock puppets, and catfishers, he had found some pretty cool people.

Some he would love to have a drink with and some he would like to do more with. But then LanaPHD had caught his attention a few weeks back: a young woman in her early thirties with an interest in ocean life, plus doctorates in biology, biochemistry, and entomology. She made him laugh, and she made him think.

"Yes, as a matter of fact I have," he said. "She's a scientist."

"Great, bring her home to Walnut Grove, I'm doing a turkey for Thanksgiving. Everyone will be here." Karen sounded excited. "Even Megan is dropping in straight after she visits you to lend a hand."

"I'll put it on the list." The ranch out in Walnut Grove had always been a great place for family events at Christmas, New Year, Thanksgiving, Easter, or just about any time. And since his dad passed away a few years back, his mom was determined to keep the tradition going.

There was only one problem bringing the mysterious Lana – he looked again at her avatar: it was of a sandy beach and blue on blue water somewhere in the tropics – he had never actually met her face to face.

Sure, his pic was of a perfect wave breaking on Australia's Bells Beach, so he guessed they seemed perfect for each other, at least on paper.

"You let me know, Matthew, and I'll set an extra place. Love you, honey, and can't wait to see you soon. Oh, and remember –"

"*No fighting*," Matt said in unison with her. "Sure, Mom, love you too." Matt rung off and then read Lana's brief message: *What are you up to? Talk to me, I'm bored.*

He grinned and slowly one-finger messaged her back. He started with: *Was just talking to my mom while I hang out with television and beer.*

He looked at it. *Too boring*, he decided, backspaced and restarted: *Planning my next getaway to find the perfect wave.*

Better, he thought, and sent it.

Matt sipped his beer again and returned to channel surfing. He finally settled on an image of seawater so clear it looked like blue glass. In the background there were cliffs, forests, and curling around the rocky point were perfect waves.

Magnificent, he thought.

He sipped beer as he let the images transport him there. Every time he saw that type of water with the sun beaming down, it made him want to dive in. And seeing a wave without a soul on it made him want to track the spot down.

The long-haired Scottish presenter pointed along a mountainous coastline that looked ancient to the point of being almost prehistoric. The man was at Milford Sound, on New Zealand's southern island's west coast, and he walked along the cliff top and then stopped to stare down at a shelf of rock. He held out both hands flat and made a rising motion.

Matt turned up the sound as the man pointed down toward the water. The camera panned around and Matt saw that, amazingly, right at the rock shelf's outer edge there was the long brown rusting hulk of a submarine.

Ping – *I want to come*, Lana messaged back.

He smiled as he replied. *Ever been to New Zealand?*

He turned back to the screen. Matt vaguely remembered seeing something on the news about this a year or so back – following a recent earthquake the seabed had been thrust up, revealing the rusted hulk of a derelict German U-boat. The Germans had removed the human remains for services back in their home country but left behind the wreck and New Zealand hadn't pushed for a clean-up.

The commentator continued in his broad accent, informing his viewers that it was the local chief, Manawa Kawheina, who had found the submarine and had agreed to allow the commentator and his team to enter his tribe's sacred marae to talk about it.

The Maori marae was a private, fenced-in complex of carved buildings and grounds that belonged to a particular tribe or important family, and it was a rare honor to be invited into one. Only the presenter and one cameraman were allowed to visit.

The tribal leader was a large man, gray-haired now, but still with broad shoulders and fearsome tribal tattoos covering his face. He reclined in a huge carved chair flanked to his left by a surly looking young man that had to be his son given the resemblance.

For all his fearsome looks the chief was jovial and friendly, and greeted his guests warmly with the traditional touching of noses. Matt was losing interest now that the program had moved away from the ocean, and frankly he didn't care that much about a submarine wreck.

He lifted the remote about to surf away again as the cameraman panned around the ornately carved room. The camera settled on a large flat green-hued stone propped at the rear of the marae, looking a little like a grave's headstone.

The camera panned in, and Matt sprayed his beer.

The slab of stone appeared to be made of some sort of green granite. The camera panned closer, and Matt's eyes widened as he tried to take it in while around him time seemed to stand still.

His phone messaged again, but he ignored it – it wasn't just the stone that riveted his attention, but the carvings, the language, and the images. He'd seen something like that before, and it sent a shiver from the base of his spine all the way up to tingle his scalp.

It was the most ancient writing in existence, and perhaps even the mother of all tongues – *Aztlantean* – and it only turned up in a few places on Earth where that long lost seafaring race visited, and also at their home, a place he had seen with his own eyes. It was buried a mile below the dark ice of Antarctica, and he was sworn to secrecy about it by the US military.

He'd seen the language and the images carved into the monolithic edifices of a crumbling once-mighty empire.

Matt hadn't even realized he had been sitting forward until his ass nearly fell off the edge of the chair.

The camera began to move on, and he quickly held up the remote, pointing it, and pressing uselessly.

"Stop."

He launched himself to his feet and stared, trance-like, as his linguistic brain immediately switched to translation mode, and began deciphering the swirls, strokes and pictoglyphs into a coherent narrative. Then the camera finally panned away from the image.

"*Shit.*"

He stamped his bottle down and grabbed a pen and magazine next to his chair and started scribbling what he remembered – it wasn't much – and after a moment he sat looking at what he had written.

They have come and they will come again. Each ending greater than the last.

"What *ending*?" He asked the empty room. The rest of the message had been lost at the edge of the stone or he'd simply missed it when the camera changed angles.

Matt stood and paced. To 99.99% of people in the world this would have been indecipherable or meant nothing. Hell, to 99.99% of linguists in the world it would have meant nothing. But the language and the implication were clearly a warning, and he had learned never to ignore warnings from this ancient race.

Plus there was something else that jolted him, and now nagged at him – he was sure he'd seen the stone before, or maybe one just like it.

His phone pinged again, and this time he picked it up and read: *Where'd you go?*

Shit, he thought. He quickly fumbled a message back: *Something's come up, chat soon, promise.*

He turned back to the TV screen, staring wide-eyed. As the presenter droned on, his Scottish accent faded into background white noise as Matt concentrated on rummaging through the attic of his memory, searching for the stone. An image formed: a photograph, not in color, grainy, and …

Matt turned and then leaped over his chair to quickly cross to a wooden chest in the corner. He flipped it open, pulling out file boxes, string-bound notebooks and then finally a battered leather folder, exploding with notes, clippings and drawings.

He took it back to his chair, sat and opened it, quickly riffling through the copious contents. It was one of his later folders that contained all manner of things associated with the mysterious Antarctic city. He soon found what he was looking for.

He gently pulled the loose page free and held it up – it was a single image, grainy and unfocused. It was from just over a decade back; a World War II artifact had turned up, a diary that was believed to be in Adolf Hitler's handwriting. The interesting thing was it dealt with a lot of the occult and spiritual things the madman was exploring toward the end of the war. The one that had caught Matt's attention was Hitler's focus on the missing continent of Atlantis.

Matt stared at the picture, refamiliarizing himself with the image. It seemed Hitler's exploration was a failure, or so the world was led to believe. But he did secure a fragment of stone that originally came from an 18th century whaler that he thought might be from the lost continent. It had caught Matt's attention then, but it transfixed him now, as it was the same as the one he had seen on the screen.

No, almost the same, he corrected himself.

They matched in that they looked to be a single large flat piece of writing stone that had either been broken in half or was like a page, or a tablet that was crowded with the Aztlantean script.

If the diary was real, then it looked like Hitler had one of the stones or one half of the whole, and now the other half had turned up in New Zealand, which was basically at the bottom of the world, and one of the closest countries to Antarctica.

Matt's gaze turned inward. It kinda all fit together: there was a World War II German U-boat that had been found after seventy-five years, obviously on some sort of mission down there. He bet his last buck that the Maori chief had secretly pulled the stone from the wreck.

The television show ended. Matt got to his feet and paced to the window and looked out over the verdant green park across the road. A few joggers moved around the tracks, and a duck pond shimmered like molten silver in the evening light.

"I need to see more," he whispered. "I *must* see more."

He glanced at the indistinct picture again and quickly read the notes underneath – the purported Hitler diary was purchased by an anonymous buyer in Germany for three million dollars, before it was even authenticated. Matt had briefly tried to search for the stone, but it never surfaced, and wasn't residing in any museum that he knew of. Either it had been lost during the war, destroyed, or was hiding in a private collection somewhere. Perhaps the person who bought Hitler's diary already had it.

That meant he had to work with what he had available. In two strides Matt was back at the side table and grabbed up his remote. He hit the info button and checked the details of the TV program.

He needed to see that stone again, and for now, he'd settle for even seeing it on screen. He needed the TV channel to send him a USB or disc with the full program on it so he could freeze-frame it, study it at his leisure, and see if there was any extra footage. They might send it to him or they might not. Or they might send it but take their damn time, and he was way too impatient for that.

Matt rubbed his chin and began to smile. What do you do when you need something to happen quickly and you don't have time to screw around? You apply brute force. And when it came to brute force, he knew just the guy.

He took out his phone and looked through his contacts, finding the one he wanted: "Uncle Jack", a direct line to Colonel Jack "the Hammer" Hammerson.

He dialed.

CHAPTER 04

The Schneider compound, Treptow, Germany

Rudolph Schneider hunched over the screen in his private vault. Over his head was a communication headset as he talked to his representative, Herr Bruder, who was out in the field to conclude negotiations.

The image displayed on the screen was of a single item – a ring; silver, not very ornate, and little more than a piece of beaten metal. Except it contained the letters "A F" in a stylized calligraphic script.

It was Hitler's ring, worn when he was a youth, and lost by the great man when he was just a boy of sixteen. And Schneider wanted it.

Schneider half turned and looked behind him, to the rear of the vault. "We've found it, my master."

He turned back to the screen as Bruder looked up from the ring to show the opposing man's face – Herr Arndt Fischer, a rare antiquities dealer.

Bruder wore a small camera just over his right ear so Schneider could see and hear everything that transpired; it also allowed him to give Bruder immediate advice.

"Up the offer to fifty thousand euros," he said softly.

Schneider's face was emotionless, but he began to feel a knot of impatience bloom in his stomach.

Herr Arndt Fischer was the current holder of the magnificent piece, but not the owner, not as far as Schneider was concerned. The true owner was Adolphus Hitler, and not this mendacious dealer in stolen goods.

Standing just behind Fischer was his bodyguard, a large thug who was undoubtedly temporary hired muscle for this meeting, and on display to either act as intimidation or be a shield.

"You joke." Fischer grinned back at Bruder and slowly shook his head. "One million." He lifted the ring and held it up. "Because it is one in a million."

Bruder sat back, waiting on Schneider's next command.

Schneider thought for a moment. The cost was high, and though still insignificant to a billionaire such as himself, he didn't like two things: *one*, that this worm would tell people Schneider was now the owner of the ring. And *two*, he would also tell people he had pushed *the* Rudolph Schneider around.

Schneider turned to the back of the vault again, and raised his eyebrows. "Well, master?" He listened for a moment and then began to nod. "Yes, of course you're right, the third option." He turned back to the screen and sat forward to lower his voice. "Kill them both."

In one smooth motion, Bruder pulled a long throwing blade from the small of his back and threw it from waist level, spearing the bodyguard in the eye socket.

Before the bodyguard had even fallen, Bruder was moving around the desk toward the horrified Fischer. From his wristwatch he pulled a long thread of razor wire, which he looped around the man's neck.

Fischer's eyes bulged and he thrashed as Bruder sawed hard, once, twice, three times. The wire cut fast and deep, and in another few seconds of tugging, the antique dealer's head fell to the table.

Bruder had been holding the body forward as the blood spurted and now he pushed the corpse to the side. He reached forward to pick the bloodied ring up and hold it in front of the camera.

"Well done." Schneider smiled. "Bring it to me."

*

Rudolph Schneider carefully polished the ring and held it up. The small item of jewelry was as unremarkable as it was scratched and dented by all the decades it had passed through.

He tried placing the ring on his fingers but found it only slid onto his little one with any comfort. The master was not a man of large physical proportions, and his fingers were refined as those befitting someone who had played the piano and violin in his youth.

Schneider pressed the button on the wall, and watched as the floor dropped and the steps cascaded down to his private room. He carefully carried the ring down and lifted the lid on a prominent glass case and placed it on a small pedestal. A down-light was already shining its beam onto the ring, highlighting the signature lettering.

He stepped back, smiled and nodded, satisfied. He then turned. "Magnificent. You always had such wonderful taste, my master."

He bowed his head and listened for a moment and then nodded. "Yes, mein Führer, our time comes around again. And this time, we will not be stopped."

CHAPTER 05

Boston, Massachusetts – later that day

Within just a few hours a courier knocked on Matt's down-stairs door with an envelope.

Matt took it and held it up. "Thank you, Uncle Jack."

He chuckled as he raced back upstairs, immediately kneeling to stick the small USB into the television port, and then he backed up just a foot or so but stayed kneeling.

He had promised to keep Colonel Hammerson in the loop if and when he found out anything. But for now it was all just exploration and academic thought bubbles so he was on his own.

Matt fast-forwarded to the scene inside the Maori marae, and as he suspected the footage hadn't been broadcast. He froze the image.

"Oh yeah." He leaned forward, letting his eyes run down the length of the ancient stone. He pointed his remote again, this time saving the image to a separate file folder. His television was connected to his internal network of devices.

He logged onto his computer and the picture was already waiting for him. He then dragged it into his image library and let the software clean up the grainy details. After a few seconds of clarification, he could see nearly the entire stone save for the edges and extreme bottom that were beyond the camera angle.

"Magnificent," he whispered as he rubbed his chin. "You came from that submarine, didn't you?"

He began the process of translating. Much he could decipher immediately, and other sections he'd need to do some research on. As he suspected, the stone tablet looked to be part of a set, like a page. There was a portion that could have been a geographical map, some that might have been mathematical symbols, and also another set of images that were rings and dots that made no sense to him – he wasn't sure if it was even part of the language string. They continued on, but the rest were lost at the break line of the stone.

He tidied up the notes he had made and then read again from the top.

They have come and they will come again. Each ending greater than the last.

Then came some new text: *Only those from the center* – or maybe *core* – *can stop them when ...*

Who's they? he wondered. Also, *what* ending? And the final piece inferring something needed or could be stopped. And by *when* – was that meant to be a time or an event?

Matt sighed. There were so many questions raised from just those three lines it made his head spin.

There were two columns of the sprays of dots, and lines that were interconnected – looking like each was having an effect on the other. They reminded him a little of pond ripples. It wasn't part of the Aztlantean language that he knew and he had no idea what it could mean. He grabbed screen images of some of the dot and ring images, and plugged them into his computer. He ran a search.

Beep, beep.

"Huh, already?" The search engine had a hit, and Matt leaned in closer.

The match came from a prehistoric astrological chart, and corresponded to the extrapolated star charts of the sky from what astrologers theorized would have been around 444 million years ago. He looked back at the images from the stone, then to the charts again.

"So-ooo, that's what you could be: star charts."

Matt sat back and folded his arms. It sort of made sense as the Aztlanteans were advanced in mathematics and also astronomy. After a moment he shrugged and plugged in the next set of rings and dots, and then the next and next. Every one of them corresponded to a star chart from a time period of extreme ancient history.

Matt scribbled notes as the information dropped: the earliest chart indicated an occurrence that was 444 million years ago that corresponded to the end of the Ordovician period. The next star chart lined up with the late Devonian age of 375 million years ago, and then another at the end of the Permian era, 251 million years ago. Those eras were when the Earth was an extremely primordial place, but for some reason they all resonated in Matt's memory.

The next hit indicated a time around the end of the Triassic period, 200 million years ago. Also another at the end of the Cretaceous, 66 million years ago, and finally, the last one he entered corresponded to the last centuries of the Pleistocene age of just 100,000 years ago.

He exhaled loudly. The damn stone ended or had broken off before it got any closer to the current time period.

"Are you some sort of long-range countdown?" He asked the screen and then turned to look for his beer, grabbed it and sipped. He grimaced at the warm brew, and lowered the bottle. "But countdown to what?"

He could see there was another row of numbers that suggested an interaction inference – something happened in one column that caused something else to happen in the other column.

Matt made a list of the dates and periods and then also ran a computer search on them to see if they meant anything. Again, his computer found an almost instant match.

His brows drew together as he read down the list with a chilled feeling in his gut. It wasn't just that they all had significant references, but what it was they were all referenced for – global mass extinctions and the percentage of creatures lost. He read on:

- End Ordovician, 444 million years ago – 86% of species lost.
- Late Devonian, 375 million years ago – 75% of species lost.
- End Permian, 251 million years ago – 96% of species lost.
- End Triassic, 200 million years ago – 80% of species lost.
- End Cretaceous, 66 million years ago – 76% of all species lost.
- And finally, the late Pleistocene that saw the demise of what was termed the mega fauna; the giant dinosaur-sized mammals.

Matt sat forward and pushed the hair back off his face. He stared at the screen, letting his mind work over the detail as he tried to make sense of it. After many minutes he gave up – because it didn't.

Matt knew the Aztlanteans were an extremely advanced race, and had sophisticated political systems, architecture, philosophy, astrology and mathematics. They had identified those dates as having meaning, but it was impossible they knew about the extinctions. So what was it that those dates signified to them?

He looked back at the stone's other column, which looked to have even more mathematical symbols embedded within it. Words, letters and their associated concepts he could do, but ancient mathematical equations he couldn't. So unfortunately they meant nothing to him, and he had a feeling that these were the concepts that might contain the key to it all.

"I don't know." He flopped back in his chair for a moment, but then sprang forward. "*Of course.*"

Matt opened a new message on his computer mail, and hummed as he first looked up the name, and then began to compose his message.

His cousin, Megan, was a mathematical genius, and one who had exposure to ancient numbering systems. In fact, Megan was one of the specialists who worked on providing an accurate number for the 2270-year-old Archimedes' Stomachion – one of the oldest known mathematical puzzles in existence.

If what he was looking at really was a set of dates, math code, or formula, then she should be able to tell him. He scratched his chin, thinking. She was probably still in the air but it wouldn't hurt to get her mind working on it already.

Matt paused his message to recheck the stone and zoomed in on the edge of the broken tablet. There was just the trace of another chart or perhaps column of numbers there. He wondered how many more charts there were, and did the predictive dates reach all the way up to today, and maybe even beyond?

Was this stone predicting, or just recording the mass extinctions? And how could they? Not even our current technology could provide predictions. Though there were many scientists talking today about current and future species tipping points due to deforestation, environmental pollution, accidental mutations, and also new viruses appearing from jungles, raw food street markets, or even accidentally escaping from research laboratories, none had ever talked about *all* of the extinctions somehow having some sort of relationship.

He sent the message to Megan and then steepled his fingers under his chin as he looked again at many of the strange symbols he couldn't identify. The more he sat staring at them the more he thought several of them might not have been linguistic marks at all, but perhaps just a representation of a particular thing.

He enlarged one that was just a fragment. "Is that supposed to be some sort of bug?" He tilted his head. *Damn nasty one if it is*, he thought. But then again, to him, all bugs were nasty ones.

Matt knew from his research that ancient graffiti wasn't out of the question – from Roman temples to Egyptian pyramid stones, strange and sometimes humorous depictions of people, places, and animals were inscribed into some texts as their version of the old: "Kilroy was here" type signature.

He sighed and got to his feet. He would love to see the stone himself and maybe even question the Maori chief. But New Zealand was at the end of the goddamn world, and he'd never get the university to spring for the extra budget.

Besides, it would probably turn out to be nothing. "Kilroy was here." He chuckled as he went into the kitchen to grab another beer.

CHAPTER 06

Khan limestone mine, Pothohar Plateau, Rawalpindi district, north-eastern Pakistan — 17 July

The noise was near deafening, the heat unbearable, and the choking limestone dust meant many of the men had cotton scarves pulled tight over noses and mouths. The scarves displayed tide-rings of perspiration, saliva, and dust.

Babar Ansari and Ejaz Fareedi were manning the cutter – an instrument that was like a giant chainsaw – as they carved out the half-ton limestone blocks for transport in the mine cart to the surface.

Babar squinted behind his goggles as they finished the last gradient slice. The blocks were always cut at a slight angle and, as the limestone wasn't a hard material to work with, the block could then be broken out like a tooth.

Pakistan was right in the middle of a building boom, and as limestone was a key ingredient in the production of cement, construction companies wanted it faster than mining companies could dig it out.

The Khan mine was a seam of limestone, dozens of vertical feet thick and maybe half a mile wide horizontally. It was a rich seam, just a thousand feet down, and was probably laid down countless millions of years ago when the area was a shallow tropical sea. The limestone was the result of pressure on crushed shells, coral, and tiny sea creatures that were buried on the sea bottom.

Babar was in charge of the directional blade and held up a hand for Ejaz to shut off the cutter as the block was finished. Immediately the noise fell away leaving just the occasional cough and muttering of the other miners, and also the occasional rare drip of water they used to cool the machines.

Natural water down here was a bad thing as the limestone dissolved quickly, the water sometimes staining and contaminating it. Best quality limestone was solid, unmarked, and medium density.

A little water was tolerated, but a lot of water could be deadly, because the water also created pockets in the stone as it percolated through, and the last thing the men wanted was for the machinery, or them, to fall into a massive sinkhole.

But there was another risk, and this time it was to the machinery. When limestone is put under extreme pressure and also subjected to heat, it can undergo a geological process called metamorphism and is then transformed into marble. As a commodity the best quality marble was also prized, but it was dense, hard, and avoided as standard limestone-cutters were no match for the attractive but solid stone.

Babar took off one of his tough canvas gloves while he waited for the extraction team to remove the block and stack it on the cart where it would wait for another of its kind before it would then head topside. He wiped his nose and then reached inside his heavily crusted jacket pocket and felt for the oversized handkerchief he kept there.

Babar pulled it out, and tipped his helmet back, pushed up his goggles and wiped his face. He looked at it; the cloth had his name embroidered there, still showing through the grime and limestone dust. His wife, Aiisha, had sewn his name on it, and he smiled as he saw the tiny heart she had finished the embroidery with.

He laughed softly, wiped his eyes with it, balled the material, and shoved it back inside his jacket. They had hours yet to go on the shift and by then the handkerchief would be stiff as canvas and look like a sheet of plaster.

"*Ya.*"

Ejaz let him know the team was out of the way and Babar prepared to start the process all over again. He maneuvered the long blade into place, deeper in this time, and he gave one last look around to ensure everyone was behind the danger point.

"Cutting," he yelled, and then powered up the spinning blade. He pulled the scarf over his nose and mouth again, and when the rotations reached their maximum speed Babar pushed the blade into the cavity.

The blade sunk quickly into the soft stone, and he first cut a four-foot horizontal line just on three feet deep. He then pulled the blade and changed the angle and pushed in again. The blade sunk in smoothly, cutting like a hot knife into butter ... until there came the god-awful sound of metal teeth striking something hard.

The rock and steel fought against each other for a moment or two as the noise grew to near deafening and the entire machine bucked like a bronco.

Men yelled from behind them, and Ejaz shut the blade down as Babar pulled it from the cut.

"*Ach.*" He spat. "I think we have marble."

He walked forward to inspect the blade, and sure enough saw that the teeth were worn down. Several would definitely need replacing.

"Well, that is us done for the day." He knew that even though it wasn't his fault, he and Ejaz would catch sorry hell for the broken equipment. It was just dumb luck, but that was the way it was here.

Babar was about to turn away, when he froze. His forehead furrowed into a deep frown.

"What's up?" Ejaz said in the silence of the tunnel.

Babar held up a hand, tilted his head, and concentrated. *There it was again*, a small click and pop like the sound ice cubes made when dropped into a glass of sweet cola.

"I think ..."

Dust softly rained down on them.

"Something there?" Ejaz came forward to join him and also leaned his head close to the wall of stone.

Marble was an unwelcome guest in limestone mines. It was composed primarily of the mineral calcite and usually contained micas, quartz, pyrite, iron oxides, and graphite. Not only was it much harder than limestone, but it was less porous, and that meant it was the perfect barrier against hidden water – sometimes lake-sized bodies of water.

The cracking started to become louder. Ejaz looked up at his friend, eyes widening. Babar returned the look. At that moment, both men knew what the sound meant. They turned to run.

The entire wall exploded in at them, and countless millions of gallons of water from an ancient underground lake came at the men like a living thing, sweeping away men, rock, and the carts.

In that freezing, black water the last thought that went through Babar's mind was that the water tasted funny.

*

On the surface all the men momentarily froze, then dropped tools, turned, and sprinted away from the mineshaft as it began to spew dust and grit at gale force. Beneath their feet the ground jumped and jerked as deep below them the earth moved, cracked, and opened even deeper vents.

Ibrahim Gardezi, the site manager, was the only one to run toward the mine's mouth but he skidded to a halt as the dust stopped spewing out, and was replaced by water surging to the surface.

"No, no, no!" he yelled, putting his hands to his head.

The geologists had assured them the ground here was stable. But then again, the government paid for the geologists, and who knew what their qualifications were. If they even had any at all.

The muddy water began to create an ever-widening pond in the slight depression at the mine entrance, and he prayed that the men down below would either be washed out, or had made it to some sort of air pocket.

He groaned, knowing that, even if they did, they would die, but just a little slower as no one would be able to reach them. The mine wasn't all that profitable or important. And now, this disaster would end it. In the growing murky pool he saw death, and also unemployment for the surviving crew.

And then something else – in the swirling water were tiny pale balls being buffeted by the surging tide. They were roughly the size of his fingernails, and there were hundreds if not thousands of them.

Ibrahim knew that in geology there were many occurrences of spheroids, some caused by concretation where sedimentary rocks are pressed into spheres or ovals, water-smoothing of pebbles, and many other reasons for the odd but natural shape. But none he knew of ever floated.

He sniffed, detecting an odd sulfurous odor. As he watched, some of the spheres washed up at the pool's edge, and he went for a closer look. They looked like Styrofoam balls or even tiny eggs and he bent forward to scoop some up in the palm of his hand.

He rolled some between his palm and finger and they felt soft, like leather, not like an eggshell at all. He held his hand up to eye level and watched as the hot sun dried their surface and they began to darken.

On the edge of the growing pond the other spheres also started to darken. Ibrahim momentarily forgot about his lost men as he stared at the tiny spheres. The dark surfaces fully blackened then began to split.

Pieces fell away – no, that wasn't right; they were being pushed outwards and then something started to emerge – long black spikes that seemed made of shining plastic. Two, then three, then four, and then the most grotesque little head he had ever seen.

Eggs, his brain screamed, *full of spiders*! He flung the handful he was holding away from him.

On the ground he saw that others were also hatching. Veined wings were lastly drawn from the eggs to lengthen and dry in the sunshine, and then strange eyes turned toward him.

He looked around – hundreds of the things had hatched … and every one of them stood on their egg casings and watched him.

The tiny wings started to vibrate. Then one lifted off, then two, and then hundreds, the sound a deep and ominous thrum.

And they all came right at him.

*

The Daily Khabrain Newspaper – 18 July
TRAJEDY STRIKES MINING COMMUNITY
A tragic day for Rawalpindi as catastrophe struck the close-knit mining community when the Khan mine became flooded after accidentally cutting into an underground lake.

All 17 miners on the morning shift are missing, and hopes are fading fast of finding survivors.

Experts believe that rescue or retrieval of any bodies might be impossible as the miners were working up to 1000 feet down in the tunnels, and the shafts had flooded all the way to surface level.

Local Mayor Hakim Hamid has ruled out calling in army divers as geologists have advised that visibility in the swirling limestone-infused water will be at zero for many more months and, further, the mine may also be subject to further collapse.

*

The Daily Khabrain Newspaper – 19 July
TOWNSHIP DECIMATED BY MYSTERY PLAGUE
Dhalla is a small mining town of the Rawalpindi district in the Punjab province and had a population of 620 people that were primarily dependent on the Khan mine for their survival.

Now, in a double blow to the town, the police are baffled by a mystery plague that has devastated the small Dhalla community. No survivors have been encountered as every person, including all domestic animals, have been killed.

The army has taken over the investigation and the small township is now cordoned off. As yet, the bodies and their autopsy results have not been released and the authorities have provided no further information.

CHAPTER 07

National Defense Command and Control Center, Moscow

General Yevgeni Ivanovich sat stony faced among all the other military heads as President Volkov roared at them so forcefully his face had turned the color of a ripe plum.

The Russian leader was already angry that his pet bear, Ursa, was sick. The Kamchatka brown bear, stood eight feet tall, and Volkov liked to have his tame press members film him wrestling the giant beast to illustrate his strength and virility.

This was just the tinder, as what came next was the spark – following their swallowing of the Crimean port with barely an international whimper, Volkov was on the cusp of his plans to force Ukraine to reintegrate with the Russian motherland as he grew his new Soviet Union. But the Americans had just approved the sale of sophisticated defense weaponry with the new Ukrainian leader – anti-tank missiles, surface-to-air missiles, and even a range of missile defense units that would complicate the Russian advance.

And worse was the American president promising to do more to support Ukraine and its new leader as he seemed to take him under the eagle's wing.

Volkov stopped yelling then, composed himself, and turned to his military leaders, his pale eyes almost wolfish as they touched on each of them. This was more terrifying than his roars, as this meant he had decided on a plan and someone was going to pay.

"The Americans need to be taught a lesson. They need to be humbled. They need to suffer a setback that will force them to focus internally ..."

He stared at Ivanovich, and the general worked to keep his expression calm.

"... so we can finish our work," Volkov said softly. His gaze was almost hypnotic. "Will you do this for me, General?"

Ivanovich shot to his feet, saluted, and held it. "Consider it done, my President."

Volkov stared back from under his brow. "Then make it happen. And make it happen fast."

CHAPTER 08

Central Scientific Research Institute, Ministry of Defense, Shchyolkovo, Moscow

Nadi Borishenko, Colonel in the Biological Warfare Unit, stood behind the thick glass window and watched the scientists work. They all wore a heavy form of hazardous materials suit, but the ones the scientists wore were more like suits of armor. Beside Nadi was the chief science officer, Doctor Mikhail Verinko, who had been tasked with leading the project.

"Begin," Borishenko said softly.

The small man picked up a telephone and spoke a few words. A group of scientists then wheeled over a coffin-sized glass case partitioned into three sections. The first contained a single white rabbit, the next a large grayish-looking snake, and the last section contained three enormous insects – *Lucanus cervus*, stag beetles, each an inch and a half long, and armored by a thick carapace shell.

They were pushed up against another tank; this one filled with black wasp-like bugs, all around an inch in length, who for now seemed dormant. The tanks were joined, and sealed.

The partitions between them slowly lifted, and after a second or two, like tiny machines, the heads of the insectoids turned. Then, as a swarm, they began to move toward the open portals in a robotic, jerking motion.

In another few seconds the enclosures of the rabbit, snake and beetles were filled. The prey ran, fought, and blundered into the glass walls, but were quickly engulfed and subdued.

As Borishenko watched he felt a curl of revulsion form in his belly as each of the target creatures became floppy and fell flat as if they were nothing more then empty sacks. The beetles, degloved from their external chitin exoskeleton, just looked like glistening puddles.

Verinko turned. "Complete extraction and consumption of all the silicon and calcium from within their bodies. Of course that means external removal for the arthropods."

Borishenko nodded slowly. It was the most amazing and horrifying thing he had ever seen in his life. "So fast."

"Yes." Verinko turned back to the glass. "They have an amazing ability to consume many times their own body weight."

"Where did they come from?" Borishenko asked.

"At the foot of the Ural Mountains. From deep underground, we think. But they are appearing in other places as well. They are extremely hardy, formidable, and aggressive," Verinko said. "Heat will slow them down. But the sort of heat required to kill them is extreme, and detrimental to everything else as well."

"They would make an excellent addition to our arsenal. If they could be weaponized." A plan began to form in Borishenko's mind.

Several years ago he had been tasked by ministerial order to work on the final stages of the Kurgan project, to create the Russian combat soldier of the future. The Kremlin had invested decades and many millions of rubles in the project and developed several soldiers all of enormous strength, speed, and intellect, and then sent them on a field test mission to an almost inaccessible mountain range in Alaska.

Their task was to recover some high-altitude surveillance data from a downed American space shuttle. But things hadn't gone to plan and it seemed overconfidence had surpassed competence.

The Kurgan came up against an American Special Forces outfit known as HAWCs, headed by Colonel Jack Hammerson. Borishenko's mouth turned down as he remembered. Their expensive soldiers had been lost. All of them.

The project was deemed a failure, and many politicians and military personnel associated with it had simply vanished. Or been made to vanish. Borishenko had only survived through rat cunning, contacts, and a honed ability to cast blame on others.

But still, his golden career path had been destroyed and to this day he had promised himself that if an opportunity for payback on Colonel Hammerson or America presented itself he would not hesitate to take it.

And with General Ivanovich calling for covert mission objectives he might now just have his opportunity. He turned to Verinko. "In twenty-four hours, you will tell me how this weaponization will be effected. This is an order."

*

Doctor Mikhail Verinko stood with hands behind his back, fingers clasped tightly as he watched through the toughened glass the next round of conditioning tests on the creatures.

Their growth rate was phenomenal; when the silachnids, as he now termed them, had been gathered they were little bigger than large wasps. But now, just a few weeks later, they were the size of alley cats.

They, and everything about them, fascinated the Russian scientist. They consumed silicon and calcium, and preferred live prey where they could inject a salivary enzyme that softened the silicon structures in their prey's bodies so it could then be sucked out via a hypodermic-like proboscis.

They were a strange mix of spider-insectoid morphology with their defined segmentation, but also had fur and scales, like some sort of hybrid mammal–reptile creature. Their eyes were hard lens coated, but not the multifaceted bulbs one would expect from an arthropod. *More mammalian*, he thought again. Though the creatures fascinated him, it was the eyes that unsettled Verinko – their gaze held a little too much intelligence for his liking.

He had read much of the documentation on the hypothesis of the existence of silicon-based life-forms, but they were expected to come from some other world, not burrow up from somewhere deep in the Earth.

The two scientists on the other side of the glass waited just outside the controlled environment room and Verinko nodded to them and then stepped closer for a better view.

One of them used a card key on a lanyard around his neck to open the door, and entered with a dish of silicon in a warm solution of water and sugar. As the scientists entered through the first airlock door the silachnids became aware of them and started to gather close by.

As the men passed through the final door the creatures surged forward. They clung to the legs of the scientists, but their sharp claws or proboscis had no hope of piercing the tough synthetic fabric of their suits.

The dish of food was placed on the floor, and immediately was overrun by the swarm. The scientists straightened and then produced slim sticks and proceeded to touch individual creatures while delivering a loud and clear command word.

Sparks flew as the shock sticks delivered their voltage. Even though the creatures were small, the charge needed was enough to stun a full-grown man; such was the toughness of the creatures and their silicon-armor plating.

Verinko smiled. The experiment was basic obedience training that worked on everything from dogs to humans – each time a command was given, if it was ignored, a shock was delivered, and if the command was obeyed, then a soothing word, and no shock. After a while, just the command was usually enough to get the creatures to perform their task, whether it was to back away, stay still, or advance.

"You learn quickly," he whispered.

Soon the creatures were all backed up against the far wall, as the scientists held out their shock sticks. Verinko still found the tiny humanlike eyes of the things most fascinating. In those tiny orbs the glare seemed to be of almost pure hatred. They were obeying, but reluctantly, he thought.

Another aspect he found fascinating was that, while the more painful aspects of the conditioning were being administered, many times every single one of the creatures would focus its strange gaze on him, Verinko, as if they knew he was the one administering the commands.

The scientist didn't like them at all. For now, Verinko knew that the creatures could be controlled. But that gaze told him that there would never be bonding between their two species. The creatures were held in check through fear and pain, and saw the humans as no more than large prey animals. Dangerous, large prey animals.

He tapped the glass and waved to the scientists. The test was successful; Borishenko would be pleased, and he could proceed to his next phase.

CHAPTER 09

"Hey, Kook."

Matt chuckled into the phone. "Yeah, hi Megs. So you got my message? Where are you?"

"I'm in a taxi, coming at you fast. And I sure did get those ... whatever the hell they were. And I've got to tell you they're the weirdest and most wonderful things I've seen in years, if not ever. So, where did you get them? This better not be a prank."

"No, no prank, they're real. They came from a television show about New Zealand's coast. I saw the stone tablet standing at the back of one of their ceremonial huts. As soon as I saw it, I knew it was special."

He looked at a pinboard he had on the wall, where he had a printout of the stone. "So, Miss Wizard of ancient numbering patterns, tell me what you see."

"You won't believe me," she said. It sounded like her mouth was shaped into a grin.

"Pfft, get outta town. I've seen things that'd make your hair curl."

"Oh really?" She laughed softly. "Like what, a language student spilling his coffee in the hallway, or perhaps the university printer running out of ink?"

You have no idea, Matt thought. "All of the above. Come on, Megan, is it a numbering pattern or not?"

"Well, uh, the best description I can give you is it's like an algorithm. You know, like on your computer."

"But it has a function?" he asked.

"Yes, I think so. I mean it has a function, but damned if I know what that function is. It's a recurring algorithm that, depending where you move it up or down a timeline, gives you back a particular date. I'm not sure what it means ... yet."

"Yeah, that makes sense. I got the right-hand column from astrological star dates. And they seem to be ancient ones. Very ancient ones."

"Of course, I thought they looked like astral patterns." She laughed. "Clever boy."

Matt thought for a moment. "Uh, any significant dates jump out? Anything interesting?"

"Yeah, ignoring the prehistoric ones, I can see that one of the columns pinpoints periods that are hundreds of years apart, almost like a timer that goes off to let people know something is *about* to happen. There are also clusters of small events and then they lead up to a large event. The last one was a major date of around seven thousand years ago, and then, get this, Matt, there's another one coming up like, around now."

"Now?" Matt frowned. "*Now*, now? What does that mean?"

"I mean this year, now. There's no obvious measurement that breaks it down any further than that. So whatever they were looking at or monitoring is happening, or going to happen sometime around now, but ..." She seemed to have a thought. "Hey, how old is that stone?"

"I don't know." But Matt could make a rough guess of when the Aztlanteans last existed. "Maybe twelve thousand years. Maybe more."

"What? Who was around then? Even the Sumerians were still a bunch of nomads." She scoffed. "Well, anyway, whoever these guys were, they were recording ancient events and also predicting new ones."

Matt heard her pull the phone away and give the driver some directions in her usual brusque tone. "Hey, Meg, can you make out the smaller cluster events with any accuracy? How many are there?"

"Maybe around twelve, but I can't make them out right now with what I've got." She paused. "But I bet I could write a subroutine that would determine what they mean or what they're supposed to point to."

"Great, do it and send them through," he said.

"*Ha*! Not a chance, buster. I want to see it, all of it. I'll write the program, but I want in. This is too intriguing."

"It certainly is," he said, his mind wandering.

"This is important, Matt, I know it." She spoke faster, "I'll be there any minute."

"Okay, fine." He barely heard her. "Create the program and we'll see what it tells us."

"Be there soon. Don't do anything without me. You promise?" Megan asked.

"Sure, promise." Matt disconnected and walked slowly to the window. He stared out over the park, his eyes unfocused. The concepts nagged at him. Megan said there were smaller events leading up to a big event. *A big event.*

That was the worrying thing, considering that some of the historical dates mentioned highlighted mass extinctions. Now *they* were big events.

How had a race that was more ancient than even the Babylonians and Sumerians worked that out? Exactly what was it they were monitoring?

Matt felt a coil of concern twist in his gut at the implications.

*

He opened the door and Megan came in fast, talking a mile a minute.

"It works, the program. I knew it would. And just as I thought, they were dates." She dropped her bag and turned. "Dates, a range of them, all leading to an end date. A *big* date." She held up her hands, arms outstretched. "We've *got* to see that stone. It's damned unique, Kooky."

"You did it already?" Matt laughed. *And that's twice*, he thought. No one had called him Kook, or Kooky, or Kooky Kearns, since he was a kid. He suddenly felt like he'd traveled back in time.

"Of course." She jammed her hands onto her hips. "Well?"

"Yeah, good to see you again too, Megan." She looked fit, a little overfed, and had on a strap tank top that displayed a matchbox-sized tattoo of pi on her bicep.

He remembered when she'd got it at sixteen, after professing a love of math. She had told him that pi was derived from the first letter of the Greek word perimetros, meaning circumference. But, more importantly, pi was also an "irrational number", meaning its exact value is inherently unknowable. And with all the solemnness of a teenager she had declared that was exactly like her.

"Well?" She demanded again.

He held up a finger. "And maybe not so unique."

"What?" she craned forward, her mouth hanging in an open smile.

"Your turn." He waggled his finger. "First, I want to see those dates."

Megan glanced about, spotted his low table in front of the television, and rushed toward it. Her nose wrinkled at all the beer bottles, empty Doritos bags, and even an empty pizza box.

"Matt?"

He shrugged. "Maid's day off."

"You need a wife." She snorted.

"Sure, but who'd have me?" He grinned.

"Probably someone who likes good-looking Harvard professors with poor hygiene." She began pushing the debris to the side.

"I'll be sure to put that in my online dating profile."

"You have one too?" She looked up, and he was sure she blushed a little. He shrugged.

"Whatever." Megan drew out a pile of folders from a satchel over one of her shoulders.

"The two strangest things are, *one*, how accurate the chronology pinpointing is. And *two*, how close those pin-pointed events are to contemporaneous time, that being, right about now." She raised her eyebrows. "You seeing that television program was pu-*uuure* serendipity."

She unfolded a hand-drawn chart. There were rings inside rings, and at its center, was something termed *Major Event*. There was also a date associated with it that was just three months away.

"Here." Megan put her finger on the chart. "Each of these rings represents an event of some sort. I can only interpret the numbers, you're the linguistic expert."

She held the edges down and then ran a hand over it, before pointing again. "This is where we are today. On the outer ring is where this cycle of events has started. I can pinpoint this to 17 July. The next is 31 July, and then 9 August. So those are the ones that have already happened."

She looked up. "Any of those dates ring a bell?"

"Nope." Matt shrugged. "Not off the top of my head, but this is probably a global thing, so think how many natural and man-made events occur every single day: hundreds, thousands." He had a thought. "Unless they were all so similar

47

that we could pick them up as a pattern." He shrugged. "We can check later."

"Okay." Megan turned to her chart again. "The events identified continue, and then speed up, so at the last few rings, they're occurring daily. Then we get to the major event. After that ... nothing but calm again for ..." She straightened. "Hundreds, thousands, millions of years, I can't tell with the fragment broken off."

She turned to him, smiling. "So ... who made it? Who created the charts and the algorithm, because it looks damn old?"

"You wouldn't believe me even if I told you." He waved the question away.

She grabbed his shirt and dragged him closer. "Try me."

Matt unpicked her fingers and then folded his arms. He looked down at the chart rings. "As always, your work is top-notch. You've still got it." He smiled, but saw his deflection didn't work. He also recognized the determination in her eyes – she was like a terrier when she wanted something.

He sighed. "I signed a confidential agreement ..." He sighed even louder. "... with the military."

One side of her mouth quirked up. "Well, I won't tell if you don't." She grabbed his arm. "Come on, Kooky, I'm here to help. The more I know, the more I can make some of those intuitive leaps you know I'm famous for."

She was right, he thought. *Who'd know?* Even as a kid she was no blabbermouth. She was also right in that she might be able to give even better insights when she knew some background.

"You have to swear to me you'll keep this confidential, okay?" He raised his chin.

Megan grinned back. "You mean, like you with the military?"

"No, better than that." He frowned.

"Sure, sure." She looked skyward for a moment.

"Okay." Matt gathered his thoughts. "About ten years ago I was sent on an expedition to the Antarctic. We found caves below the ice and, well, to cut a long story short, we found a civilization buried there, miles down."

"No. Freaking. Way." She gawped at him for a moment and then grabbed his shirtfront again. "Come here." She led him to a chair, pushed him back into it, and then sat opposite. Megan leaned forward and stared intently into his face. "Go on."

"You can't tell anyone, Megan, promise me?" He pleaded.

"I already said okay. Come on, fess up." She grinned.

He sighed. "The people who once lived there called the place Aztlan, and themselves Aztlanteans."

"Aztlan? *Aztlanteans?*" She grinned. "Are you saying it was Atlantis?"

He looked her in the eye. "No, yes, maybe."

She nodded slowly. "So cool ... if true."

He didn't really care if she believed him or not. In fact, he hoped she didn't. He continued. "They had their own language and writing that predated anything I had seen before anywhere in the world. It was a root language and possibly even the mother tongue that gave rise to everything from Sanskrit, Egyptian, and even to the Olmec pictoglyphs systems." He looked up. "I've since encountered that language several times – from a temple in the Amazon jungle, and also in the Iranian desert where they called it the *language of the angels*. And now here, from a fragment of stone that was retrieved from a sunken German World War II U-boat off the coast of New Zealand."

She lifted a finger. "Which just happens to be one of the closest places on Earth to Antarctica."

"Correct. They were a brilliant and advanced seafaring race, and it seems they had a message for us." He stared into Megan's face. "I think they wanted us to know that something is catching up to us, and it's coming fast."

Megan's mouth hung open for a few seconds before it snapped shut. "I fucking love you." She pointed at his chest. "Take me with you, I know you're going there, please, please. We need to see that stone tablet, find out what's going on. We need to be in New Zealand like ... yesterday."

"What?" His brows shot up. "What about your mathematics convention?"

"Oh forget that, this is way more interesting." She nodded. "So, are you going?"

Matt shook his head. "I've been thinking about that. And the bottom line is, I don't think the stone is of such great importance. The writing on it is. Where it came from is. And importantly, where the other half is. Those are the things we need."

"*We*. I like that." She sat back. "You said it was in a Maori chief's hut – we can talk to him."

He shook his head. "Nah, he won't admit it, but I bet all he knows is it came from the submarine. And in the program they said the German war office had no record of the voyage. Whatever that U-boat was doing down there, where it had been, and what they planned to do with the stone has been kept secret. And now maybe those secrets are lost."

He smiled at her. "But ... I believe they were on that mission at the personal behest of Adolf Hitler, as part of his *Übernatürliche Kriegsführung*, that is, his supernatural warfare unit. And if Hitler did send that U-boat it'll be in his secret diary."

"Hitler had a secret diary?" Megan clutched her chest and pretended to faint. She slowly sat back up and held out her arms, showing him. "Look, I've got goose bumps." A smile spread on her lips. "If old Adolf put the mission in his diary, then it's simple. We need to see that diary."

"Yeah, simple." Matt laughed. "Small problem there: I don't know who has it, or even where it is." He flopped back in his chair.

Megan seemed to think for a moment before clapping her hands together. "If the Aztlanteans had an important message for us, then we need to know what it was." She tapped her chin for a moment before springing forward.

"Okay, here's what we do: for now, we work with what we've got – we see if those near-term dates relate to any event that's happened, or if anything leaps out at us. Then we can put a trace on that elusive diary. Deal?"

"Okay," he replied, carried away by her enthusiasm.

"First thing we need." She pointed at his empty beer bottle. "Beer."

After Matt grabbed them some beers, he and Megan spent the next forty minutes scanning the internet. As they expected, on the dates they searched there were too many events to count. They excluded anything modern like plane, train, or car crashes, as well as terrorism events, and tried to narrow it down to natural things like floods, fires, or earthquakes, meteors, or even the damned inexplicable.

They tried to narrow the field and only search for events of the last month. And that's when they got their first hits: earthquakes followed by local towns being wiped out.

Matt stopped on one describing a place in Rawalpindi district, north-eastern Pakistan – there was an earthquake followed by an entire town being decimated.

In addition, there was an eyewitness who was locked in a car and said that the people in the town were killed by a plague of giant, horrifying bugs.

Matt read the last sentence out. "… killed by a plague of horrifying bugs … that ate their bones out." He raised his eyebrows.

"Yeah, nice." Megan blew air through pursed lips. "And here, another one corresponding to one of the stone tablet's dates, from an outback Australian town. Once again, an earth tremor in a place that didn't usually have them and then followed by the nearest town being wiped out."

"Earthquakes, towns decimated, and all corresponding to a pinpointed date of the Aztlan calendar stone." He turned to her. "*Bam.*"

"Calendar stone, huh?" She raised an eyebrow. "Seems to be an extinction stone rather than just a diary, if you ask me."

"With the bugs more like an extinction plague," Matt said. He went over to his wooden chest and riffled through his notes until he found some printouts he'd made of the stone's details – he quickly located the carving of the strange insect-looking thing. "Look." He showed it to her. "Another coincidence?"

"Too many of those happening here." She took the page and stood, pacing as she examined it. "Something weird is going on. We need to know more, but we don't even know where to start or even how to start. That Hitler diary might be anywhere in the world by now." She sat back down heavily. "So what now? We just sit on our ass, and watch and wait for these events to just happen?"

"We couldn't locate the diary by ourselves, and even if we did there's no guarantee we could even get close to it." Matt sat back, thinking.

After a moment, he held up a finger. "But I know someone who can." He picked up his phone and dialed Jack Hammerson again. After all, the colonel said he wanted to be kept in the loop.

*

"No," Jack Hammerson replied.

"Jack, this is important, and I know right now I can't prove there is a direct relationship, but the circumstantial evidence is overwhelming." He turned to Megan and shrugged.

"Matt, son, I like you ..." Hammerson began.

Matt looked heavenward and sighed.

"... but a few earthquakes dotted around the world and a Nostradamus stone hinting it could pinpoint them is way out there. I can pick a few dates anytime, and I bet you could find some sort of weird-ass thing going down on that day somewhere in the world."

Matt half smiled, knowing Hammerson was probably right. But he had a gut feeling about this. "Jack, there's something strange going on, and in a few months time it points to something big happening."

Hammerson remained silent.

I'm losing him, Matt thought. "And just preceding the pinpointed event date, we have minor earthquakes, and then the nearest town gets wiped out. Jack, there's a witness saying there was a plague of bugs."

"Very biblical," Hammerson replied distractedly. "You said you had a witness?"

"Well I don't, but over in Pakistan they do. Look, Jack, it was also imprinted on the stone. The bug thing, I mean," Matt said. "This is a warning to us from the Aztlanteans, to everyone."

"Is it bad actor, or terrorist inspired?" Hammerson asked.

"No, no ..." Matt frowned.

"Is it a direct threat to the United States, its interests, or its allies?" Hammerson pressed.

"Undoubtedly. Well, it could be. I think this thing is only just ramping up. We've got to get ahead of it, right now. If we leave it be, it might be too late, maybe for the world."

Matt knew it was hopeless with a man like Hammerson who dealt in facts, not theories, and the more he pressed on the more he sounded ridiculous even to himself. "Look, Jack, we just need –"

"Matt, stop talking." Hammerson's deep voice was soft but cut across him. "It certainly looks like you might have a puzzle there. But there are too many pieces missing." He exhaled. "Let's agree to put it on a watching brief. You said another one of the dates is coming up. Well, you keep watch, and then, like I said, keep me informed."

Hammerson rang off and Matt tilted his head back for a moment and sighed. He turned to Megan.

"No go, huh?" She laughed. "You've sure gotta lot of pull there, Kooky, I'm impressed." She put her hands on her hips. "So what now?"

Matt drummed his fingers on his table for a moment and then looked at his watch. "What now? Now it's dinnertime, and I know this great little place that serves the best chicken quesadilla this side of Tijuana. And best part is, it's just around the corner. I can get us in no matter how busy they are."

Megan's face brightened. "I take it back, cuz, you do have some impressive pull around here after all."

CHAPTER 10

Blessing, Matagorda County, Texas – 9 August

Margaret watched her two daughters peddle furiously up the wide tree-lined street. There were few cars out any day of the week, but Sundays were especially quiet.

It had been a good church service that morning, and Father Patrick Montgomery was at his best, being both humorous and authoritative with the added advantage of having a fine singing voice. He wasn't at all like old Father Hennesy who yelled a lot and scared the children witless.

Margaret sighed as the warm sun made the skin on her neck feel tight. She loved living here, always had. Blessing was a lovely town, and it was unfortunate it was shrinking.

Blessing had a total area of just two square miles and at last count there were 861 people residing here; down on last year, and on the year before that as well.

Her family had lived here for generations – ever since the town had its start when the railroad finally extended out into the heart of Texas. The first settlers accepted the name "Blessing" after their first choice of "Thank God" was deemed unsuitable by postal officials.

Imagine that, she had thought when first learning that fact. People asked where you lived, and you could respond: *Thank God, Texas*. She smiled broadly as she kept an eye on her girls weaving back and forth across the road.

Margaret placed a hand over the back of her neck to shield it from the bite of the heat. They had little here beside God, sunshine, and a little mining work. But it was enough for most people. After all, a simple life is a healthy life.

As she walked slowly down the street she waved at some folk out watering lawns and washing cars. She knew everyone, and everyone knew her. It was one of the benefits of being in a small town; everyone was friends with everyone else, and everybody was there to help.

She squinted in the heat – the air seemed to shimmer around her girls and she wondered about her eyesight as it certainly wasn't hot enough to create a heat mirage just yet.

Then she saw little Sophia fall to the ground as the entire road jerked one way then the other. There came a sound like distant thunder, but it didn't come from the sky – it seemed to come from somewhere down deep. Maisie got off her bike to help her little sister.

Margaret held her arms out to the sides to keep her balance, as the shaking grew worse. Beside her she heard breaking glass and the thud of falling objects from within some of the houses. People rushed outside looking bewildered and a little frightened.

A large cloud was rising up in the distance, and as it drew nearer she was able to make out *things* within it – specks, or blobs of blackness now coming down the center of the highway.

Margaret felt as well as heard the deep *zumm* as the cloud approached and she ran to her daughters to throw her arms around them.

They arrived then in their dozens, then hundreds, then thousands, massing on everything, and seeking out anything living.

A plague from hell coming to torment Blessing, Margaret thought, as the first of them alighted on her back. She gathered her daughters in under her as they shivered and screamed under the wings of her arms.

More things landed on her, then more. The cloud darkened the sky and the deep zumming filled her world. Their tiny legs dug into her flesh and then into her daughters'. Margaret opened her eyes – they looked like huge wasps, but there were too many spidery legs, and what might have been scales glistening on their carapaces.

Many turned their nightmarish faces to her and, instead of the multifaceted or bulb-like insect eyes, they were like those of an animal. Tiny frilled mouths attached to her skin and what felt like needles pierced her flesh. She gritted her teeth as she sensed she was being flooded with acid.

She hugged her girls as they screamed beneath her, agonizingly, as they too had the things on them. Just faintly over the chaos she heard other voices, screaming as well, and Margaret could make out the shapes of people rolling back and forth in the street as though to put out flames. It wasn't fire they were covered in; they were crusted with thousands of hard, bristling bodies.

She had to clamp her mouth and eyes shut as the hellish bugs found her face. Margaret prayed, *Please take us to you quickly, Lord.*

Her arms fell away from her girls and flopped bonelessly by her sides. The pain she felt was unbearable but it was nothing compared to the knowledge that she couldn't protect her children.

Around them the warm sunlight was totally blacked out as the three females were now covered in a bristling, moving mound of segmented bodies.

*

Umberto "Bert" Terracini of the National Guard let his eyes move over the landscape. Blessing was a sparsely populated town, dry and well maintained, all of which was expected. But what was out of the ordinary was the deathly silence. And the emptiness.

Terracini held up a hand, and concentrated, listening for anything. But since he and his team had arrived they hadn't seen anything living at all, not even a single bird trying to dine on the dropped cookies and sandwiches scattered on sidewalks.

He turned to his team: five men and women, ranging in ages from forty to twenty-two. Their eyes were wide and wired, and they perspired heavily from the heat. It was no wonder as they were all wearing full tactical gear: helmets with goggles, body armor, and each carried black, skeletal-looking M4A1 carbines, held perhaps a little too tightly.

Terracini waved them on and they turned into Hickory Street. Their destination was St Peter's Church, the one structure large enough to hold at least a hundred people.

He swallowed dryly. There were over 850 people in Blessing, and they had to be somewhere. But it was as if everyone had simply been beamed up into space.

The Guard had been sent in rather than the local police following a frantic call from the local mayor, yelling to high heaven that they were under attack. There were screams, chaos, and then all communication was lost.

The original expectation was there would be an ongoing hostage situation and Terracini was prepared for armed resistance. Outside in the streets there were definite signs of panic with tables and chairs knocked over, food left uneaten on the street, and a sea of broken glass. But there was no blood, no bodies, and no stragglers hiding in bushes or under cars.

The church was right in front of them and, like a single, many-legged creature, the small group of soldiers surged forward. Terracini could see that all the ground-floor windows were smashed inwards or had golf ball sized holes in the remaining panes of glass as if someone had thrown rocks through them.

They stopped before the large wooden front door that was ajar, and Terracini spoke in clipped tones back to his headquarters. "Entering now."

Terracini turned to his team and held up three fingers, counting them down. He made a fist and kicked the door, exploding it inwards. His team went in, some to the left, some right, and a few going to one knee with eyes down over the sight of their machine guns.

"Clear." From the center.

"Clear." From the left, and the same from the right side.

Then he saw them. "Got 'em," Terracini said softly. He stared, and gulped. "I think."

"Any survivors?" His supervisor immediately asked into his receiver.

"Checking," Terracini replied.

He grimaced as he gaped, and then thought: *I hope not.*

There were dozens of bodies, many up against the walls and in clumps as though they had been forced back by some attacking force. But it was the state of them that stretched his sanity.

Terracini had seen bodies torn up before, but these were all flattened as though they were empty sacks. When he and his team prodded at them, they were soft.

One of his team used the barrel of his gun to lift one woman's arm. The slim silver bangle she wore slid off the end of her empty glove-like fingers and clattered to the marble floor. The flaccid arm draped over the gun barrel as if it were just an empty sleeve of clothing.

"I think the bones are gone." Terracini stared.

"Say again, team leader," his superintendent queried.

"The bones, all of them, taken out, somehow." He looked around slowly. *Nothing but empty suits*, he thought.

Fluid leaked from some of the bodies. He guessed that, with the bones gone, the liquid-filled organs were no longer supported by their calcium scaffolding and so were releasing their moisture from the closest orifice.

"Even the teeth are gone." One of his men was using a finger to lift the gums of one flattened face. He turned. "This is bad shit, man."

Terracini nodded. *Bad shit was an understatement*, he thought, and was glad he had on breathing equipment, as he was sure the smell of bile, undigested food, urine, and feces filled the air. He had no idea what could have caused it.

From under the pile of bodies he caught a hint of movement, and then burrowing out came a bug. It was about two inches long, glossy black, and glinted like hard plastic in the light. Terracini put a boot on it. Under his sole, it refused to crush and felt more like a rock. He applied more weight and finally its shell crackled like breaking glass.

Fucking roaches already come to feed on the bodies, he thought.

"They're all dead in here, no survivors. Assailants or cause unknown." He swirled his finger in the air as he and his team started to back out.

More bugs started to come out of the cracks and crevices of the body pile to investigate the new arrivals.

"Please confirm this is a non terrorist-related event, team leader."

"I cannot confirm that, Superintendent – maybe a chemical or biological agent was used. But it might also be one for the National Center for Rare Diseases." His lip curled. "One more thing: there's weird bugs everywhere."

"Get a sample, over."

Ah, fuck it, he whispered, not wanting to touch anything. He exhaled. "Yes, sir, roger that."

Terracini stared at the mass of bodies again. He had no idea what had happened but he wanted to be home. This was way above his pay grade.

He pointed to one of the bugs. "Someone catch a few of those critters so we can get the hell out of here."

CHAPTER 11

"The entire town is gone," Hammerson growled the words. "Every man, woman, child, and damn dog and cat is dead."

"Just like the stone predicted," Matt replied softly.

Hammerson sounded like he spoke through clenched teeth. "Yeah, I was wrong. And that pisses me off."

Matt had the phone on speaker and kept his mouth shut as the HAWC Special Forces Colonel continued.

"We have some biological samples which are being analyzed as we speak."

"The bugs?" Matt asked.

"Yeah, the bugs. If that's even what they are. No one has ever seen anything like them before." Hammerson sounded like he swore again under his breath. "We need to get ahead of this. You called it and I didn't listen. Seems like there might be something in that analysis of yours that we need to check out."

"Good." Matt felt a swell of vindication, but wished he didn't. "There's missing pieces of the puzzle. We need to see that New Zealand stone and the Hitler diary, and hope it leads us to the second half of the message stone, which has vanished somewhere in Europe."

"Agreed. So three things are going to happen real quick," Hammerson declared. "One, I'm dispatching a team to track down that missing diary. We have a lead on that already and I want you there to verify its authenticity and also interpret the contents. Two, we're going to retrieve that stone from New Zealand. And three, we're going to analyze this weird bug thing we caught."

"They're going to let you borrow the New Zealand stone?" Matt asked.

"Sure they are. They can have it back safe and sound when we're finished."

"That's good of them." Matt was constantly impressed with the colonel's influence.

Hammerson went on. "We're moving quickly on this, Kearns. The clock is ticking on those dates you gave me."

"Problem is, the half of the stone we've seen only says when, not where," Matt said. "If we can determine that, then we may be able to save some lives."

Megan leaned over the phone. "Yeah, but first prize should be stopping these events from happening in the first place, right?"

Matt winced. There was several seconds of silence over the line after she spoke. Then the colonel's words came low and slow.

"Who the hell have you got with you, Kearns?" Hammerson demanded.

Matt grimaced theatrically at Megan who put a hand over her mouth. He was sure she was smiling behind her hand.

"*Uh*, a colleague, Jack. Well, actually my cousin, Doctor Megan Martin. She helped with the analysis of the stone's numbering patterns. She has a PhD in pure mathematics and is a genius." Matt squeezed his eyes shut as he waited.

"Professor Kearns, take the phone off speaker." Hammerson's voice had a menacing edge.

Matt gulped and did as the colonel asked. Megan frowned and mouthed: *What's up?*

She then tried to put her ear up closer to the phone, but Matt pushed her back, got to his feet, and walked a few paces away.

Hammerson sounded like he had the phone real close to his mouth. "Professor, I like you, and you've been very helpful to us in the past. And that's why I'm only going to give you a warning about breaching your confidentiality agreement with us. Because if I didn't like you, or stopped liking you, then you might find yourself in the darkest, deepest lockup we have in the country. Do you understand me, son?"

"I think so, sir, yes, sir." Matt's heart rate increased.

"Professor, do not tell anyone, even members of your family, of the work we do together. Do not tell them who we are. Do not tell them of past missions, and do not tell them you even know what a HAWC is. Everything we do is of vital importance to national, and sometimes global, security." Hammerson's voice got even lower. "This is me being nice, Professor. Do you understand?"

"Yes, sir."

"Can I come?" Megan asked.

Matt shook his head and waved her away.

In typical bulldozer fashion, Megan made a guttural sound in her throat and grabbed the phone from his hand. She put it to her ear while keeping the other on Matt's chest to fend him off.

"Hello, General?" she winked at Matt. "This is Megan. You need me because –" She stopped talking and listened.

Matt felt a knot grow in his stomach.

"Don't you dare." Megan's eyes widened.

"But –" Her mouth snapped shut.

"Prick." She tossed Matt the phone.

Matt fumbled it out of the air and put it to his ear. "Hello, Jack?"

Hammerson sounded like he'd sat forward. "She's your problem, Matt. Don't let her become mine. She's out of the loop, keep her out, and that'll keep her safe."

"I get it, sir." Matt turned to Megan who glared at the phone and gave it the finger.

Matt silently laughed. He didn't know what Jack Hammerson had said to her, but he'd never seen his cousin shut down so effectively.

Matt turned away and walked to the window, lowering his voice. "Jack, one more thing – those bugs, where'd they go?"

"Last seen heading north." Hammerson exhaled loudly. "Damndest thing, they decimated the town and then vanished. We're still searching."

Matt frowned. "Could they have died off?"

"We don't think so," Hammerson replied. "We'll find them."

"Okay, good. So, what now?"

"In two hours a car will be out front. Travel light. You and the team will be paying a visit to Herr Rudolph Schneider, a collector of World War II memorabilia."

"Is he expecting us?" Matt asked.

Hammerson laughed, slow and deep. "Unlikely."

*

An hour and a half later, Matt had thrown some gear together and shut everything down. He still had about thirty minutes until pickup, and he decided to ping Lana, hoping he hadn't insulted her with his last abrupt message.

Hi Lana, sorry for getting dragged away. Something urgent came up – going to be out of town for a while. He sent it.

He waited for several moments, but his phone remained lifeless. He checked his watch and exhaled through pressed lips as he surveyed his now empty apartment. He had lied to Megan. She had asked him if there was anything to worry about and he'd said "No". These things usually sorted themselves out, he'd told her, and she should just forget about it.

So she had decided to go to her mathematics convention after all, and told him to go to hell with his bullshit stories. Next time he needed help, she'd said, he should ask one of his military bullyboys. He just hoped he could smooth things over with her when he got to his mom's place at Walnut Grove.

His phone vibrated, and he was thrilled to see it was from LanaPHD.

Hi Matthew, don't sweat it, I fully understand. I also have been requested to get involved in something urgent and extraordinary. Might be hard to catch me for a while.

Oh great. Matt felt even more depressed. Was this a brush-off? Or maybe payback because she thought he had shut her down a little too brusquely?

Everything okay? He messaged.

The response came back immediately.

Of course. By the way, you'd better ask me out for drinks or dinner soon ... or else.

Deal, just say the word, he sent. He waited, but she was gone. He didn't know if he felt better or worse.

CHAPTER 12

Milford Sound, New Zealand west coast, the Maori marae

It had just gone 1 am and Roy Maddock entered the marae and stopped just inside the door. He turned slowly and changed vision spectrums from light assist, to amplification, and then to thermal, sighting the many sleeping bodies flaring with an orange glow. He changed back to light assist, and then saw the stone exactly where it was supposed to be.

The full infiltration suit he wore was matte black and absorbed ambient light, making it a smudge in the darkness. But its technology also gave the wearer mechanically assisted power, while delivering the silence of a wraith.

He held a duplicate stone under one arm. The objective was to retrieve the original, replace it, and then leave without trace.

As Maddock crossed the marae, he detected movement and one of the figures came at him like a charging bull.

The infiltration suit had numerous sensors to deliver a 360-degree defense field – a form of "eyes in the back of his head". Plus the hydraulics gave the wearer the power of three men on top of the already above normal strength of the Special Forces soldier.

He shot out an arm, grasping the throat of the charging Maori warrior and closing off any yell. The burly young man still managed to throw a punch with enough force that it would have felled a normal man. But Maddock barely flinched from the impact.

He let the replacement stone slide gently to the floor and pulled a long-barreled gun from a holster on his thigh, aimed it at the young man's stomach and fired. The ice dart entered the skin, immediately melted, and in a few seconds the man's struggles slowed and then stopped.

One-handed, Maddock carried the 240-pound man back to his sleeping place and carefully lay him down. By morning it would seem nothing but a bad dream.

Captain Roy Maddock stood silently, watching for a moment, but no one else woke, so he reholstered the dart gun, lifted the replacement stone again, and went to where the original stone sat behind the throne.

He picked up the age-old 150-pound tablet and tucked it under one arm like it weighed nothing, moved the replacement into place, and then silently exited the marae.

In another five minutes he was heading over the cliffs in the stealth helicopter for a rendezvous with a boat waiting just half a mile offshore.

CHAPTER 13

"Take me through it." Colonel Jack Hammerson put the scientists on speaker as he watched their live feed.

"Yes, sir. Basically, this is the most amazing thing Doctor Miles and I have ever seen ... *anyone* has ever seen." Phillip Hartigan was one of the chief military biologists working at USSTRATCOM, and he led the analysis project of the biological sample brought in from the devastated town of Blessing.

"This thing is a biological wonder, and absolutely unique. Frankly, Colonel, it shouldn't even exist."

"Looked like one hellova big ugly bug to me," Hammerson replied. "So we agree it's weird and ugly – what else can you tell me?"

"For a start, it might not be a bug at all," Hartigan said. "We're simply fascinated –"

"Then what is it?" Hammerson cut him off. "And where'd it come from, or where's it been hiding?"

"Images coming through now," Hartigan said.

Hammerson's screen pinged as the scientist's image folder appeared. He opened it and looked through the magnified images of the bug thing, in various states of dissection.

"So, like I said, it's a big bug." Hammerson squinted. "With extra legs ... that attacks people?"

"Yes and no," Hartigan said. "It certainly has arthropod morphology, but it doesn't correspond to any entomological classifications that we know of. And there's no match in the historical or fossil records that we can find, although insectoids didn't tend to fossilize all that well. Anyway, I want to direct you to image one." Hartigan waited.

"Got it." Hammerson stared at the spread-wide creature with a slide scale next to it. The Blessing specimen was around two inches in length and shiny black.

"Doctor Miles." Hartigan handed over to his assistant.

Hammerson heard the young woman's voice take over. "Colonel, on first pass it does look like an insect due to its exoskeleton and segmentation. But the first anomaly apparent is it has eight legs, more like an arachnid, and it injects a form of venom, also like a spider. However, as well as having a carapace exoskeleton, it also has scaling. Interestingly, the scales are epidermal, like those of a reptile rather than a fish. Plus there is a downy fur on its underside."

"It's a damn bit of everything." Hammerson grunted.

"Exactly our thoughts," Hartigan agreed. "Like evolution took a bit of everything along the way to establishing its form. But all of that pales into insignificance to what we found next."

Hartigan paused, perhaps for effect. Hammerson didn't have the time. "Let's keep it moving."

"Okay, well, everything on Earth, from the lowliest bacterium to the most sophisticated mammal, is a carbon-based life-form." Doctor Miles sounded a little breathless. "This thing isn't."

"Wait a minute." Hammerson sat forward. "What are you saying, it isn't from Earth?"

"No, no, I think it definitely had a terrestrial evolution, but its basic structure is silicon-based. Every scientist involved in evolutionary biology has theorized this possibility."

"My understanding is silicon is a hard chemical element, something like quartz. Is that what these things are?" Hammerson frowned.

"Not quite. But you're right in that silicon is a chemical element acting as a hard and brittle crystalline solid. But it's one that's an essential element in biology." Hartigan sounded excited. "You see carbon is the backbone of every known biological molecule. Life on Earth is based on carbon, likely because carbon atoms are well suited to form the long chains of molecules that serve as the basis for life as we know it, such as proteins and DNA." He cleared his throat. "Are you still with me, Colonel?"

"Of course, go on."

"Well, the thing is, carbon and silicon are chemically very similar in that silicon atoms can also each form long-chain bonds. Moreover, silicon is one of the most common elements in the universe. Did you know that silicon actually makes up almost thirty percent of the mass of the Earth's crust and is roughly one hundred and fifty times more abundant than carbon in the Earth's outer layer?" Hartigan sounded a little awed.

"No, I didn't. But I see what you're getting at – why didn't life start out as silicon-based rather than carbon-based?"

"Exactly." Hartigan sounded like he'd slapped a tabletop. "Life had all the raw materials there for it. It's always remained an open scientific question why life on Earth is based on carbon when silicon is more prevalent in the Earth's composition. And now maybe we have our answer."

Hartigan took a deep breath. "This specimen seems to have moved along an entirely different evolutionary path to what we know. It feeds on and converts organic silicon into its own physical structure."

"Bones." Hammerson breathed. "The bones in the bodies were missing."

"Not just bones," Hartigan said, "but hair, teeth – anything that has organic silicon would have been consumed. It latches on with hook-like teeth around the mouth parts, and then uses a hypodermic-like feeding apparatus that we believe injects a substance that liquefies its chosen food source and then simply sucks it back out."

"Those poor folk," Hammerson muttered.

"Yes, those poor folk … over eight hundred of them. Plus every horse, dog, cat, cow, sheep, and wild critter in that town was consumed. Or at least the parts of them these things prefer," Hartigan said. "There must have been thousands of them, many thousands of them, Colonel, to consume so many organisms in such a short period of time. So, the million-dollar question is, where'd the swarm go?"

"Where indeed?" Hammerson asked softly.

"That's all we've got on the sample analysis so far …"

"Okay, very good, Doctor Hartigan. Continue with your investigations and I'll be in touch." Hammerson moved to disconnect the call.

"One more thing, Colonel," Hartigan rushed in.

Hammerson waited.

"The sample creatures you brought in – they were splitting down the back, naturally, as if they were outgrowing their shell." Hartigan sighed. "I think they were about to molt, and to get bigger."

They're growing. Hammerson ran a hand up through his iron-gray crew cut. "How much bigger?" He turned.

"Who can tell?" Hartigan shrugged. "But the Permian, about three hundred million years ago, was referred to as the age of insects. Bugs were enormous, spiders the size of hubcaps, dragonflies as big as eagles, and millipedes ten feet long."

Doctor Miles sounded like she came closer to the speaker. "And then there was an anomaly unearthed in China in 1984 – a sample cast in amber from late in the Permian period, just a fragment, mind, but it was clearly insectoid." She gave Hammerson a crooked smile over the video link. "It corresponded to some sort of beetle-like creature that stood six feet tall, and might have weighed two hundred pounds."

"Could these things get that big?" Hammerson asked.

"At this time, we can't answer that, Colonel." Hartigan's face was deadpan.

The silence stretched for a few seconds as Hammerson processed the information. Like Kearns had said, time was catching up with them.

"Thank you, doctors." He disconnected the call and leaned back in his chair.

Colonel Jack Hammerson looked at the creature's image on his screen, and felt a primal horror. These things were beyond deadly, but he couldn't imagine how much worse it'd be if they got bigger.

And Hartigan was right – *Where are they now?* was the million-dollar question. But right then, not he, or anyone else, had even a two-bit answer.

CHAPTER 14

Treptow, Germany

Matt looked down the cabin toward the three huge elite Special Forces soldiers, called HAWCs, which stood for Hotzone All Warfare Commandos.

There were two men and one woman, and he didn't know any of them. But he knew their boss, Jack Hammerson.

He kept watching them for a moment more; right now they were in civilian dress, but had kit bags that had their "work gear" inside. Plus, Matt bet they had more weapons than he could count.

The biggest and oldest of them, who looked to be in his late thirties, and was their team leader, was Roy Maddock. He was coal dark and shaven-headed and had shoulders that strained his bomber jacket. He talked softly to the other two, giving instructions by the look of it.

The other male smiled easily. He was the youngest-looking and lantern jawed. Vincent "Vin" Douglas could have been on any starter's lineup for a college football team. Instead of tackling and running, his training was probably how to kill you quickly and silently in a hundred different ways.

The woman was Klara Müller, a German speaker who was ice blonde with the palest eyes Matt had ever seen. It made him wonder whether she was part albino. Once she had looked down the cabin at him, and he smiled and nodded in return. But she just stared back the way a cat intensely studies its prey before pouncing. She never blinked and, after a while, Matt simply looked away. She was the only one that unsettled him.

What had struck Matt about these types of Special Forces soldiers were they were a rare combination of intelligence, tactical thinking, and deadly brawn. You were only invited to join HAWC after proving yourself in the SEALS, Rangers, Green Berets, or even in one of the other foreign Special Force units. Working with them made him feel safer, knowing that they were on his side.

"Ten minutes." The pilot's voice was low and calm.

Matt rubbed his face, already weary from the traveling. Hours back they had arrived in Ramstein Air Base, one of several US airbases across Europe and the headquarters for the United States Air Force in the continent. But then they had immediately left the plane and sprinted across the cold tarmac and jumped into a dark insignia-free helicopter.

Its blades were already turning but were whisper quiet. Onboard there was just a single pilot who checked his instruments until Maddock drew the heavy door shut and the chopper immediately lifted off.

Now they were on their way to Treptow, known as the billionaire's borough. Matt had been there once before – it was a place of huge parks, houses behind ten-foot fences, and more Rolls-Royce and Mercedes limos than you could poke a stick at.

It was also where Herr Rudolph Schneider – property mogul, software importer/exporter, and collector of World War II memorabilia – lived. And hopefully Schneider was still the current holder of the secret Hitler diary. At least he was according to Hammerson's intel.

He glanced at his watch – Megan had calculated they had two more days until the next event. And at this point he had no idea how the diary was going to help.

Roy got to his feet and sauntered down the cabin and sat beside him. "How you doin'?"

"I'm okay." Matt sat back.

Maddock continued to stare at Matt for a moment longer. "This diary must be important, huh?"

"Yeah." Matt thought for a moment. "Hitler was researching the supernatural for ways to give him the edge in the dying days of the war. Somehow he planned to use the tablet stones, and I believe the diary will tell us how."

"Use the stones like a weapon?" Maddock asked.

"Possibly, but he must have thought he could control whatever they unleashed." Matt turned to look at the huge man. "Maybe *exactly* like a weapon."

"Control the plague events." Maddock's eyes narrowed. "Yeah, we need to see that diary." He looked past Matt and out of the window onto the dark forest below. "Heads up, Professor." He got to his feet and ordered his team to prep for disembarking.

Vin had pulled out a computer tablet and brought up the schematics for their target – Rudolph Schneider's compound. It was a huge mansion set on several acres and backing onto parkland. When Schneider looked out from his upper floors it would look like he was living in a never-ending countryside, with his own waterfall, rivers and lakes. It was a secluded paradise for the mega rich and uber famous.

For the HAWCs it was perfect – they could land in the secluded and darkened park, and strike out from there. Matt watched as the soldiers seemed to agree on a plan and he sat forward.

"What do you want me to do?"

"You're coming in with us," Maddock replied. "I've got your kit, and you're going to suit up now."

Matt groaned, but already guessed he wasn't here just to make up the numbers.

"We want to be in and out, and on our way home in two hours, well before the sun comes up." Maddock threw him a pack that thumped heavily at his feet. "Let me know if you need help."

"I've done this before." Matt opened it, and found the same night-black clothing the HAWCs were putting on.

The pilot must have switched over to silent running mode as the sound of the already quiet chopper blades vanished completely. Maddock turned out the internal lights.

Matt touched his chest, feeling the solid plating over the pectorals; he rapped on it with his knuckles. He also wore the head and facial unit that were of a light material with lenses over the eyes that illuminated ambient light sources.

Maddock held up five fingers as the craft came down feather light and Matt felt his heart rate kick up. Maddock counted down from five, four, three, two, one – he pulled the door back as the wheels were only just settling, and they all leaped to the ground.

They were in Treptow Park, not far from the Schneider compound's fence-line, a ten-foot concrete wall running all the way around the perimeter of his estate.

Matt knew the plan – once they scaled the wall, they were to quickly locate Rudolph Schneider who would be inside a house that covered over thirty thousand square feet, had over fifty bedrooms, packs of patrol dogs, seven fully armed guards, electronic surveillance and was also heavily fortified – simple, really.

In a few minutes the team was at the wall. Vin went up first, reaching back to grab Maddock's hand to haul him up. Then came Klara and finally it was Matt's turn.

They dropped lightly to the grass on the other aside and Matt marveled at how quickly and efficiently the soldiers worked.

Klara and Maddock pulled telescoping rifles from over their shoulders and lay down flat. Vin took out a small device the size of a laptop computer and opened it up. A small lens telescoped out from its front and he angled it toward the massive house.

Maddock lifted his head from his scope. "Here comes our welcome party – the mobile bear traps." He sighted again. "Let's put 'em to sleep."

Multiple dogs bore down on them, and Maddock and Klara fired off several well-placed shots. The sprinting animals were all hit; they slowed and then simply toppled onto their sides.

"That's them out of the way for a few hours." The pair compressed their tranq-guns and slid them up over their back again.

"Walls are fortified, but we still have good clarity," Vin said. "Eight bodies inside, five downstairs, and three up. Only one seated – gotta be our guy."

Maddock nodded. "Good." He reached into his pack and pulled out a small dark box. He opened the lid to display a touchpad and began to key in some data, and then enabled it.

He waited for a second or two until he was satisfied with what the machine was telling him. "Confirm, comm-net now enabled over the compound – their communications will be down for sixty minutes." Maddock got to his feet. "Kearns and I will go in on the first-floor balcony. You two introduce yourself to the muscle on the lower floor."

"Roger that." Vin closed his scanner and then he and Klara sprinted for the left-side corner of the huge mansion. Maddock waved Matt on to follow him and they moved toward a smaller structure attached to the side of the main building. It was possibly a gymnasium or indoor swimming pool.

Maddock scaled the building like a mountain goat. And even though Matt was extremely fit from years of surfing, he found it difficult to keep pace with the HAWC.

In another few leaps Maddock was hanging on the outside of the large upper balcony, and he reached back to haul Matt up beside him. He put a gloved finger to his lips.

There were two men slowly walking along the balcony edge, and Matt and Maddock pressed themselves flat to the railing. As the guys went past Maddock leaped up and over, and slammed a flattened hand in underneath one of the men's ears. He fell like a rock. The other big man turned, and Maddock lashed out, firstly to his throat, immediately cutting off his voice with a blow to the larynx.

But the guard was a professional and had time to reach inside his jacket and drag out a gun. He was fast, but the HAWC was faster, grabbing his wrist, removing the gun, and then using his elbow to jerk it back and catch him under the chin, snapping his head up. He too fell backwards.

In a few seconds, Maddock had plastic-cuffed their hands behind their backs and then also cuffed the hands to one of their legs. He lastly taped their mouths, and then waved Matt closer.

Matt was both impressed and surprised. HAWCs were the most lethal forces on the planet, but Maddock had chosen to only incapacitate the guards, even though it had slowed him down. Matt could only guess that these men had received special treatment because Germany was an ally.

The pair then went to one of the window-doors and peered in. It was a grand bedroom, but looked empty, so they guessed it was an unused guest room. Maddock quickly ran a pencil-like device around the outside of the door – taking out any alarms, Matt assumed.

Maddock pushed it inward, and they entered.

Then from downstairs there came a shout of alarm. Maddock and Matt froze.

*

Vin turned to Klara. "Orders are non-lethal."

The female HAWC looked briefly at her younger teammate. "Objective is to secure the floor, with overriding priority to obtain the target. Non-lethality depends on them." She then focused her pale, laser-like gaze on the room's golden interior.

Everything seemed to be gilded, crystal, marble or have a rich burgundy material covering the furniture's cushioning, rugs, and drapes. It was a veritable palace.

Vin held up his wrist using the same device that Roy Maddock had used on the upper balcony doors to deactivate any alarms. He then drew forth another pencil-sized instrument and inserted it into the lock. There was a hiss and a click and the door was open.

With one hand on the door handle, he counted down from three, and then went in low and fast. Klara followed.

The large entertaining area they crossed was lit up like a stage, so they changed their lens type for normal vision. Klara saw the guard as he came into the room and went to one knee. Vin didn't.

The guard saw the young HAWC and his eyes widened in surprise.

"*Target*," Klara said, causing Vin to turn.

For Klara, the guard was behind a column. He grabbed at his gun, but had to spend an extra second unclipping it from its underarm holster position.

Vin spun and fired, striking the guard in his gun-arm shoulder and spinning him around. He yelled a warning as he went down.

"Shit." Vin cursed his luck.

He turned to Klara, who muttered something, just as the other four guards poured into the room. This time they already had guns drawn and pointed them dead on Vin.

Klara pulled her second gun and stepped out. Machine-like, she shot each of the men in the forehead, the suppressers on her guns sounding like someone softly coughing.

The guard that Vin had shoulder-shot on the ground yelled again and she turned to him. She stared down with half-lidded eyes for a moment. And then also shot him in the head.

"Non-lethal takedowns," Vin hissed.

"He was alerting our primary target." She reholstered her gun, and then turned her laser-like gaze on the younger HAWC. "Lift your game."

*

Maddock pulled Matt closer. "We're outta time, stay behind me." He went through the door fast.

Matt followed on his heel, trying to keep up as the HAWC sprinted forward while trying to see everywhere at once. He had his gun up, and went into the hallway, moving along an opulent artworks-lined corridor.

From their reconnaissance they knew where the master bedroom and study were, and Maddock headed there first. All of the super-wealthy expect that there may be kidnap attempts, and so guard themselves accordingly. To that end they create defensive and offensive capabilities within easy reach.

As Matt and the HAWC leader burst into the enormous golden room a huge steel door was already closing at one end, and a wall covered in paintings was now concealing it perfectly.

The remaining guard was waiting for them, and swung to them with his handgun up.

"Down!" Maddock yelled.

Bullets flew and Matt dived to the side. Maddock threw himself forward, also firing. He was faster by a quantum and a lot more accurate, and he hit the guard in the meat of the bicep. The man was spun around and his weapon flew from his deadened hand as he hit the ground.

Maddock went and placed a foot on the guard's wrist who glared defiantly up at the HAWC. He half turned to Matt.

"Translate for me." The HAWC stared back down at the man. "Do you want to live?"

Matt translated into perfect German. But the man's lips pressed shut and just continued to deliver his incendiary glare. Matt bet if he could he would have killed Maddock a dozen times over in the worst ways known to mankind.

"I don't have time for this." The HAWC team leader lifted his gun and shot the man in the other bicep. He spoke to Matt over his shoulder.

"Repeat."

"Do you want to live?" Matt repeated again in German, but the guard just emitted a strained but furious growl.

"Not much work for security guards in a wheelchair." Maddock pointed the gun at his knee.

"Wait." Through gritted teeth the guard nodded once. It had obviously dawned on him that his wages weren't worth permanent disability or a death sentence.

"Can the room be opened from out here?" Maddock moved the muzzle of his gun to point at the man's groin.

"*Nein,*" the man hissed and closed his eyes.

The HAWC fired a shot between the man's legs, nicking the material of his pants but not the flesh.

"*Nein, nein,*" the man yelled.

"I believe you." Maddock quickly cuffed him and then taped his eyes and mouth. The HAWC then stood and turned, lifting his chin.

"I know you can hear us, Herr Rudolph Schneider. You are probably thinking right now that you are safe, and the authorities are coming to rescue you. I assure you, they are not."

Behind them Vin and Klara entered the room, and nodded to him. Maddock turned back to the sealed door. "All your guards have been neutralized, and your communications are down. It's just you and us now."

Matt repeated the words in German.

From a speaker overhead they got their reply, in English. "I care not, I have stored supplies for a month. Do you have that much patience? I think not."

"No." Maddock smiled. "Not that much patience. But we do have cutting tools and just enough time to pry you out of your steel box like a pearl from an oyster."

"Who are you?" Schneider asked.

"People who don't want to hurt you," Matt said. "We don't even want *you*, just something that you have in your possession. And we'll return it after we've studied it."

"So, you are criminals or terrorists, and I do not negotiate with either." Schneider snorted. "See you in a month."

Maddock turned to Vin. "Cut him out."

"On it." Vin exited the room.

*

The young HAWC knew he had to move quickly. Though they had taken out the guards and also disabled the compound's communications, Schneider being offline for any period of time would raise red flags somewhere.

But the thing about safe rooms or panic rooms, and any vault-like space designed as a siege shelter for human beings, was they always had one wall a little weaker than the rest in the event that the occupier became incapacitated and needed to be retrieved.

Vin counted paces along the hallway. He stopped, took off his bulky backpack and removed a series of metal poles, clear tubes, boxes and electronics. He set to assembling something on a tripod. It was a steel box, glass tubes, and a series of lenses. Then he attached several steel pipes to the front.

The finished product looked like some sort of futuristic tripod mounted gun. He switched it on, and the insides lit up. He spoke into his mic.

"Cutting ... now."

A beam of thin red light was emitted from the front and struck the wall; it smoked and a tiny flame appeared before it burrowed into the panels. He already knew the paint, plaster, and wood paneling was only an inch thick, and behind it was the armored steel. Everywhere else the shielding was two inches thick, but his earlier soundings had told him that here was the weak point.

He hummed as he gradually moved the beam in a line along the wall.

*

Maddock smiled after receiving Vin's message. He put his hands on his hips and lifted his chin once again.

"So, Herr Schneider, I would suggest you move away from the center of the room, so as not to be cut in half by our laser. The one that is now opening the western wall of your steel box."

Maddock turned about for a moment. "Your opportunity to negotiate as equals is rapidly deserting you."

Matt shook his head. "Herr Schneider, I assure you, we mean you no harm. We just want the diary."

"The ... diary?"

Matt turned back to the hidden speaker. "Yes, Hitler's diary that we know you purchased over ten years ago from a local auction house. We know you have it. There is something in it we need to see."

Matt waited but there was nothing but silence. "Please, Herr Schneider, negotiate while you still have something to negotiate with."

"The diary contains nothing but fairy tales. Made-up stories by a great man under enormous pressure," Schneider replied.

"Probably, but I must read it. Sir, work with us, before you are forced to, and it all gets … messy," Matt implored.

"Whom am I speaking with?" Schneider's voice was quiet.

"Don't," Maddock ordered Matt.

Matt turned away. "I'm just a scholar searching for the truth. We believe that the diary might hold answers to some deadly events taking place right now, globally."

"The plagues, yes?" Schneider asked. "And if it doesn't?"

"Then it doesn't," Matt replied. "We all go home."

"If you stop your cutting, I will speak to you, Professor, and you alone. But I will not come out." Schneider sounded resolute.

Maddock looked up at the speaker briefly, and then to Matt. He nodded once. He then pressed the mic stud at his ear, and from outside they heard Vin's laser cutter shut off.

Maddock turned to Klara. "Let's go." He turned to Matt. "You've got five minutes." The pair went to step out of the room, but Maddock paused. "If anything happens to my man, then for you, Herr Schneider, it will be extremely painful." They stepped out of the room and shut the door.

Matt looked up at the speaker. "Okay, we're alone. Where's the diary?"

"Stand back please," Schneider said.

There came the whine of hydraulics and then the floor to one side of the room started to drop, cascading down to form a set of steps. Matt went to the top and stared down as lights came on.

"It's my private gallery," the German billionaire said.

Matt went down, and was followed by Schneider's voice, guiding him. As he reached the bottom, spotlights came on all around the large room.

"Oh wow," Matt whispered as he let his eyes run over the magnificent artifacts – on a tiny plinth there was a battered silver ring, there were German uniforms, medals, bars of gold pressed with the iron eagle symbol. There were hundreds of pieces. There was also an entire wall filled with items associated with Adolf Hitler. Matt had a creeping feeling that Schneider was a bit of a fan.

"What the ...?" Matt stopped in his tracks as he saw what was under a sealed bell jar. "You have got to be kidding me." He shook his head.

"Oh, I assure you it's real," Schneider said with a smirk in his voice.

There was a red velvet chair pulled up in front of it, as if someone had been sitting there simply gazing at the object.

Matt knew Schneider was watching him somehow, and he stepped closer to the container. The thing made him feel a little squeamish – not so much by what it was, but *who* it was.

Under the glass dome was a mummified head, grayish-brown hair was parted on one side and small bristling toothbrush mustache was under the flaking skinned nose.

"Adolphus Hitler, Führer und Reichskanzler of the Nationalsozialistische Deutsche Arbeiterpartei, and once almost ruler of the entire world." Schneider sounded triumphant.

Matt leaned forward, staring into the desiccated face. The eyes were half lidded.

"I thought Hitler and Eva Braun's bodies were both burned up," Matt said. "After they committed suicide in the bunker."

"Shot, hung, burned, but not destroyed," Schneider replied reverently. "Toward the end of the war Hitler embarked on a voyage of the supernatural world. Whatever he was doing imbued him with significant, how shall we call it, *staying power*. They say he had to be beheaded before they thought he was truly dead."

"They thought?" Matt reached out to lay a finger against the glass. It was freezing. "You're keeping him – *it* – cold," he said.

"Yes, he prefer –" A clearing of the throat. "It slows down decomposition," Schneider replied.

Matt squinted in at the half-lidded eyes, and he could just make out that the sclera were still white and not shrunken back at all. He shivered slightly as he looked at the ghastly head.

Please don't open your eyes, he prayed.

"I bought him from the Russians. It cost me ten million euros in gold bars. A bargain, I think," Schneider cooed.

"Yeah, right, bargain." Matt backed up a step, wiping his hands on his pants and feeling a little unclean. He looked about. "The diary?"

"In the long glass case to your left."

Matt saw the small red leather book immediately. He went to it, carefully opening the cabinet's lid and reaching in.

"You should really be wearing gloves. That item is *unique*." Schneider sniffed.

"I know, sorry." Matt started to flick through the pages, checking its authenticity.

"I could lock you in, you know. Your friends would never get to you." Schneider's voice became crafty.

Matt looked up to where the voice floated from. "But they'd get to *you*, and believe me, you wouldn't like that. They can be very ... brutal. Is that the sort of trade you'd like?"

There was silence for a few moments, and then: "I will not be expecting a receipt."

Matt held the diary up, satisfied with it bona fides. He was about to head up the steps when he paused. He looked around, quickly scanning the shelves, cabinets and walls.

"Hey, one more thing ... did you ever find the stone?"

Schneider snorted. "The *aussterben steins*? Like I said, the diary is a book full of fanciful dreams. So, no, I didn't even bother looking for something that was probably never real to begin with."

Matt mentally translated his reference – the *aussterben steins*: the extinction stones. *Same as what Megan had said,* he thought.

"Okay, fine."

"Professor," Schneider whispered.

Matt paused.

"I think you are a believer, yes, Professor?"

Matt nodded.

Schneider sighed. "Then I wish we could have met under different circumstances."

Matt reached the top of the steps and the gallery entrance began to close. He looked up. "I'm also sorry we had to meet this way. One more thing, Herr Schneider. Please don't come looking for us – these guys play for keeps." Matt headed out into the hallway.

"Of course," Schneider whispered. "But it is a small world, is it not, my friend?"

Matt paused, looking back at the speaker. He was sure there was amusement in Schneider's words.

He found Maddock, Klara and Vin waiting for him outside the room. He waved the small red leather book at them. "Got it."

Maddock snorted and held out a hand.

"Damn." Vin slapped a fifty-dollar note into it.

"Never doubted you for a second, Professor," he said to Matt and waved them on.

The group traced their steps back to where they came in over the wall, and collected their hardware as they went.

Outside, Matt jogged beside Maddock through the dark forest-like park. "Like you planned, all over in under two hours. What now? Head home?"

The HAWC team leader turned to him and half smiled. "Our job is far from done just yet, Professor."

"Huh? We got the diary," Matt replied.

Maddock bobbed his head. "It's like this: you walk into the hardware store to buy a shovel. Is it really the shovel you want?"

Matt frowned, but then got it. "No, no, it's not. It's a hole I really want. The shovel is just a way to get there."

"Correct." Maddock smiled.

Matt half smiled. "We have the diary, but need to use it to find the missing stone, right?"

"That's my orders. We'll leave the base and head somewhere secure while you work out where we need to go to find that stone. Nothing else matters right now." Maddock faced front and lifted his speed a little.

"And if I can't?" Matt tried to keep pace, but struggled.

"You will, Professor. I have great faith in you." He looked over his shoulder. "Plus I have another fifty riding on it." The man continued to power ahead.

*

Rudolph Schneider had exited his safe room and now sat at a console desk that had a wall of screens in front of it. He hummed a stirring Wagnerian tune as he accessed the Interpol global search engine.

Schneider had friends in high places. He also had them in low places. And one of them had sold him the Interpol-protected password used by the Kommando Spezialkräfte, the German Special Forces.

After the group of intruders had left, he had seen the bodies of his guards laid out in the living room on his internal monitors. He sighed and let his mind work for a moment.

He then stood and crossed to his man still bound and gagged on the floor, bleeding from twin wounds in each shoulder. He ripped the tape from his mouth.

"Ah, Bruda, a bad day."

"Sorry, sir, they were too quick." Bruda grimaced from the pain, and his face was already pale from blood loss.

Schneider used a finger to pull back the material of the man's shirt to examine the wound. "Nine millimeter, Glock, I think."

He eased back. "All the others are dead. What do you think we should do?"

"Police. Stop them from leaving." Bruda grimaced.

Schneider grunted and got to his feet. He opened a desk drawer and searched through his gun collection, selecting a Glock. He took the weapon back to Bruda and pointed it at his forehead.

"Wrong answer."

He shot the guard dead.

"Failure is not tolerated in the new order."

He replaced the gun in his desk and sat down. He'd use another of his black book contacts to call in a team of cleaners to tend to the removal of the bodies. No trace of them would ever be found, and no questions ever asked. After all, the last thing Schneider wanted was to be queried on why the group had targeted him.

Schneider used the recordings of the four intruders to search global audio files. As expected, the soldiers came up blank. But he got an immediate hit on the academic.

He sat back and read the file: Matthew Kearns, professor of paleo linguistics at Harvard university. He read the personal profile, found his home address, phone numbers, and even his social media data.

"You're a believer indeed, Professor. And an intelligent one, I see." He nodded. "You may just get the job done for us, this time."

Schneider had searched for the *aussterben steins* for many years. He'd told Professor Kearns that he thought they were a fantasy. But he had always suspected they were real. And now it seemed the Americans had some sort of new lead.

Schneider steepled his fingers under his chin, as he thought through his plan. He'd expended millions of euros and many years on a fruitless search. But now he had a team that would do it for him, and for free.

He grinned as he logged into another application. A global map showed a small red dot moving fast out of Germany. The tracker he had inserted in the diary when he acquired it would allow him to follow this team anywhere, as they chased down their lead to the missing stones.

He briefly glanced again at the rapidly cooling bodies of his guards, and shrugged. "Worth it."

Schneider then hit a few keys on the console, and the floor began to drop again. Downstairs he crossed to the west wall to press a hidden stud. A panel slid back revealing a screen that showed the world map. Small lights highlighted major cities and readouts displayed their populations.

There was a countdown clock set into the bottom that was nearing zero. Schneider smiled and nodded.

"The great extermination is almost upon us. But we must help it along to ensure it is fully successful." He turned to the bell jar with the mummified head inside. "And we must also ensure that the right people survive to rebuild."

He smiled as he seemed to listen, and then turned back to the screen, tracing a hand down along the east coast of America. "I agree. Our problem before was our exterminations were small-scale and artificial. So now we will leave the job to the expert – nature."

Schneider crossed to the bell jar, lowered his head in a small bow, and then went to one knee. "And I have great news, mein Führer. It seems the Americans can lead us to the stones."

He looked up into the flaking face. "They thought the thousand-year Reich would come to an end, but your disappearance was a mere bump in the road to your plans being enacted. We will rebuild a world in your image. This time, unbound."

Schneider's face lit up. "Thank you, my master. It is my honor to serve you." He then stood ramrod straight, and lifted an arm, hand flat. "*Seig heil, Seig heil, Seig heil.*"

In front of him, the ghastly head remained impassive.

CHAPTER 15

Matt sat with the diary open and a bright light shining down on it. He moved through the small pages that were filled with the Führer's ideas, jottings, drawings, doodles, and, on one page, even a flowery poem he had written to Eva Braun.

When the German leader was writing, his mind seemed like a pinball bouncing around all over the place. But the one thread that held it all together was an unshakable belief in myth and magic, and especially the dark occult.

He spent a fortune in stolen gold searching for a supernatural edge, and no artifact was off-limits – the spear of destiny, or the arc of the covenant, and then there were the mysterious *aussterben steins*: extinction stones.

Matt came across the image he had seen from long ago: a photograph, black and white and very grainy, of a stone similar to the one in New Zealand. It was obviously its other half or twin.

Klara sat close to him and motioned to the diary. "Everything you hoped for?"

"No, I can't read it," he grumbled.

Matt looked back at the woman who smiled, causing tiny lines to form on each side of her mouth. He looked into her eyes. They were luminous pale blue but with hints of frozen ice. He bet they almost glowed in the dark.

"The diary?" She frowned. "I can read German."

He grinned. "So can I, and all of the dialects. It's the stone's carvings I can't read. I mean, I could if they were clearer, but the image is too grainy."

"We have software programs that can clean it up," Klara said.

"No, you don't. Not this language," Matt replied. "No application is ever going to be able to clean up a language it doesn't recognize to begin with. If I had a few months I might be able to generate a program to recognize the symbols and make a best guess as to what they are. But time is not something we have a lot of."

She nodded. "So has it helped at all?"

Matt turned to her. He wondered whether it was just her turn to act friendly to him or if she was really interested. *It didn't matter*, he thought.

"Somewhat." Matt exhaled through his nose and went back to examining Hitler's words that surrounded the image of the stone.

"The original stone he had in his possession was definitely moved. And he hoped to retrieve the second half to ..." He frowned. "Initiate a targeted event, maybe." Matt turned to Klara. "How could he do that?"

"Create a targeted event? Like a targeted strike on his enemies?" she asked.

He nodded. "It confirms what we thought: Hitler imagined these stones could be wielded like some sort of weapon."

"A mad plan." She half smiled. "From a mad man."

"We won't know that for sure until we understand the stones a little more," he replied. "One thing that's coming through from his notes is that he was convinced he had something that would win him the war."

"We'd better find it then." She continued to watch him. "You're very intriguing, Professor Kearns."

He turned and her unblinking eyes bore into his. "Er, thanks."

She continued to stare, and Matt wondered whether she was expecting a return compliment. But then, was she really complimenting him?

He pointed at the diary, and she finally released his gaze. "Look here, this reference: *die Berge der Nachtvögel*. The only notation written in red ink."

"The mountains of the night birds." She frowned. "What does that mean?"

"It means the Owl Mountains."

Matt jumped at the HAWC team leader's voice. Roy Maddock had come up behind them so quietly it was like he had just appeared out of thin air.

"Jesus, man, a little warning next time," Matt said. "The Owl Mountains ... I've never heard of them."

"I'm not surprised," Maddock said. "But as World War II was ending, they were a hive of activity, albeit an extremely clandestine one. Let me see that."

He came in closer to crouch beside them and look down on the diary. Matt held up the small book.

"Not much to go on. But it is something." Maddock rested his forearms on his thighs.

"They were significant?" Matt asked. "How?"

"At the time, very significant," Maddock replied. "In 1944, Hitler authorized work on several huge bunkers, basically hidden underground lairs, that were to be his emergency bolt-holes. The best known was the Wolf's Lair, in Pullach, Eastern Poland. But by far the most secretive was the Riese bunker deep inside the *die Berge der Nachtvögel* – the Owl Mountains. He diverted twenty-eight thousand laborers to the job."

"Holy crap." Matt's mouth hung open. "How did he keep it secret with that many laborers working on it?"

Maddock smiled ruefully. "They were slave laborers, prisoners of war, and no one came home. The rumor is when their work was done they were all buried inside the cavern system in the mountain."

"Those bastards! That's one way to keep a secret," Matt seethed.

"Unfortunately, very true. But these were massive projects and the construction required three quarters of a million cubic feet of steel-reinforced concrete, over hundreds of thousands cubic feet of tunnels, and hundreds of miles of pipelines. These fortified hideaways were so important to Hitler that he diverted more concrete to them than was used for the entire German population for the construction of air-raid shelters."

"Holy shit." Matt was awestruck.

"They might have worked, kept him safe and hidden except for one problem." Maddock half smiled. "In January 1945, the Russian Red Army overran Eastern Europe, heading straight for Berlin. In panic, an SS Unit in the Owl Mountains ordered the tunnel system bricked up and sealed over, and all entrances hidden." He shrugged. "And that's when up to twenty-eight thousand POWs vanished."

"Have any of them been found?" Klara asked.

"No." Maddock scoffed. "But it's not surprising. At last estimation, there were still over a quarter of a million feet of tunnels, rooms, antechambers, and whatever else is down there, still unaccounted for."

Matt turned to Klara. "Then that's where it is, that's where the lost extinction stone has been hidden. I just know it."

Vin had joined them. "Maybe, like the legend goes, it's part of the Nazi treasure still buried in the Owl Mountains, including missing riches from all over Europe."

Maddock shrugged. "Nazi gold hunters started looking for the missing tunnels as soon as the war ended." He smiled flatly.

"Nearly eighty years." Matt groaned.

"We don't have decades, Professor." Maddock rose from his crouch.

Matt nodded. "There must be a clue in here somewhere." He sighed and looked back at the small red leather diary. "All we need to do is find it."

CHAPTER 16

Gorban sugar beet farm, Lviv district, Western Ukraine

Vasily Gorban and his sons worked the field. The ground was hard, the work backbreaking, and the sun beat down mercilessly, but Vasily couldn't help smiling as he watched his two boys rake, shovel, and gather in the dark red beets.

Andrei moved quickly, like a machine that never seemed to tire. But his younger brother, Bohdan, looked like he forgot why he was even there half the time.

But he loved them both, and they never complained of the hardships they faced since the seeming never-ending conflict with their huge neighbor that had dragged on for years now.

Vasily straightened and looked over his fields; they were scarred with old bomb craters that he knew he'd need to fill in one day. At least nothing had fallen for over twelve months, and the new Ukrainian president had opened dialogue.

He wasn't hopeful of an equitable outcome as he knew that Russia held all the cards. Ukraine had much national pride, but sometimes it was better to be satisfied with fifty percent of something, rather than end up with one hundred percent of nothing.

Vasily's trained ear picked up the sound of the airplane high above them. He craned his head back to hold a hand over his eyes. The dot in the sky seemed to be dropping something and, as he continued to watch, he saw the speck's rear bloom open with the canopy of small parachutes.

He frowned, not knowing what it could be. But it was passing directly over them, had dispatched some of its cargo right over their farm, and it was going to plummet to the Earth in his fields.

"Hey, what is this?" he asked.

Andrei and Bohdan lifted their heads and turned to him. They then followed his gaze.

Bohdan placed his hands on his hips as the thing descended. "Supplies? The new president said he was going to look after the farmers, remember?"

"I was not informed," Vasily replied, but felt his spirits buoyed at the thought of receiving something for free.

"Well, it's coming down right here, so maybe we should take a look?" Andrei dropped his rake and set off.

"*Stop!*" Vasily yelled, but the boys were already jogging to the package's arrival place.

In a few minutes he caught up and the trio stood on the edge of a shallow depression where the package had thumped to earth. They stared down into the crater at a large canister, with red blinking lights on its side. There were no markings, no letters, numbers, or anything to identify it.

Vasily frowned down at it, but Bohdan grinned. "I think it is something valuable." He turned back. "We will need the truck and a rope."

"Wait, look." Vasily pointed.

The red blinking lights on the canister turned green, and there was an audible click and hiss as an area along the side popped open. A cloud of vapor escaped.

Bohdan eased down the loose soil and crouched to lay a hand on the canister. He jerked it back. "It's cold. Maybe it's refrigerated food." He carefully put his fingers inside the lid section and prized it open further.

More gas escaped. At first the three men could see nothing as the clouds of gas were so thick. But in a few seconds the gas dissipated and they saw that the canister was filled with a glutinous liquid with small things packed in tight.

Bohdan squinted. "I think it might be olives or large nuts, or something."

In the warmth of the sun, the fluid began to agitate and then exploded into a thousand separate entities.

"Ah, god, cockroaches." Bohdan scrambled backwards.

Warmed and dried by the sun, the swarm poured out of the canister. Many took to the air, and it became thick with the deep *zumm* of glistening wings, and the clack of hard bodies as they jostled against each other.

Bohdan screamed as he was enveloped, and Vasily turned to his other son.

"Run."

The boy hesitated.

"*Run!*"

This time the boy turned and sprinted back toward their house. Vasily slid down the dirt slope toward his other son, who was screaming as though in the flames of hell.

It was then that the first of the bugs alighted on him. In seconds he too was covered, and the pain was like fire and needles all at once. Even though his brain gave commands for his arms to lift to try and ward the creatures off, his limbs refused to obey and just hung like long hairy sacks at his side.

The old man screamed from the agony. Thankfully it didn't last for long.

CHAPTER 17

Central Scientific Research Institute, Russian Ministry of Defense, Shchyolkovo, Moscow

Lead scientist Mikhail Verinko waited as Colonel Borishenko sat with his fingers steepled and watched the satellite footage of the results of their "seeding" program in the Ukraine. The town of Bibrka in the western corner of the Lviv district had been totally decimated.

Borishenko spoke without turning. "You have exceeded my expectations."

Verinko exhaled with relief and nodded so deeply he almost bowed. "Thank you, sir. The creatures are extremely voracious and efficient."

Borishenko grunted and turned back to the screen. "And where are they now?"

Verinko hesitated and Borishenko turned, casting pale eyes over him. The military man made him nervous and seemed to be able to smell falsehood, weakness, or indecision. After a moment, Verinko bobbed his head.

"We think the swarm might have died out."

"You know this for sure?" Borishenko asked, still pinning the scientist with his gaze.

"We believe so, but as you would expect we can't exactly send a team in there right now." Verinko waited, holding his breath.

Borishenko smacked his lips and stood. "So, all you know is they've vanished, yes?"

Verinko nodded.

Borishenko seemed to think about it for a moment, and then shrugged. "I don't care. If they do what is expected of them, and then all commit suicide, maybe it is for the best."

"Yes, sir." Verinko stepped back.

Borishenko headed for the door and paused with a hand on the handle. "Continue with your testing."

"Of course, sir." Verinko gave him a stiff salute, and turned back to the screen. He bit one of his nails as he stared at the Ukrainian landscape littered with bodies that were grotesquely flattened.

It was a horrible way to die, and even though as a scientist he was usually able to distance himself from the human cost of a weapon's field test, he couldn't help feeling a sense of unease.

He'd told Borishenko that the creatures had probably died, but he didn't really think that at all. They were still there ... somewhere.

CHAPTER 18

USA – USSTRATCOM Headquarters

Colonel Jack "the Hammer" Hammerson read quickly through the reports coming in that matched the characteristics of the massacre in the small town of Blessing.

Across the world, the profile and the aftermath were always the same: small, localized earthquake, followed by people, and every other damn animal, being killed. *Obliterated, more like*, he thought, furiously.

Except for in the Ukraine. For some reason, the small town of Bibrka was an outlier in that the swarm appeared without any previous quake. A new pattern emerging? *Still far too many unknowns*, he thought.

Hammerson looked again at the pictures of the corpses; for someone who had seen it all, and all manner of degradation that could be inflicted on the human body and soul, even Hammerson's strong stomach rebelled at the images of the bodies that had been *deboned*.

"Fuck it," he whispered. Those poor souls had been just left as bags of meat. He wished to god they died quickly. But he had already been told from the autopsies that many died from heart failure or suffocation, meaning they lived through the attack. Afterwards, their bodies couldn't function without bones. They couldn't breathe, and their hearts labored under the weight of their sagging flesh.

So far their investigations had located what they thought was the primary event in the Pothohar Plateau, Rawalpindi district, north-eastern Pakistan. The small town of Dhalla had been attacked, and over 600 people had been exterminated.

That was two weeks ago. But then a week later, just fifty miles to the north of Dhalla, the town of Munjindi had been attacked. This time some 5200 people were wiped out. The plague, invasion, or infection was spreading, and getting stronger. And from the body count, it seemed these things were getting hungrier.

CHAPTER 19

Halloday homestead, Brewster, Nebraska

Big Jim Halloday stepped out onto his porch and sipped from a huge mug of coffee. Sun was just coming up, and he knew the slight chill in the air would vanish real quick, leaving them with another dirt-dry, stinker of a day.

Been a while since rain, but last season was okay and the tanks still have plenty of water, so we'll be okay, he thought.

Jim was going to be sixty in a few weeks and was born and bred here. The town had grown around him and, unlike a lot of the nearby Texas towns, was holding its own on population growth – 2425 people last count, and even growing a little.

As the sun came over the top of the orange trees in his front yard the shadows started to retreat. He sipped and then clicked his tongue against his cheek.

"Damn gophers."

There were mounds everywhere. He frowned. Damn *everywhere.* And the more he looked the more he could see them pocking his front yard, all the way down the scrubby path to the road.

"What inna rat's ass?" He stepped down on the grass and walked toward one of the baseball-sized mounds. The dirt looked soft, as if something had been burrowing in just recently. He found a stick that was around three feet long.

He approached the mound again and began to stab into it. The stick sunk into the soft soil. He pulled it back out, looking at the tip, and then stuck it back in, a little deeper this time. He hit something hard, and he wiggled it around. The stick jerked, and then was tugged, almost from his hand.

"Don't like that, *huh*?" He grinned and pushed down hard on the twig and then jerked it back and forth, using the old toilet plunger technique. He drew it out and checked the end looking for some evidence of the thing, but there was nothing. He went to stick it back in again, even deeper. He paused. The soil was starting to lift out and the critter was coming on up.

Jim gripped the stick as the soil fell away, and then a black head emerged that was the size of a child's clenched fist. Jim's eyes widened when he saw it was no gopher. In fact, it was no creature he had ever seen before in his life.

The sun was up high enough now to spill over all the mounds in his yard and, as if receiving the same command at once, they erupted like tiny volcanoes.

The creatures fully emerged and shook themselves down. Jim could only stare at the thing in front of him. Its eyes looked eerily human and stared back.

The creature had to be eight inches long, solid, and resembling a massive hairy wasp with extra legs.

"Aw, Jezus, man." He backed up onto his front porch holding the stick out in front of himself. "You fellas just stay there now."

He had a twelve gauge on the rack just inside the doorway and thought he might just need it. As he watched, the first thing to emerge twitched and its wings unfolded.

Run for it, Jim's mind screamed. Big Jim Halloday, aged fifty-nine years, eleven months and twenty-two days, turned and fled.

There was a deep *zumm* and then the creature hit him and stuck to his back – scaring the living shit out of him.

"*Get the fuck offa me!*" He screamed, flapping big beefy arms up over his shoulders.

Its needle like legs clung to him, and then something like fire latched to his neck and burrowed in deep. But it was nothing compared to the pain that followed.

CHAPTER 20

Entering Polish Airspace

Matt pored over the small diary. The pages were cramped with Hitler's tight, forward-sloping handwriting. Pictures drawn in ink were interspaced with notes, references to other books, and personal quotes.

There were many from a Professor Rudi Hokstetor, and Matt assumed he'd been tasked with deciphering the unique language carved into the stone.

The things that Hokstetor had deciphered were obviously enough to convince Hitler to dispatch a U-boat on a secret mission to the farthest corner of the world to procure the other stone. It seemed he was building his future war effort around using whatever it was the stone promised.

Now and then Hitler had drawn some of the symbols, obviously from the stone he had, and Matt translated them.

"They have come and they will come again."

Matt straightened. It was exactly as he had deciphered from the other stone. But Hokstetor had added some of his own text: "They can be used."

"They can be used," Matt repeated softly. "So it *is* a weapon."

He sat back and rubbed his face, feeling the fatigue around his eyes. He closed them for a moment, and let his mind relax. He took himself back to calm beaches and waves that broke in blue tubes calling for him to ride them. He could almost smell the sea salt in the air as the wave broke onto a sandy beach somewhere in the tropics, and it became Lana's profile picture.

He jerked forward and quickly pulled out his phone. He messaged her.

Hi, miss you. What're you doing?

He sat waiting and watching the small screen. And waited some more, and then some more. But it remained mute.

A shadow fell over him and he tucked the phone back in his pocket before looking up.

"Supposed to be a comms blackout, Professor. Don't you know that?" Klara squatted in front of him.

"Yeah, don't worry, it was nothing." He sighed. "Just something I think I lost."

"Are you working with someone else? Spying on us, Professor?" Klara looked at him from under her brows, and her lips just curled at the corners.

"What? No." But for some reason she made him feel guilty. "That's just dumb."

"Don't make me torture you." She stared.

Matt peered back into her pale eyes and swallowed. "What?"

She held his gaze for a moment, but then broke into a low chuckle. She gripped his forearm. "I'm only playing with you. I know you're okay."

Matt swore softly and shook his head.

Klara rested her arms on her knees. "So, are you managing to pull anything else helpful from Adolf's personal thoughts?"

"Well, he definitely thought the stones were going to reveal to him some way to win the war. Something he could use as a weapon. Then when things were all going to crap for him, he hid the one stone he had in his possession somewhere in the Owl Mountains. We think."

Klara held out her hand and Matt placed the small leather book in it. She flipped some of the pages back, and then forwards. "I think the stone was too valuable to him to just leave it to someone else to hide without him keeping a record of where it was."

Matt threw his hands up. "I agree, but there are no coordinates. No map. Maddock tells me the tunnel system was numbered but there's not even a secret code I can find. I've translated all of the German I can see here, and even the areas where he has included the Aztlantean interpretations." Matt sat back. "Nothing but bad spelling, erratic thinking, and random marks and doodles while he planned his mass genocides."

She held the small book up. "Yeah, but this diary, this particular one, meant something to him. You said it was the *one* diary he kept with him at all times in the last few weeks of the war." She rubbed the cover with her thumb for a moment. Her mouth quirked up. "I think it's time you got inside his head."

Matt turned to her. "You know, I had the chance to do that last night ... get inside Hitler's head, I mean." He chuckled, darkly.

"I'm serious." She reached out to take hold of his arm again. "In the rules of engagement, when trying to understand a madman, use a madman's logic."

Matt nodded. "Okay, go on."

"Maybe there is a code hidden in here but not as you'd expect." She reopened the diary, flicking through the pages. "At the end, Hitler was paranoid, so he might have obscured important elements of his thoughts. Maybe some words written across several sentences that form a single important sentence? Something hidden right in front of you – you said yourself there were misspellings. Perhaps they weren't misspelled at all."

Matt sighed, and took the diary back. He stared down at the page again. After several minutes he began to shake his head and then used his thumb to fan through the pages. He stopped dead. Matt frowned and craned forward. "Hey." He quickly began to skip back and forth on the pages. "I think you might be right."

He smiled. "He *did* leave clues that are maybe more like a signature of sorts." Matt flipped some of the pages back again and then pointed to one of the doodles in the top right corner. "See this?"

There was an image of a rounded-looking cross, like a curved swastika.

"Yeah, I recognized it. It was one of Hitler's favorite doodles," Klara replied. "He started drawing that long before he even came to power."

Matt flipped the page. The image appeared in the top right corner again. He flipped the next page.

"And here." He turned more pages. "And here, and here, and then ... *look*."

On the next page the image had changed. This time it was like a tree, except the lines were straighter like a many-pronged trident or fork.

"Yeah, it's different," she observed.

"It's the only one like this and I don't think this is a doodle." Matt felt his excitement bloom in his chest. "I think it's a map. It's our way forward."

Klara leaned toward the page. "Holy shit – one of the prongs, just one, has a *dot* at its end." She looked up at him, her pale eyes blazing. "The Owl Mountains. If we knew where to start, we might be able to follow it."

"Many of the tunnels have been found, so I'm sure you guys could get some sort of schematic. That'll give us a scale, and also allow us to see what's already been located and mapped."

She nodded. "And if that particular tine of the fork hasn't been found?"

Matt sat back and folded his arms. "Then we just located the missing tunnel, and perhaps the lost extinction stone."

CHAPTER 21

Copernicus airbase, Wroclaw, Poland

Matt stamped his feet to keep warm as they waited for their new chopper to refuel. He watched as the pilot, a local, climbed into the cockpit. They also kept a lookout for a guide that Jack Hammerson had arranged to take them into the Polish interior.

The man was Alojzy Mazur, a retired military reservist and someone who supposedly knew the Owl Mountains like the back of his hand. Matt hoped he had big hands as the Owl Mountains covered an area of nearly eighty square miles.

Alojzy had apparently also acted as a guide for several of the larger companies and outfits that had searched for the missing Nazi gold and other looted treasures inside the tunnels.

The refueling was soon done, and Roy Maddock approached Matt.

"Our boy is late." Maddock looked over the mist-heavy airport. They were waiting at the far end of a runway, well away from any public scrutiny. As far as everyone knew they didn't exist and their mission wasn't recorded in anyone's book or flight system.

"I know it's a big area, but can we go on without him?" Matt asked.

"Sure," Maddock replied. "If we want to spend days just searching for the correct entrance." He exhaled, his breath escaping in a stream of vapor. "I spoke to the colonel, there's been more attacks. Whatever these things are, bugs or whatever, they're growing in size and number. Moving to bigger and bigger towns throughout the world. We need answers, Professor, and at this point all we've got is a 75-year-old diary, and a map based on a madman's doodling."

"Better than nothing," Matt shot back.

"It better be. Lives are at stake. Lots of them," Maddock countered.

A car sped onto the rear of the tarmac, causing Vin and Klara to ease back into the shadows and draw weapons. The car pulled up next to a maintenance shed, and the driver got out and waved.

"Stay cool," Maddock said.

The guy threw a pack over his shoulder and jogged toward them.

Klara and Vin reholstered their weapons but remained focused on the approaching figure.

"*Halooo!*" the guy waved.

Matt saw that he seemed to be mid-fifties, broad-shouldered and with a beard and mustache shot through with silver. He looked from the HAWCs to Matt and must have decided that Matt looked a little more approachable than the soldiers so made a beeline for him.

"I am you guide, Alojzy Mazur." He grinned, his teeth showing white through his thick beard. "Hello." He stuck out a large hand.

"Matt." Matt shook the hand and then pointed. "And –"

Maddock glared.

Matt continued, "… my friends."

Alojzy nodded. "I understand. Secrecy is important."

"Good man." Maddock waved them toward the chopper. "Give the pilot the coordinates of our destination and then we can brief you as we go. Time is catching up to us, so let's get moving."

The five people loaded into the helicopter, and in seconds they were away. The Sikorsky UH-60 Black Hawk, purchased from the US military by the Polish armed forces, could travel fast at around two hundred miles per hour so it would take them just forty-five minutes to reach the heart of the mountainous timberlands. The same journey by foot would take a week.

Matt looked out of the windows as they passed over the beginning of the woods. The Owl Mountains were situated in an ancient forestland of spruce, natural beech and yew. He'd done some quick research and read that the massive green mountains sometimes looked blue in the morning mist and they covered an enormous amount of wilderness.

It was an area of almost mythical beauty and, with its forests, mountain peaks, and dark valleys, was mostly inaccessible to even the most experienced hikers. Plus the geology was old: Precambrian gneiss rock that was hard and cold, and the perfect place to hide a person, or an entire system of caves and tunnels stretching hundreds of miles.

The four-bladed, twin-engine, medium-lift helicopter could seat a dozen fully equipped combat soldiers, so they had room to spare. Matt and the HAWCs were seated on each side of Alojzy in the rear cabin as he spread a map on a small portable table. Even with the sound muffled by the armor plating, they had to shout.

"Here." He tapped the map. "Here is the entrance to what was called Project Riese."

Maddock traced the map with his fingers for a moment, as though trying to memorize the topography. "What are our chances?"

Alojzy looked up and grinned. "There were seven underground structures located in the Owl Mountains and also beneath Książ Castle in Lower Silesia. Most have been found. But the historical experts believe there are still many miles of tunnels that were expertly sealed over and hidden." He tilted his head. "And believe me, many, many have looked for them."

Vin gave him a gum-chewing grin. "But we got something all those other suckers didn't have." He thumbed at Matt. "This guy."

"No pressure," Matt shouted back. "Do you have any sort of schematic of the already found tunnel systems?"

Alojzy nodded and pulled out a roll of paper that fitted over the map. It was a clear paper that showed through the mountains' topography as if X-raying the area. It was marked up with the tunnels – branching tree shapes in several places.

"Perfect." Matt produced a sketch he'd made of the diary drawing of the tree. "This is widely out of scale. But this is what we're seeking." He laid it beside the tunnel system, and began to slowly move it around, comparing to what was there.

"This one." He pointed.

"The Sokelec system." Alojzy nodded. "Could be. But there are differences."

Matt looked up. "Exactly. And it's the differences we're interested in." He looked at Maddock and raised his eyebrows.

The HAWC leader sat back. "Alojzy, give the pilot the coordinates of the Sokelec system. That's where we'll start."

*

It was mid-morning when the chopper lowered them into one of the few level areas where it was able to touch down.

Matt was first out and his cheeks prickled and his breath steamed in the amazingly cold, clean air as he waited. The land here was heavily forested and the geology so uneven it bordered on primordial. It seemed as far from human contact as was possible.

But it was in this very area some seventy years ago at the end of World War II, thousands of prisoners of war, plus German engineers and Nazi military personnel, built one of the most elaborate and sophisticated tunnel systems ever created.

The land had obviously healed. Or perhaps it had just grown scar tissue over the corruption still buried beneath its earthen flesh.

The rest of the group jumped down from the chopper with their kits, and all assembled around Roy Maddock as they waited for the machine to lift off. In seconds it had vanished over the treetops.

Maddock looked around slowly, sniffed and listened for a while. The other HAWCs did the same. Matt knew they were probably smelling for wood smoke, tobacco, or even aftershave, and perhaps also listening for any sounds of habitation. A helicopter touching down would undoubtedly intrigue anyone in the area, and the HAWCs didn't want company.

Maddock turned to their Polish guide. "Alojzy, we're in your hands. Take us in, sir."

Alojzy checked a small GPS device and then motioned with a flat hand. "This way." He led them into some of the thickest forest Matt had ever seen.

CHAPTER 22

USA – USSTRATCOM Headquarters

Hammerson held the phone from his ear for a moment as he read from his screen about the latest reports from mainland China. It seemed they were carpet-bombing large areas of their countryside with high-intensity thermite ordnance.

He knew what they were doing – cauterizing an infection. Just like in a lot of other areas of the globe right now, the weird bugs were surfacing and ravaging the countryside. Everything living was being sucked dry.

Bone dry, he mused darkly.

He put the phone back to his ear. "The Chinese are cleansing their countryside with thermite. You told me these things are almost impervious to heat. Will it work?"

Phillip Hartigan, one of the senior scientists working at the biological warfare section of USSTRATCOM, ummed for a moment.

"They're impervious to extreme temperatures, but if you use enough heat then anything can be incinerated, melted, or transformed. But broad carpet-bombing is hardly a precision tool, is it?"

"No, it is not, so I'm assuming there's no live bodies in their kill zone. And if there were survivors before, then they're not survivors anymore," Hammerson replied evenly.

"There are other options for dealing with silicon-based life-forms," Hartigan said.

"What else have you got, because I'm reserving recommending carpet-bombing our home territory for a last resort and even then I can't see the president ever signing off on it." He sighed. "Until it becomes inevitable."

"I've been running tests on the sample specimen. The carapace is mainly a biological silicon chitin. It's very tough and more similar to a form of super-tough glass than the long-chain polymer component of exoskeletons of arthropods such as crustaceans and insects."

"Yeah, and?" Hammerson wished these guys could say something in five words instead of fifty.

"Acid," Hartigan replied. "To be precise, the best acid to dissolve silicon-based compounds is hydrofluoric."

Hammerson groaned. "Hydrofluoric acid? Seriously?"

"Yes, I know it is dangerous to work with. But it'll give you the best and fastest results. Risk verse return, Colonel."

Hammerson tilted his head back for a moment. "We tried that for chemical weapons decades back, but abandoned it." He sat forward. "The damn stuff remains suspended in the atmosphere for days and will permanently damage lungs and eyes. But the main reason we junked it was if it gets into the waterways, it can stay there for years and also becomes aqueous hydrofluoric acid. It's a contact poison that has a nasty habit of hanging around and giving you deep epidermal burns and necrotizing tissue death. I'd rather a fast and clean burn than using that."

"Colonel, my job is to give you some options. Use them or not," Hartigan retorted.

The scientist sounded offended; Hammerson couldn't care less. "That's not enough. Bottom line, we need more information.

There's a major swarm moving over Texas, and smaller swarms starting up in Wyoming, North Dakota, and Ohio. At this point the National Guard is the first line of defense. But I don't think simple man-power is enough, do you?"

"Probably not, sir." Hartigan said slowly. "Colonel, one question: which direction are the swarms headed?"

Hammerson thought for a moment, and then tilted his head. "Not in the same direction, and in no pattern we can discern."

"Could they be converging?" the scientist asked.

"Unknown at this time. And on what?" Hammerson leaned forward.

After a moment, Hartigan shook his head. "Interesting."

"Interesting?" Hammerson's jaws clenched for a second and then he leaned forward onto his elbows. "Listen up, I want to know all about these things' breeding cycle, lifespan, internal organs, where they're from, and then a million other things in between. I want to know everything about them so I can freaking wipe them out, faster, more completely, and without rendering swathes of our countryside uninhabitable."

Jack Hammerson rubbed a hand through his iron-gray crew cut. "And before they goddamn wipe us out first."

CHAPTER 23

The Sokelec system, the Owl Mountains

Matt paused to suck in a deep breath. They'd been trekking for an hour along the side of a small forest-clad mountain with the trunks of the trees so thickly pressed together that even in the late morning sunshine it was still little more than twilight.

The air was cool and dry and, coupled with the exertion of the hike, quickly dried the mouth and throat. Though they expected to only be searching for a few days, Matt knew they'd need to preserve their water.

They came to a ridge, and Alojzy consulted his GPS once again. Matt stood beside him and followed his gaze – down in the gorge there was a small valley with what looked like a dry river course at its base. But other than that he saw nothing.

"This is it," Alojzy announced.

"It is?" Matt squinted. "I was expecting a huge tunnel mouth or something."

Klara scoffed. "You remember that bit about them being hidden tunnels, right?"

"Yeah, I knew that." He rolled his eyes. "I'm just saying there's hidden, and there's invisible."

"This way." Alojzy led them down the slope, and in another ten minutes they were at the bottom of a gorge. The ground was unnaturally level and hard packed, and gravel had been pressed into it.

"This was a path or road once," Maddock observed. He pointed to the left and right flank and Klara and Vin spread a little wider.

Though Matt doubted the HAWCs expected to run into any opposition, there could have been treasure hunters, squatters, or local survivalists about, and in Poland many of them were bad-tempered and well-armed.

The path ended at a cliff face with trees standing at its base, and a sheer granite wall rising hundreds of feet above them. Alojzy took them in and then turned to grin back over his shoulder.

"Here."

Set in among hanging vines and drooping branches were two massive green-tinged iron doors, twelve feet high and twenty feet wide, that were partially swung inward. The designers had known that doors that open outward can scar the ground and leave telltale signs for searchers from above.

Maddock nodded to Klara and Vin who switched on their rifles' barrel lights and headed in.

"*Clear ... clear,*" came echoing voices from inside after a few moments.

"Shall we, Professor?" Maddock turned with a small smile to Matt. "I believe this is where you take the lead."

The group switched on their flashlights and headed in. Matt sniffed, and smelt rusting iron, dank earth, and a hint of something like ammonia that might have been animal droppings. *Probably bat shit,* he guessed.

"Any bears around this part?" he asked.

Alojzy shrugged. "Yes, but very rare here." He lifted his brows. "Wolves, we have plenty of."

"What sort of wolves?" Matt stopped.

"Little ones, like poodles." Vin winked.

"Wolves prefer smaller dens, not big open tunnels. They'd be more wary of bears than we are." Maddock waved them on. "Let's go, Kearns."

Matt conferred with the Polish guide for a moment and they worked out the point of intersection where Alojzy's map said there was nothing, and Matt's drawing hinted at another tunnel.

After another moment Alojzy looked up, got his bearings, and then headed in deeper.

There were pools of water, and the sound of dripping. It was cool and became even colder the further inside they went. After only a short distance, their breath steamed in the beams of their lights. The tunnels were wide – big enough for a jeep to travel along the pathway.

There were also smaller side tunnels, and some looked to have housed barracks or maybe sleeping quarters. Rotted furniture lay in corners, and in one room, Matt backed out slowly holding his breath. He bumped into Vin and put a finger to his lips.

"Wassup?" Vin whispered, lifting his gun. Matt simply pointed to the roof.

Vin looked up. Overhead the tunnel was crowded with hundreds of bats, all jostling and fidgeting but silent for now. The smell from the ammonia of their concentrated urine made Matt's eyes sting. On the floor and in among the bat droppings, huge carnivorous beetles rummaged and searched for any bats that fell to the ground from old age, disease, or an unlucky dropped youngster.

Matt and the others continued on, and came to several areas with fresh-cut rock. In one place there was a large area of blackened stone with vein-like cracks running through the ceiling and surrounding walls.

"Looks like someone started to do some exploring," Maddock observed.

Vin poked his head into one of the new excavations. "Nothing. Looks like they came up empty here."

"Came up empty everywhere, that was the problem," Alojzy replied morosely.

They continued on, and found more excavations, even some in the floor. After another twenty minutes, Alojzy started to slow.

"Coming to last big junction of tunnels." He turned to Matt. "Let me see your map again."

Matt held out the drawing and the Polish guide studied it for a moment more. "At the last junction, this says there should be another tunnel." He exhaled through his nose. "I know this area, and there is no such tunnel."

They walked another few thousand feet and the air started to grow thicker. Finally they reached a large chamber that had further branching tunnels.

"Smells like a garbage dump," Vin observed.

"Is that good or bad?" Klara asked.

"Here." Alojzy turned. "This is where Professor Kearns' map says is start of hidden tunnel."

The group stopped and shone their lights in all directions. The excavated room was large, at least one hundred by eight hundred feet. The single tunnel they had come from branched into three more tunnels at its northern end.

"According to the picture from the diary, the missing tunnel opens up from in here … *somewhere*," Matt pronounced.

He still felt confident and enthusiastic as he panned his light about. There were excavation areas on many of the walls, indicating that others had been here before them, digging, maybe even searching for the same thing.

"What exactly are we looking for?" Klara said.

Matt exhaled through his teeth. "Something that the others missed. A push-stone, lever, code word, or even an area that sounds hollow when we tap it. It's gotta be here."

Maddock pulled his knife and flipped it in his hand. "Good place to start. Everyone pick a quadrant and give it the tap test."

In seconds the tunnel was filled with the sound of thumps and taps against the cold stone walls.

Matt looked across to Klara, who caught his glance and winked back at him.

She tapped: *tap – tappy – tap – tap*.

He couldn't help replying: *tap – tap*. He grinned back.

"Anything?" She asked.

"*Nada*." He looked at his section of wall. "Just plenty of graffiti."

"Yeah, everywhere," she replied.

Many areas had words, names, and curses chipped into and scrawled on the walls. Some of it in German, some in Polish, French, and even English. All of it related to the hopelessness of the plight of the prisoners forced to work in the darkness and the constant falling rock dust.

But none of it indicated an entrance. It took them twenty minutes to go all the way around the walls and meet up again.

"Nothing," Vin said.

Maddock clicked his tongue against his cheek. "Hundreds upon hundreds of miles of tunnels, and millions of tons of rock above and below us. We need some better clues or we'll be searching for years."

"And could still come up empty," Vin added.

"Welcome to my world." Alojzy shrugged his bear-like shoulders.

"Come on, Professor," Maddock said, "you brought us here, so you need to read the signs, and give us something to work with. We're standing in the center of a mountain with nothing but flashlights and shitty moods."

Matt nodded and looked around again. He began to pace, circling the huge room. He stopped and turned. "In the center of a mountain."

The silence stretched as the group waited and watched him.

He held his flashlight out and panned it around. "We've looked all around the room, on a horizontal perspective. But there could be an entrance above or below us." Matt lifted his light.

"How we gonna tap the roof?" Vin looked up at the ceiling two feet above his head.

"Look for a sign first," Matt replied. "Anything that shouldn't be there, or looks out of place. We start high, then we look low."

Once again the group circled the room, lights slowly moving over the ceiling. When that was completed, they moved to the floor. This was a little harder as there were pools of dank water, or a layer of dust that had turned to a slimy glue-like mud.

"Last throw of the dice," Maddock said.

The group tapped, kicked, scraped, and tried to wipe away as much of the ground scum as they could. But the surface area was large, and in the darkness the murky water kept refilling any areas that had been wiped out.

Just when Matt thought the map he had made from the diary was wrong, Maddock clicked his fingers.

"Professor."

The HAWC team leader was near a wall that ran with dark water. He scraped a boot along the ground and then stood back, pointing his light down.

Matt saw what he was illuminating – one of the curled swastikas, almost flowery in its design and no bigger than a watch face. The murky water quickly covered it over again.

"Hard to see." Maddock smiled.

"I'm betting it's supposed to be. And why it's been overlooked." Matt grinned back and then scraped his boot over it, exposing it briefly once again. "Hitler's personal mark."

Matt went to his knees. He used the side of his hand to push more of the sticky mud out of the way so he could inspect a greater area, but the curled cross was the only mark there. He then started to hammer with the hilt of his knife. After a moment he looked up.

"It's a solid surface, like a skin, but I think it might be hollow underneath."

Roy and Vin joined him, doing more tapping and marking out the size of the hollowness beneath them. After another few minutes they had marked out a square roughly eight feet wide.

"So, the missing tunnel is underneath us. Has been the whole time." Alojzy chuckled. "I think we might get rich soon."

"Now what?" Matt stared at the tunnel floor. He couldn't help feeling vindicated.

"We blow it," Klara said. "Shaped charges at the edges."

"Hang on, we could collapse it," Matt replied. "Cave everything in on top of the tunnel."

"Start small, shaped charges, blow a layer away at a time," Klara countered.

"I agree," Maddock said. "We didn't bring a jackhammer, and if this is an artificial floor then it won't be solid granite. We use small shaped charges and see what happens." He nodded to Klara. "Make it happen."

Without a word the tall woman dropped her pack, removing a plastic box that contained several foil-wrapped packages, plus slim, battery-sized rods. She expertly peeled away pieces of the putty-like substance and placed them in an x-shaped pattern across the sealed entrance. She finished by sticking a detonator into one of the blobs and also a small timer.

She leaned back on her heels. "Should just lift away the top layer, I guess." She turned to wink at Matt.

"Give it one minute," Maddock said.

Klara nodded and set the dial, then stood.

"Let's go." Maddock began to jog back along the tunnel and Matt headed the other way.

"*Hey*, you!" Maddock yelled. "This way. If the tunnel collapses, you want to be on the exit side."

"Shit." Matt sprinted back toward the group. He rounded a bend and Klara grabbed him and pulled him in behind the wall.

"Three, two, one ..." Klara stared at him, her eyes almost luminous with excitement.

The thump wasn't huge and they felt the ripple pass through the stone under the soles of their boots.

Klara poked her head around. "Clear," she announced, and let Matt go.

The group headed back in to see smoke rising from a shallow pit where the female HAWC had planted the explosives.

She nodded with satisfaction. "X marks the spot."

The top layer of stone had been exploded away exposing a huge metal door.

Roy nodded. "Well done, Professor, seems you might have found us our missing tunnel."

Matt fist pumped. "Yes." He felt Klara rub his back, and he turned to see her nod at him.

"We a very good team." Alojzy clapped his hands together. "And maybe soon a very happy team." He held up a hand and rubbed a finger and thumb together.

"That's not why we're here." Maddock turned to Vin and motioned to the door. "Get that open, soldier."

The young HAWC used the hardened steel blade of his Ka-bar to first work around the outside of the steel plate. Though the steel was age-darkened it was in surprisingly good condition as it had been protected from the air by the granite cement mixture that had covered it over.

Vin paused. "Can't see any locking mechanism, so ..."

He grabbed hold of a foot-long bar handle recessed in one side of the door and then tugged. Nothing moved even a fraction so he repositioned himself and tugged again. Still nothing happened. He looked up, grinning and red-faced.

"Little help here, guys."

"Wait." Alojzy had a looped length of climbing rope in his hand. "Tie the end to the handle.

Vin did as asked and then stood. "Okay."

Alojzy held up the rope. "Everyone grab on, and we'll pull it open."

One after the other the group grabbed the rope.

"On the count of, one, two, three, *pull* ..." Alojzy with the group behind him tugged on the rope. Nothing happened for a moment, but then the steel door popped open like a tin can lid, and the iron slab clanged heavily to the ground. The group approached.

CHAPTER 24

Matt immediately threw a hand over his mouth and nose. "Jesus." He grimaced and backed up. "Gas."

A sickening stench escaped from the dark void they had just opened.

Alojzy also backed away. "Could it be some sort of leftover nerve gas, like as booby trap?"

"Masks on," Maddock said.

The group pulled on their gas masks, except for the Polish guide who just tied a spare t-shirt around his mouth and nose, and stayed well back.

"Not a chemical attack but I've smelt this before," Maddock said. "When I was in Syria we uncovered a mass grave that had been baking in the sun for several months. Hundreds of bodies in that one."

"Corpses?" Matt grimaced.

"Yeah," Maddock said. "We should have expected it. Remember around twenty-eight thousand laborers on this project disappeared. We might have found their final resting place, and their reward for all their work."

He pointed his light downwards. "Steps." He waved Klara with him. "We'll take a quick look. Everyone else hold positions."

Matt watched as Maddock and Klara vanished into the dark hole. After another moment there was no sound or light coming up out of the pit. He looked to Vin, who held up a finger, and then pointed.

Sure enough, in another moment Maddock resurfaced standing half out of the hole. "There's a huge tunnel stretching both ways. But a few hundred feet in one direction there's another door." He spoke directly to Matt, and then Alojzy. "But everyone better steel themselves for what we see down there."

"Bad?" Matt asked.

"*Oh yeah.*" Klara's voice drifted up from the darkness.

Maddock turned back, facing down. "Let's do this. Klara, lead us in. Matt next, and I'll bring up the rear. Vin, you get to stay here and cover our rear."

"Got it, boss," Vin said.

"I would very much like to see," Alojzy pleaded. "I have searched for these tunnels for nearly half my life."

"Not without breathing equipment, you wouldn't last thirty seconds. The air is off the toxicity scale," Maddock replied.

"Hey Alojzy." Vin took off his mask and tossed it to the Polish guide. "You owe me one."

"Thank you, Mr. Vin." Alojzy pulled it over his head. "And now I am ready."

"Then you go in front of me." Maddock eased aside. "Let's go, people."

Klara headed back down, with Matt close behind her. Once they were below the floor level and in the new tunnel, Matt's beam seemed to pick up veils of a miasmic mist hanging in the air. As he stepped off the last step, his foot squelched into a glutinous mud.

"Ah shit." He sank to the ankle.

Matt slid to the side; feeling sharp sticks and objects hidden within the thick mud as he waited for the team to join him.

He shone his torch at the ceilings and walls and then toward the end of the tunnel that was still lost in darkness. Closer to the walls there were mounds of something that looked like stacked kindling.

"Massive," he said. "Wonder what it was used for?"

Maddock stepped down last. "I know what its final use was." He shone his light downwards and moved his boot through the muck. Something large and round surfaced: a skull. "A kill zone."

He lifted his light higher so the powerful beam shone down along the tunnel illuminating the seemingly endless river of death. "And there." He lifted his light to one of the mounds against the wall.

Matt saw now it wasn't kindling at all, but piles of age-browned bones. Bodies, dozens of them, and further down there were many more piles. "Oh god no, the missing prisoners of war," he whispered.

"I think so." Maddock toed through the sticky slime. "And this ... this mess we're standing in is what happens to bodies that are left to rot in dripping water."

"People soup," Klara said.

"There were nearly thirty thousand of them," Matt said. "Please tell me they were dead before they were sealed into the darkness."

"I think so. Those piles of bodies were probably machine-gunned." Maddock swept his boot to the side again lifting another bone shard. "This is like the other bones I've seen – it's been splintered. I think they might have thrown grenades in here and blown the rest up."

"They could never kill them all with machine guns and grenades," Matt replied.

"No." Maddock shook his head slowly. "And at the end of the war ammunition was becoming scarce and expensive."

"These poor souls were condemned to work like slaves. And their final reward wasn't freedom, but this." Alojzy made a guttural noise in his throat. "Those devils."

Maddock turned away. "Come on, let's get this over with."

The group continued on slowly, carefully placing one foot after the other. The sludge deepened to mid calf and Matt didn't look forward to when they left and took their breathing equipment off – it would undoubtedly smell like corruption and ancient death. And he bet it'd be even worse as it warmed up.

Matt had been around dead bodies before, and there was something about old death that stuck to you. Whether it was the fats in the human body starting to liquefy or other bodily fluids becoming toxic, it usually meant the smell stayed with you. More often than not, clothing had to be thrown out or burned.

It took them nearly an hour to reach the next junction point, which was another huge door blocking their way. In its center was a huge eagle with wings spread wide, holding a globe that held the Nazi swastika.

"This looks promising," Matt said, and then looked closely at the handle. "Uh-oh, this might be a problem."

It was locked and, even though the chain and locking mechanism was bubbled with orange corrosion, it looked professionally made and the steel as thick as two fingers.

"Blow it," Maddock said.

"On it." Klara stepped forward.

"What about methane ... you know, from the bodies?" Matt asked.

"Should have oxidized and dissipated to below five percent by now," Klara said over her shoulder. She turned. "And if not, kiss your ass goodbye, Professor."

"Great, we'll join the body pile." He looked to Maddock who just shrugged.

Klara snorted and went to work, packing and shaping the plastic explosives around the lock and then inserting a detonator pin.

"Back up fifty feet and turn away." She set the timer and slide-walked back toward them. When she reached the group she faced away and counted down from five, and then ...

The explosion was more a metallic pop, but Matt still felt the percussion wave travel down the tunnel to press on his eardrums. Small pops of light went off around them as obviously the more concentrated bubbles of methane ignited in the air. He gritted his teeth and held his breath, but they quickly vanished.

When they looked back the smoke haze was already dissipating, but the lock had crumbled.

Klara was first back and grabbed the huge bolt that was now unencumbered by the chains and lock. She slid it back with a deep and solid *thunk*.

Maddock joined her and both of them leaned into the iron door. "Count of three, two, one – *heave* ..."

The metal door sounded like it screamed in agony as ancient steel hinges worked for the first time in around three quarters of a century.

The door opened a few inches, then a foot, and then two feet before Maddock called a halt. "That'll do." He waved Matt forward. "You're up."

"Cool." Matt hurried forward, not even thinking about any risk as his curiosity and excitement were through the roof.

Maddock swapped his powerful flashlight for Matt's so he had the big one. Matt switched it up to maximum illumination and shone the brilliant pipe of light in through the gap in the door.

He slid in and eased his foot down. "First bit of good news, it's dry in here." The floor was dust-covered but thankfully the sludge hadn't made it into this section. His light didn't extend to the end of the massive tunnel-like room. But the second bit of good news was that it wasn't empty.

"It's a warehouse," he said softly.

"What do you see?" Maddock yelled.

Matt grinned. "Wonderful things." He thought it appropriate he echo the words of the great Howard Carter from nearly a century ago, the famous archeologist who was the discoverer and first inside the tomb of the great pharaoh, Tutankhamun.

Matt shone the flashlight beam slowly around the huge warehouse-type room. Gold glinted back at him. Bars of it, stacked on crumbling wooden pallets and rising in blocks six feet high.

Thankfully, this room had been sealed and was watertight, so the artworks lined up against the wall were still vibrant, and those containing human visages stared back mutely from the shadows. Matt wondered about the things those painted eyes had witnessed before the iron door was sealed up for so many decades.

There were crates, some coffin sized, and some only a few feet in length, all marked with the German Reich's eagle. Among the treasure there were racks of wine, and tinned foods – ham, fish, caviar – undoubtedly the supplies that were to keep a fleeing Hitler in the luxuries he was accustomed to.

Matt tried to see how large the room was but his light couldn't possibly reach down to the end. He took off his mask and sucked in a deep breath and let it out.

"Air's okay," he said over his shoulder, and in another moment the entire group was inside the underground warehouse.

Alojzy immediately hefted a bar of gold. "I have searched for this half of my life. It is a pirate's buried treasure and Aladdin's cave all at once." He looked like he was about to stick the bar in his pack.

"There's blood money, and then there's corpse gold. I'm betting this treasure was formerly wedding rings, gold keepsakes, and maybe even gold teeth once." Matt didn't look at the Polish guide. "If I believed in curses, and some I do, then I would think this treasure is tainted by the death of millions."

Alojzy dropped the bar and it thudded to the ground. "I'm sure there are others who deserve it more than me." He shrugged, but kept staring down at the golden brick for another moment.

Maddock raised his voice. "This will all be for the Polish and German governments to sort out. But for us, there is one thing and one thing only we are interested in."

"The stone tablet," Matt finished. He turned to the group. "We've all seen what the other stone we have in our possession looks like, and we know what the one from Hitler's diary looks like – it'll be around four feet high and three wide. It probably looks like a green-tinged headstone." Matt turned to look down along the dark room. "I just hope it's not boxed as that will be –"

"Impossible," Klara finished.

Matt turned to her. "Not impossible. Just time-consuming, when we don't have that much of it. It means we'll need to rely on luck as well."

"Okay, people, we'll all take a quadrant each, fifty feet square and begin our search. But first, Professor Kearns, I want you to do a quick reconnoiter up along the tunnel length. I'd sure hate to spend days opening boxes, and then find that this sucker is leaning up against a wall a quarter mile down the tunnel."

Matt grinned. "Yeah, good idea." He started to turn away.

"And, Professor ..."

Matt turned back. The HAWC team leader half smiled. "Don't do anything dumb."

"Me?" Matt chuckled. "Impossible."

Matt headed on down the long central space between the shelves and stacks. Behind him he heard Maddock giving orders.

Wish I had a pushbike, he thought as he flicked his light to the left to a shelving system of smaller boxes. His curiosity was screaming at him to look through a few – *just a peek*, it whispered.

What could he find, he wondered as he shone his beam onto a stack of iron-cladded crates.

Hitler's *Übernatürliche Kriegsführung* – the supernatural warfare unit – was rumored to have located and retrieved wondrous things. There were bound to be items in these boxes that might blow his mind. Hitler spent millions of marks, plus the last few years of his campaign, searching out artifacts that were occult based and he believed might give him a military edge or even win him the war. Maybe he found some. Maybe he found a lot.

Matt's light illuminated a magnificent golden harp. It was breathtaking. Most of the items would be returned to their owners or their estates, if they could be identified. The gold that was untraceable would be absorbed into the Polish and German gold reserves.

But the artifacts, the mysterious and magical things, would probably just vanish. The government might study some, and if they could determine what the things were or how they worked, then they might try and make use of them.

Much as that pained him, he knew he needed to focus. They were here to do a job because there was some bad shit going down outside and people were dying. Lots of them.

He remembered the quote. *They have come and they will come again. Each ending greater than the last. Only those from the core can stop them, when ...*

The quote scared the hell out of him. Something big was coming, and it was his job to help understand it, and then, if possible, stop it.

CHAPTER 25

South-west of Walnut Grove, Redwood county, Minnesota

Private 1st Class Tony Bianchi tilted his helmet back and wiped his brow. Full kit, plus armaments was damned hot when it was eighty-five degrees in the shade. Plus it was only mid-morning. By early afternoon it'd easily slide past one hundred.

He and around five hundred other guardsmen had been called out and assembled in a broad battleline formation. As yet, they had no idea what it was they were supposed to repel or defend against. Their superiors, if they knew, would only tell them that they'd know it when it came.

Big help, he thought.

But the guys talked among themselves, and some mentioned a swarm, or plague, or something that wasn't people. That had to be dumb considering him and most of their forces had standard armaments such as M4 carbines, a shorter and lighter variant of the M16A2 assault rifle.

Tony gripped his a little tighter, feeling the heat of the steel on his hands. The M4 was top of the line: an air-cooled, direct impingement gas-operated, magazine-fed carbine, with a 14.5-inch barrel and telescoping stock. He felt he could have taken down a rhino with this baby. But a swarm of bees or sumthin' ... like, what the fuck?

But then again, not all of them had carbines: a few of his buddies had been ordered to fix M320 grenade launcher hardware, and the grenade rounds were the new mini thermobarics, called heat blasters. That was a little better. But the real kicker and strangest call-up he'd ever heard was the requisitioning of flamethrowers.

Those bad boys had been abandoned as a weapon of war in the US for decades, but in many states it wasn't illegal to own them. They could still be seen in use for land clearing, snow melts and rubbish burn-offs.

The brass had called for them, the public responded, and now they were fueled up, tested, and on the front line.

Swarm of bees, huh? Tony's breath hissed out through clenched teeth. Yeah, coz somehow he didn't think the adversary they were called to stand against with goddamn flamethrowers was going to be Jack Frost or an army of White Walkers.

Tony glanced left and then right; his military unit was eighty strong, and was spread in a skirmish line on one side of a small creek. It was to be their drop-dead zone – nothing was to get past them.

Behind him there were military transport vehicles, plus around twenty M1161 Growlers, or ITLSVs, Internally Transportable Light Strike Vehicles, all fitted with M2HB fifty-caliber BMG machine guns – they were light, fast, and packed a serious punch.

He shifted his feet, hoping it was all part of a war games trial, or maybe even a readiness test. But the looks on the faces of some of the brass, as well as the stories he heard of towns being wiped out, gave him a cold, leaden feeling in his gut.

Tony felt the trembling beneath his feet and, looking down, saw tiny pebbles jumping and bouncing on the hard-packed yellow dirt.

"What's going on?" His buddies beside him started to look one way then the other.

"Tanks maybe?" one of them asked.

The vibrations felt a long way off and after a moment subsided. There was nothing on their far horizon and, just as he started to settle into his sweaty boredom again, one of the growlers started to move past them from behind. Major Terry Thorne was standing in its rear, yelling commands.

Their group leader, 2nd Lieutenant Foley, listened to his radio for a moment before yelling for them to form up. Apparently, HQ had just picked up an approaching *mass*.

"A mass? What the fuck is a mass?" Tony muttered.

Beside him, big Hamish McDonald grinned, showing a mouth full of crooked teeth. "Ten bucks says it's all gonna be a drill."

"Yeah, I hope so," Tony whispered.

"*There*," someone said from behind him.

Tony's head whipped around to see a smudge on the horizon that looked to be a growing cloud, or, *mass*.

"Ah, fuck." Tony grimaced, wishing he had been away on holidays when the guardsmen call-up came. "That don't look like no drill to me."

The cloud grew, rising to about a hundred feet and filling the horizon for half a mile. It came fast, and as it approached, Tony began to hear the deep hum and then also feel its vibration right to his back teeth.

"It's like a chainsaw," Hamish observed and pulled his helmet down a tad.

"A cloud of chainsaws." Tony squinted. "And coming at us fast."

"*Hold the line,*" Second Lieutenant Foley yelled from the bed of the growler behind them. "They're just critters, and they are not going to get past us to bother the good people of Walnut Grove."

"Critters? Like bugs?" Tony felt a little relieved. "Maybe like a locust plague." He nodded. "That's why we got the flamethrowers, right?"

"We'll barbecue 'em." Hamish grinned and held up his gun with his hand now on the grenade launcher trigger. "Come git some, little buggies."

The cloud grew darker and more ominous as it approached. Tony could feel the hum deep inside him. It made the inside of his ears tickle and reminded him of a model airplane he had as a kid.

"There's lots of them," he said, but probably just to himself.

"On my order. Target where they are at their thickest." Foley's voice was a roar, and thankfully it remained strong and calm.

Tony felt his heart hammering in his chest and he was getting a little out of breath. He began to count down the swarm's approach: ten and nine and eight and seven ...

"*Fire.*"

Foley's yell was drowned by the roar of the gunfire, grenade launching, and heavy machine guns from beside, behind, and all around him. It submerged the hum of the approaching bugs and almost immediately the air became filled with orange blooms of heat and flame.

Clouds rose from the guns and also from the swarm as it entered the wall of bullets and fire.

If it slowed them, it wasn't by much, because out the other side of the gouts of smoke and flame the bugs came through. Then they found the first of the guardsmen.

They're so fucking big, Tony thought. And there were more bugs than soldiers. A lot more.

It wasn't long before the gunfire began to peter out as soldiers now wrestled on the ground – firstly with a few of the things, and then they became subsumed by them.

Tony felt one clamp onto his leg. He looked down, not believing what he was seeing was even real. It was the size that freaked him out: it was as big as a cat and clung to him with too many long sharp legs that pierced his tough pants. And the freaky bug's eyes were more human than insectoid. They swiveled up to his face.

Then something hit the back of his neck and stuck. Something hung there like a hot pinch and then he felt a spike or needle immediately pressed into his flesh. He took a hand from his gun to reach back and take a grab at the thing.

He gripped it; it was huge, hard and sharp, and immensely strong. The wasp-like creature felt more like a machine than a living creature, and refused to let him go. Its sharp legs tore at his skin.

More and more slammed into him. Beside him, his big buddy Hamish writhed and screamed on the ground, and the last thing Tony saw was his friend being fully cloaked in black, bristling bodies.

Tony first went to his knees, and then fully collapsed. Not so much from the weight of the monstrosities, but because it felt like his legs were gone. His once muscular legs, which he was told looked great in shorts and had at one time won school sprinting races, were now spread beneath him like empty pipes of meat.

One of the things moved to his face, and the eyes looked directly into his. Tony believed in the devil, and he knew it was looking at him right now.

Mercifully, consciousness left him as the light was shut out when the noise and the pain became his entire world.

*

"We believe they're all dead, sir." Hammerson gripped the secure phone hard as he spoke to five-star General Marcus Chilton. "The machine guns, thermobaric grenades, and flamethrowers didn't even slow them down."

On the line it sounded like the general growled for a moment. "How many?"

"Five hundred, general. We're sending in drones to do a low altitude check right now. But satellite says the area is cold," Hammerson replied. "Reports are coming in from all over the world. These weird bugs are destroying everything biological they come in contact with. And they are on the move. China, India, European states all want to talk, to pool ideas and resources."

"Jesus Christ, Jack." Chilton exhaled. "And where are we on that – ideas, I mean?"

"The science teams have some suggestions, but as yet they are just theories. There's more they don't know than they do know, right now. Maybe India or China knows more."

"Unlikely. They wouldn't be coming to us if they had the answers," Chilton said. "What's Russia doing? Strange that we haven't heard from them."

"I don't know. Maybe they want to wrestle with it themselves for a while," Hammerson replied slowly.

"I don't like it when those guys run silent. Could it be an attack?" Chilton asked.

"The swarms seemed to have initiated organically, and there's no evidence to suggest there's an external genesis to these events, sir." But Hammerson had wondered the same thing. Especially after hearing about the Ukraine incident.

"Okay, Jack, but keep your eyes and ears open, I don't trust those guys." Chilton sounded like he sat back. "We always wanted to unite the world, but not like this." Chilton cleared his throat. "Where are the swarms now?"

Hammerson was ready for the question but hated it just the same. "We don't know. They just vanished."

"How? In your briefing notes you estimated the swarm at being around ten thousand individual entities. Plus they're now the size of a dog."

"I know, Sir. Like I said, these things are like nothing we've ever seen or encountered before. We're learning as we go." Hammerson rubbed his chin, the stubble making a rasping sound. "We've begun an emergency evacuation of Bay City, all eighteen thousand of them."

"Good." Chilton sounded like he leaned forward as his voice grew louder. "Just remember, Jack, we can't keep retreating. Sooner or later we'll end up with our backs against the wall. One more thing. Initial reports stated these things were tiny, and now they've grown and are growing. So just how big are they going to get?"

Good question, Hammerson thought. "Going to have to add that to our list of unknowns, sir."

"Get those answers, and get 'em fast, Jack. A military leader's deadliest adversary is the unknown."

"Yes, sir. I'm on it." Colonel Jack "the Hammer" Hammerson heard the line disconnect.

Hammerson knew he was *on it*, but not *on top of it* – big difference.

*

The aerial drones hovered over the field of death. The ground was littered with corpses, and they were all flattened like empty suits of clothing laid out to dry in the sunshine.

Even the hairless and toothless skulls were shapeless bags, with the open eyes still glinting glass-like in the sunshine. There would be no crows, insects, or other vermin to pick at them as they too had been consumed by the plague swarm.

Hammerson sat still as stone, his gaze unwavering as one of the drone operators detected movement and zoomed in on one of the bodies.

It was a man, or once was. And like the others, his body was spread flat like a rug. But the camera zoomed in, and then zoomed in even further, just on his face.

The eyelids fluttered. The muscles still working, and not needing the scaffolding of bones to support them.

"God damn." Hammerson breathed.

The HAWC leader straightened. "Acquire target."

On the screen a red bombsite targeting system appeared, and also a grid system.

"Quadrant F4."

The bombsite moved until it was centered over the flat skull.

"Discharge one."

From the drone, a single nine-millimeter round was fired, penetrating the soft skull. The eyelids stopped fluttering.

"Forgive me, son." Hammerson leaned forward to put his head in his hands.

*

"You asked me were the swarms converging; we now believe they are," Hammerson said evenly. "The major swarm is moving up from Texas, a rapidly growing swarm in Wyoming is moving east, North Dakota's swarm is moving south, and Ohio's is moving west. Plus dozens of smaller outbreaks."

"So there is a pattern. I knew it." Hartigan nodded. "Where are they headed?"

"Our plotting software can only make a best guess at this stage, and so far it suggests either Wisconsin, Iowa, or Minnesota. Lot of territory."

"Too much," Hartigan responded softly.

"How do we narrow it down? We need somewhere we can focus our damn efforts," Hammerson seethed.

"I don't know, Jack. Let me think on it for a while." Hartigan exhaled through his nose. "But it'll became clearer as they progress, I should think."

"Obviously. Then for now, all I can do is try and get people out of their way." Hammerson hated retreating, but his job was to protect the innocent, and sometimes that just meant getting them out of the way.

"Keep at it." He signed off.

CHAPTER 26

The Sokelec system, the Owl Mountains

Alojzy, Maddock, and Klara used their knives to pry the tops off crates, large and small, and then peer inside.

Alojzy hummed as he worked, enjoying the task. He had hunted for the missing tunnels and their mythical treasure haul for decades, now he felt vindicated for all the time, effort and money he had put into it.

So many had laughed, he thought. *And now, it is proven, so many were wrong.*

The search had cost him his wife, his money, and his former job. It had become his lifelong obsession. Though he had dropped the gold bar before, one thing for sure, he wasn't just going to hand everything over to the authorities and see it all crated up and packed off to some other hidden vault, possibly to the benefit of the Germans who were responsible for looting it all in the first place.

He prized the lid off another crate and held up his flashlight to peer inside. There were small black cloth bags tied with drawstrings at the top. He reached in and opened one and tipped it out.

"Nice," he whispered. It was jewelry. Beautiful, magnificent jewelry.

He checked a few more of the cloth bags and found more of the same – gold coin, bracelets, necklaces, some with precious stones and some with diamonds that glinted in his light like chips of fire and ice.

Alojzy slowly turned his head, checking on Maddock and Klara and found them still fully occupied with their own investigations. So he snuck a bag in each of his pants' pockets.

He was about to move off, but paused and carefully checked on the soldiers again. Satisfied, he quickly snuck another bag into his coat breast pocket and one into his back pocket. They were heavy and dragged on his pants, threatening to pull them down.

"Shit." He tucked his flashlight under his arm and stepped back to adjust his belt in another notch.

"Mr. Alojzy ..."

Roy Maddock's loud voice startled him and made him momentarily cower.

"... do not even think of pissing in here."

Alojzy exhaled, feeling relieved. He shrugged and turned to grin back sheepishly at the soldier. "I will wait then ... or go outside in the mud tunnel."

Maddock glared for a moment. "Just keep working, we've got a lot to check – quick glance, if it's not what we're looking for, then move on to the next crate."

"Yes, yes." He saluted with his flashlight and turned back to the crates.

After another moment he heard Maddock had gone back to his own investigations and he chuckled softly.

I'll be pissing gold tonight, he thought. His only concern was if the soldier wanted to do a check on them before they left. The bags were heavy and difficult to hide, at least until he could get them into his pack, which he'd left topside with Mr. Vin.

Alojzy opened more crates, finding endless boxes of silver plates, candelabras and cutlery sets – probably the results of looting the wealthy houses as the Nazis swept through their conquered cities' suburbs. Or maybe they simply cleaned out Jewish people, taking everything from family heirlooms to children's picture frames.

He finished his first section and moved onto the next. These crates were more secure, and some of them were constructed of solid iron, heavy riveted, and more like ammunition boxes. Some were even secured with padlocks, although the locks had corroded so he knew a few sharp strikes with the hilt of his knife should break them open.

Alojzy laid his hands on the largest of them and thought he felt a tingle run through his fingertips. The box wasn't big, but seemed to be the most securely fortified. There was the eagle crest of the Nazi SS brigade and writing indicating it had been taken from a collector in Greece in early 1944.

The Polish guide lifted his blade and struck down several times, each time making the locking mechanism shower rust, then warp, and finally break open.

He smiled and quickly jammed his knife back in its scabbard and lay his light down on the shelf pointed toward the top of the steel box. He lifted the lid.

Alojzy exhaled almost dreamily. The light made the gold glint, and large precious stones sparkled like carnival lighting. It was a single necklace in beautifully wrought gold in the shape of two serpents whose open mouths formed a clasp. Along its length it was inlaid with various jewels – he picked out sapphires, rubies and emeralds, and the snake's eyes were the clearest diamonds he had ever seen, both the size of peas.

Alojzy's mouth puckered into an "O" as he silently whistled. He chanced a quick look over his shoulder – Maddock and Klara were still working like machines on their own tasks.

He looked back and his smile pulled up even higher. The single piece would be worth a king's ransom ten times over. He quickly stuck his hands in his pockets and removed the bags of gold and piecemeal jewelry, preparing to place them in the box in exchange for the magnificent necklace.

In one hand he took hold of the necklace to lift it out and with the other he placed the bags in its place. Once again his fingers tingled as though there was a mild electrical current running through the gold.

Most beautiful thing I've ever seen, he thought. It was obviously ancient and he wondered what royal goddess wore this in some long-gone century. And the best thing was, he could wear it, and therefore not burden his pockets. Maddock might make them empty their pockets when their work was done, but he doubted the man would make them strip down.

Alojzy undid the clasp and quickly looped it around his neck and then pulled his collar up over it. He stroked it under his clothing, smiling contentedly, and then gently closed the lid of the iron box.

"Dressed in the adornment of the gods," he whispered. *This will change my life forever.*

He felt the tingling again, this time emanating from his neck and right through his chest. He hummed as he moved to the next box.

*

Matt saw the dustcovers over the items against the wall, some being the approximate size of the stone tablet he sought. He crossed to them and pulled them away. He could only stare. And then he began to chuckle.

"So, this is where you ended up." He backed up. "The Eighth Wonder of the World."

In the glare of his flashlight the huge panels glowed like golden honey, and he now saw they filled a hundred feet of one entire side of the chamber.

He stepped forward, laying his hand gently on one of the ornate panels. It was the Amber Room from the Catherine Palace in Saint Petersburg.

He ran his fingers along the smooth surface, and then stepped back to let his light move over the amber blends: some fiery red, some golden honey, and some creamy white. It was said to be so beautiful that simply standing before it made people weep from its magnificence. And he could see why.

The 300-year-old amber artwork was estimated to be valued at a billion dollars, and had been missing since the war.

"Missing no more." Matt breathed, almost reverently.

He went to lay his hand on one of the panels again, but pulled back. *Focus*, he demanded.

Matt turned back to the tunnel depths, and his light illuminated more items of gold and silver – it was the treasures of empires.

He continued on until he arrived at an empty section of tunnel. Almost empty. Because there, leaning against a wall and covered by a dust cloth, was something that looked like a gravestone.

Matt walked toward it quickly, keeping his light trained on it – he ripped the cover away, fanning the cloud of dust out of the air as his smile began to split his face.

It was a single slab of greenish-looking stone, covered in the familiar pictoglyphs, images, and writing style he had expected and hoped for.

Matt nodded. "So, you're –"

"*Kearns!*"

The sharp, echoing shout from back down the tunnel jerked his head around.

Roy Maddock prized lids from crates, took a quick look inside, didn't find what he wanted, banged the lids back down, and moved to the next. Further up the tunnel in her own quadrant, Klara did the same. The pair worked like machines, the treasures meaning nothing to them.

Behind him, Maddock heard Alojzy working, but much slower. He sighed. He knew the guy was probably filling his pockets, and wondered whether he should give a damn. The thing was, it was a HAWC mission, and so Alojzy looting the already looted goods was really on Maddock's head. Still if the guy just grabbed a few gold coins after seventy-five years it wasn't going to kill anyone.

He heard Alojzy getting slower, and then he sounded like he stumbled into the shelves he was working on. Maddock turned to check on him, and saw the man was leaning against the crate he was working on as if all tuckered out.

"Okay back there?" He yelled and shone his beam back at the guide.

Alojzy turned and nodded slowly. Oddly, his hair looked longer and also seemed to be run through with white. Even his frame looked a little shrunken inside his bulky clothing. Maddock frowned and stepped back from his work.

"Hey, Alojzy, you okay?"

Klara stopped her work and now also turned to watch.

Maddock slowly began to approach the man, keeping his light focused on the frail-looking body. He saw that the guide rested his arms on one of the shelves and as Maddock watched his head drooped forward.

"Are you sick?" Maddock stopped just a few paces from him. "Please step out here."

Alojzy turned and moaned, long and low. He then staggered out from the alcove where he had been working.

"Ah, shit." Maddock's brows snapped together and for the first time in his career he was confused and frozen with indecision.

The Polish man had somehow aged, and now looked to be eighty years old. His hair was white and thin, and his skin was like old yellow parchment stretched drum-tight over a skull covered in liver spots.

He held up a bony hand in front of his face. "What's … happening … to me?" He staggered closer.

Infection, Maddock thought. The man must have opened a crate that the Nazi war machine had stored some biological or chemical agent in. Maddock pointed. "Alojzy, stay where you are, we'll get you help."

"Tired. So tired." Alojzy ignored him and staggered on, now just a dozen paces away.

Klara joined Maddock and had her gun drawn. "He's infected by something." She aimed at his chest. "Say the word, boss."

They didn't need to. Alojzy's hair now grew past his shoulders, but then in the next instant it all simply fell out like strands of fine silk. His tiny wrinkled head and neck seemed to swim in oversized clothing that had fit his large frame snugly only minutes ago. His rheumy old eyes pleaded with them as the man sunk to his knees.

Maddock sucked in a breath and turned to yell over his shoulder: "*Kearns!*"

"Help me," Alojzy rasped as he continued to shrink before their eyes.

"What the hell is wrong with him?" Klara gripped her gun tighter.

On his knees, he managed to continue to crawl toward the HAWCs.

"Stay the fuck back." Klara's gun was now held tight in two hands as she drew a bead on his wrinkled forehead.

"Hold fire," Maddock said.

Alojzy's mouth hung open and his teeth began to fall from his jaws to sprinkle on the ground around him and skitter away into the shadows. He slowly held up his hands as if they weighed a hundred pounds each. "It ... hu-*uuurts*." The man looked at the gnarled and liver-spotted claws and began to softly weep.

"Get Kearns, *now*," Maddock said to Klara.

The female HAWC holstered her weapon and sprinted down the tunnel.

Maddock crouched in front of the Polish guide. "Alojzy, stay with us. Tell me what happened."

He knew what he was witnessing was impossible as the figure looked to be the oldest human being he had ever seen in his life. His small yellow eyes remained fixed on the HAWC leader, but they shrunk back into his skull and Maddock doubted whether the man could see or even speak anymore.

Behind him he heard the sound of running feet and then Matt Kearns skidded to a stop beside him.

"What the hell? Is that ...?" He went to approach.

"Stop." Maddock threw out an arm. "Yeah, Alojzy. He must have come into contact with something in one of those crates."

"Holy shit. What ...?" Matt stared, open-mouthed.

Maddock just shook his head.

At first it looked like smoke started rising from the little old man, but then Maddock knew it was really his skin as the guy turned to dust.

Alojzy opened his mouth, but no final words came, as his tongue was shriveled and black inside his mouth. The flesh flaked from his reptilian-looking hands and face and in another few seconds, the tiny frame collapsed in on itself and fell forward.

The skull clacked on the concrete ground and then rolled free, and Maddock saw that, still hanging around the yellowing vertebrae of the neck, there was a magnificent golden necklace.

"He wasn't wearing that before," Klara observed.

"No, I'm betting he found it in one of the crates." Matt approached and waved away some of the floating dust. He crouched in front of the pile of empty clothing and bones. Maddock joined him.

The HAWC saw that, even now, the bones continued to age, going from a yellow-white, to brown and then the color of the earth. He had no doubt that in a little while all trace of the man would be gone forever.

"What just happened here?" he asked.

"Give me you knife." Matt held out his hand.

Maddock drew it and handed it to the Harvard professor. Matt then leaned forward and used the long blade to lift out the necklace from Alojzy's decaying bones. He held it up for a moment and then turned.

"It's supposed to be just a myth." Matt looked at the dangling golden jewelry. "In fact, five minutes ago, I would have said it *was* a myth." He snorted softly. "But not anymore."

"Would someone like to tell me what the hell is going on?" Maddock asked. "And whether we're at risk of the same fate as Mr. Mazur here?"

Matt turned and gave him a half smile. "It would be mine or your fate if we wore this." He glanced over his shoulder at Klara. "But not hers."

"What is it?" Maddock stared at the jewels glinting in their light beams.

Matt held the necklace up on the end of his knife. "It was handcrafted by the great Hephaestus, blacksmith of the Olympian gods. He made it for his wife, Aphrodite. He also made Zeus's thunderbolt spear, and Poseidon's trident."

He smiled up at it. "It's the Necklace of Harmonia." He turned to Maddock and raised his eyebrows. "And Hephaestus cursed it."

"Cursed, yeah." Maddock thumbed at Alojzy's moldering bones. "I can see that."

"Curses are real things?" Klara shook her head. "This is bullshit. How do you even do that?"

"Magic of course." Matt turned to give her a flat smile.

"Oh, of course." Klara's lips pressed together.

"There's a whole world of things that is well beyond any normal person's comprehension." He turned back to the jewels. "I've seen things that defy physics and would tear at your sanity."

"So, the mad Führer wasn't so mad after all?" Maddock held up a hand flat in front of the necklace. "I can feel it, like static electricity."

"Yeah, I can feel it too," Matt replied. "It is said that any woman who wears the Necklace of Harmonia will remain young and beautiful forever."

"That doesn't sound like a curse,' Maddock said.

"Not for the woman," Matt replied. "But there was a sting in the tail; a trap. Apparently Hephaestus found out that his wife, Aphrodite, goddess of love, was having an affair with Ares, the god of war. He became enraged and vowed to avenge himself."

He turned to Maddock. "Never piss off a god or demi-god. Crafty old Hephaestus knew that Ares had a taste for adornments, so expected that Aphrodite would let him wear the magnificent jewels."

Matt turned the necklace a little. "You see, the necklace's granting of eternal youth to women means it's got to get the essence of youth from somewhere." He chuckled. "So it takes it from men. Hephaestus hoped to turn Ares into an old man. But the curse was too broad, so *any* man who wore it lost his youth. It never worked on Ares." He tossed it back onto the pile of moldering clothes. "But looks like it really does work on anyone else." He sighed. "Poor Alojzy."

"The punishment was a bit over the top, but the thief deserved it," Klara scorned.

"Lighten up." Matt scowled. "No one deserves that."

"Yeah? And what if he pulled out something that killed us all?" Klara's chin jutted.

"That's enough." Maddock got to his feet and turned about. "What other horrors are waiting for us in these crates?"

"It doesn't matter." Matt stood and handed back Maddock's knife. "Now for some good news." Matt flat smiled. "I found the stone."

CHAPTER 27

Central Scientific Research Institute, Ministry of Defense, Shchyolkovo, Moscow

Colonel Nadi Borishenko let his eyes run down the list of interested parties for his weaponized silachnids: Iran, North Korea, Pakistan, and even a number of South American countries had displayed interest.

The conditioned silachnids were going to be worth hundreds of millions, maybe even billions. Borishenko smiled; it'd be a nice little side-deal to the mission plan he was working on that would be the culmination of his work. Once undertaken, Russia's main adversary would be hobbled, and the devastating value of the bugs would be displayed for the world to see. And then that's when he would set a price.

He changed computer screens. Borishenko steepled his fingers under his chin as he reread his mission profile; he'd already performed his target assessment, and the lethality impact, and also chosen his delivery mechanism. The only question remaining was whether there was going to be a second-wave attack, or if things went wrong, a political need for plausible deniability.

He snorted; nothing could go wrong. After all, a plague outbreak in the center of a major metropolis would be catastrophic. When the silachnids were finished, the city would be a war zone, or empty of life. Who'd be left to ask questions?

He had one last thing to do; the Russian hummed a soft tune as he prepared for the most important meeting of his life.

CHAPTER 28

Vin was waiting for them up top, and helped haul the slab of granite out. When he was told about Alojzy he just grunted and took it in his stride. Matt knew that these soldiers dealt with death every single day.

When they finally exited to the forest again Matt sucked in a cool draft of frigid air, and filled his lungs, cleansing them.

"Hey!" Maddock drew his gun, pointing it upwards.

In a flash, both Klara and Vin followed suit, and when Matt looked upwards, he thought he saw a dot disappear over the treetops.

"What was it?" he asked.

"Drone, I think." Maddock seethed. "We've been made."

"By whom?" Klara asked, and then slid her gun back into its holster.

Maddock did the same. "Doesn't matter now." He pointed. "Let's get back, double time."

The hike back to the pickup point seemed more arduous than the walk in, and not only because they did it at speed. Though it took less total hours, it was done in near total silence, and that made time stretch.

Once onboard the helicopter, Matt felt elated they'd achieved their objective and also simply that they'd been able to get the hell out of there – the entire place had a lingering feeling of death hanging over the landscape. They all knew that there were the restless ghosts of nearly thirty thousand men, women, and possibly children still trapped below the ground. The bodies' state of decomposition and degradation meant they'd probably never be identified.

"Well, Professor, we've done our bit in getting you what you need. Now it's up to you," Maddock said. "It'll take us a full day to get back home, but your work starts now."

Matt nodded, barely hearing the soldier. He kneeled before the stone tablet and used a rag to gently wipe away the dust in the tiny grooves and crevices.

They still hadn't taken off and the Polish pilot moved about securing the cabin for takeoff. He gave Maddock the thumbs-up, and then, as he passed by Matt, leaned over him.

"I think you go long way for gravestone."

Matt looked up, just as the pilot dropped his hand and stuck it in his pocket. Matt nodded. "Yes, a long way in distance and time."

The pilot hovered for a moment more, and Matt looked back up at him. He made a small sound in his throat and headed back to the cockpit. "Takeoff, two minutes," he said without turning.

Matt went back to his work. He ran a hand down the side of the stone, feeling the rough edges.

"I don't think it was broken off the other piece. But more like a separate page," he said over his shoulder. "But the messages overlap, from one tablet to the other."

"Looks like the same markings and certainly contemporaneous," Klara observed.

"Yes, and I'm betting same astronomical signs and formulae." He traced some of the runic-style designs. "Could be a map." Matt made some notes. "It has to be, and coordinates in a fashion."

"A map to what?" Maddock asked.

"That's the question, isn't it?" Matt faced him. "I'll need to have the stones side by side, but from my previous notes, the first stone outlined the problem. Remember the quote: *They have come and they will come again – Each ending greater than the last – Only those from the core can stop them, when ...*"

"Uplifting," Klara replied.

"Given the plague that's occurring all over the world, I'd say more prophetic," Matt retorted. "The first stone even had an image of one of those strange bug-like things. And this second stone works with the first one, creating a cross-referencing answer to the problem. Or at least I think it does. Once I have both pieces of the puzzle, I can start to draw out the meaning. Maybe even find out where they're pointing us toward. And to what."

Klara squatted beside him. "It looks so old. And you said it predates any other civilization known?"

"Yes, the Aztlanteans were in existence when everyone else was still in nomadic tribes hunting the last of the mega-fauna mammals. About ten to twelve thousand years ago, maybe even older," Matt replied.

"That might be a problem." Maddock slowly turned. "If those symbols really do turn out to be map coordinates then they were in existence at the end of the last great ice age, which only ended around eleven thousand years ago." Maddock raised his eyebrows.

Matt shrugged. "And so? It was a lot cooler then. Humans adapted to snow and ice with little problem."

"Snow isn't the problem. But ice is. You see, more freezing cold means more ice. More ice, means more seawater locked up in the caps. More ice locked up in the caps, means ..." He lifted his chin. "Get it now?"

"Oh shit, of course." Matt put a hand to his forehead. "More seawater locked up means more landmass exposed, so sea levels were hundreds of feet lower." He pushed his long hair back and then looked up at the HAWC. "Let's keep our fingers crossed that wherever this is leading us is well inland. But if not, then what?"

A corner of Maddock's mouth lifted. "Underwater, in a desert, or buried under ice – we'll find it and get to it. "

Matt held up a finger. "Unless it's inside a volcano. I ain't going inside a volcano again for as long as I live. Or under ice for that matter." He chuckled. "And I'm skipping jungles as well from now on."

Klara half smiled. "You really have used up eight of your nine lives, Professor." Her smile dropped. "Stay lucky."

"Don't envy me, I've seen too many good people die," he replied.

"Everyone dies." Klara's eyes were glassy and dispassionate.

Matt wondered if there was something personal behind the comment. He watched her for a while, but she seemed to have closed down.

After a while Matt's eyelids began to droop and he felt he'd drawn out about as much as he could from the stone. So far it indicated that there was a place where a solution, or answer, or maybe even a cure, for the plague existed. But the wording was complex, in that it referred to the solution in terms of it being something like an adversary, and he didn't know whether that meant to them or the bugs.

He looked at his watch – it was already twenty hundred hours, eight in the evening, and he didn't think he had slept in two days. He was hungry and so tired that his vision was beginning to blur.

"Can't do any more here. I'm calling it a night. Tomorrow we'll be back home and when the stones are together, I can begin again."

Matt lay down across a row of hard seats, folded his arms across his stomach as though hugging himself and closed his eyes. "Wake me for breakfast."

He yawned and started to dream of monstrous bugs, hidden caves, and a world without people.

*

Rudolph Schneider rubbed his hands together as the images arrived on his computer. There were only three photographs, but he complimented the pilot for being able to get such clear and complete shots.

He rubbed his chin as he sat forward and began to unravel the inscriptions. After another few moments he eased back in his soft leather chair.

"Interesting."

CHAPTER 29

The War Room, USSTRATCOM

The massive room was a hive of activity. The two dozen technical specialists and an equal number of military personnel generated a groundswell of noise as information was collected, analyzed, collated, and then summarized for one man.

Colonel Jack Hammerson stood at the center of the information vortex, directing the information traffic as he coordinated the mission project.

Bottom line was they were at war, and as yet, they knew little about their adversary – which was a fatal flaw in any conflict theatre.

On the fifty square foot wall before him was an image of the globe spread out in two dimensions. It was a composite image taken from their satellites and collected into a single real-time mosaic by their computer systems.

Hammerson's jaw clenched as he watched the monstrous orange nuclear flowers blooming around the world – one over northern China; one, strangely, deep in the Siberian Lake Baikal; another in Pakistan; and a final one, smaller, identified as a Massive Ordnance Air Blast, or MOAB, in eastern Australia – that one ate up oxygen in a designated area and burned with the intensity of a sun.

Hammerson knew exactly what those countries were doing – trying to cleanse their landscapes of the swarms. It'd probably work, as nothing could survive that heat. But the problem was the swarms had multiplied, and some covered huge areas. Plus the damn things got bigger and more voracious, and now consumed entire towns, and anything else too slow to get out of their way. And the price was high if there were still survivors in the overrun zones.

Hammerson knew that no country was going to be able to continue nuking its own territory. There had to be a better way.

He turned to another of the huge screens – their sophisticated artificial intelligence MUSE system tapped into every foreign power's security database to see what they were using, where they were using it, and when. If any one of them had found a solution to the swarm that didn't involve weapons of mass destruction, he'd adopt it. So far they had the same as he did: *nothing*.

Their own swarms were now moving at will over Texas, Oklahoma and Arkansas, with smaller ones over Mississippi and Missouri. Reluctantly, he'd taken Hartigan's advice and used crop dusters to spray them with hydrofluoric acid. On contact it melted the bastards right out of the sky. But it also poisoned the landscape. Plus, seeing it was a contact toxin, they could never hope to physically hit every single one of the damn things.

"Fucking bugs," he muttered. Some were calling it the return of the biblical plagues.

Extinction plagues, Hammerson thought as he exhaled through clenched teeth. The difference was, where the locust plagues ate the crops, these horrifying sons of bitches went after the people and ate the bones right out of the flesh.

"Colonel."

Hammerson turned.

"Professor Kearns has arrived."

Hammerson nodded. "Take them to laboratory two, and see they've got everything they need. I'll be there in thirty minutes."

Colonel Jack Hammerson headed for the door. Hartigan had something to show him in relation to the bugs. Somehow he bet it wasn't going to be good news.

*

Jack Hammerson ignored the cold of the refrigerated room and focused on the long metal table with four large foam blocks at varying intervals.

Doctor Phillip Hartigan stood rod straight, arms by his side, and a colleague at each shoulder.

Hammerson looked from the trio to the blocks.

"Ladies and gentlemen, at ease." Hammerson nodded. "I hope you've got something for me."

"We have, but unfortunately nothing good."

Hammerson snorted. "Why did I expect that?"

Hartigan stepped toward the long steel bench. "We've shown before that the silicon entities are growing, and evolving."

"Evolving? First time I've heard this." Hammerson frowned. "How? I thought it took hundreds if not thousands of generations for an evolutionary change to become apparent."

"That's true. But we know with biological entities like these that have a sped-up metabolism and lifespan, generational change can occur very quickly. Look at *Drosophila melanogaste*, the fruit fly. In four years it can have had over two hundred generations."

"So they're like large fruit flies?" Hammerson looked up, waiting.

"No, their lifespans are longer, and the changes are more significant. Something else is promoting the alterations. Maybe it's the solar energy, or something else in the atmosphere or environment. But whatever it is, these things are rapidly changing."

"How?" Hammerson asked.

"Becoming more formidable for a start," the small scientist beside Hartigan added.

Hammerson recognized the woman. "Doctor Miles." He nodded to her. The young scientist was Hartigan's specialist entomologist. Hammerson had read some of her analytical work previously, and recognized she had a top-class mind.

"More formidable? Well that's just great. We're already having trouble stopping them now."

Hammerson stared down at the steel tables and their four passengers. On the first foam block was the original specimen, roughly the size of a hornet. The next showed a specimen about the size of a fist. On this one it was easier to pick out the anomalies from normal hexapod invertebrate creatures, such as the eight legs, scales and tufts of fur underneath.

The third block had a grotesque insectoid-looking thing that was around a foot in length. It hardly looked real – its carapace looked like black plastic. But he could see the eyes looked more human than insect, and Hammerson immediately felt a visceral revulsion for the thing. He couldn't imagine being out in the open when a swarm of these descended on you.

This specimen had half extended the needle-like proboscis that it used to pierce its prey, inject the digestive enzyme, and then later suck out the liquefied calcium and silicon compounds.

Hammerson turned then to the last specimen.

"Jesus," he whispered, and folded his arms as he stared at the thing tied to the block. It had been captured just a few hours ago, and had to weigh in at forty pounds. The damn thing was nearly three feet long.

The eight legs were spread wide, and on the end of each there was a branching that made it look like there was a tiny hand complete with fingers. The face now looked like some sort of human-insect gargoyle mix and it made the skin on his scalp crawl.

"Why does it look like that?" Hammerson asked softly.

Hartigan shrugged. "Maybe its diet is influencing the way it looks. Maybe eventually, when it reaches its final form, it plans to try and blend in with the herds of its prey ... us."

"Be a cold day in hell." Hammerson ground his teeth.

"Hell is right." Hartigan nodded. "Its evolutionary changes are alarmingly fast. But though its appearance is quite disconcerting –"

"Disconcerting?" Hammerson frowned. "You think?"

Hartigan flat smiled. "Just distancing myself scientifically from the horror of the silicoid creatures, Colonel."

"*Silicoids*." Hammerson snorted.

Doctor Miles took over. "Its external appearance is certainly alarming, Colonel, and with its silicon armor plating, and biomechanical exoskeleton it is extremely strong for its size. But it's the internal changes that concern us."

Hammerson laughed softly. He knew that if it concerned these guys, it probably was for damned good reason. "Tell me," he said softly.

Using gloved hands, she grasped the head of the largest creature and removed the top of its skull. The exoskeleton plating had obviously been separated before, and now lifted like a lid.

Beneath there was a pulpy pink-gray mass showing the gyrus and sulcus folds.

"It has a brain?" Hammerson waited.

"Oh yes, all insects have primitive brains. Though the insect brain does not play as important a role as human mammalian brains do. In fact, an insect can live for several days without a head, assuming it does not lose a lethal amount of hemolymph, the insect equivalent of blood, upon decapitation."

Doctor Miles pointed. "The previous versions of the silicoids had a more normal brain for arthropod creatures in that it was little more than a brain stem. Like a spinal cord with a lump of neuron clusters at one end."

She walked along the table, pointing to each specimen. "In each version or iteration, its brains grew exponentially, and with it we assume its intelligence." She stopped at the largest version. "Neurons vary in number among insect brains. The common fruit fly has one hundred thousand neurons, while a honeybee has one million neurons – they are regarded as the smartest insects and have fantastic memories."

"As a benchmark, a human being has eighty-six billon neurons," Hartigan added. His lips set in a grim line as he stared down at the creature.

"And these things?" Hammerson asked.

"This guy here, about fifty million. See those tiny digits on the end of its arms? They're fully dexterous." Lana looked up. "They're problem-solvers now, Colonel." She stepped back and took off her gloves. "For now, they're not even as smart as a dog. And that's a good thing. But each version is hundreds of times smarter than the previous version."

Hammerson exhaled through his nose. "How long?"

"Until they're as smart as we are?" Hartigan's eyes were resigned. "Possibly three more iterations. In about five they'll be *smarter* than we are."

"And possibly a lot bigger." Hammerson began to turn away. "Keep working, time is growing short."

Hammerson felt a little lightheaded. The iterations were occurring cyclically at around one every two weeks. In less than two months their adversaries would be their equals. In another month, the bugs would be their superiors.

"One more thing, sir."

Hammerson turned, his mind still whirling with what he had just heard.

"You asked why the silicoids seemed to be converging." Hartigan walked forward.

"And *where* they were converging. Go on." Hammerson waited.

"Silicon, of course," Hartigan replied. "They're primarily made up of it, they ingest it, they seek it out. And where are the largest silicon mines in the US?"

Hammerson slowly nodded. "Minnesota."

Hartigan gave him a crooked smile. "It's a theory."

"It's one that makes sense. Well done." Hammerson gave him a small salute. "Keep at it."

Hammerson headed for the door. He had plans to make and a million things to do. Priority one, the president needed to know where they were up to, and the risks and options, one of them being nuking swathes of their own countryside. It wasn't a call Hammerson was looking forward to making.

CHAPTER 30

USA – USSTRATCOM Headquarters, sub-level 1 laboratories

Matt stood as Jack Hammerson entered their laboratory facility. It had been a while since he had been in the tough HAWC leader's physical presence, and the first thing he noticed was the man still looked as bull-necked and formidable as ever. But the second thing he noticed was his eyes looked tired as hell.

Hammerson gave Matt a flat smile and shook his hand. "Well done on the stone retrieval." He crossed to where the two large slabs had been laid side by side. "Let's hope you can make something of them." He turned. "Have you been brought up to date?"

Matt shook his head. "We came straight from the landing pad. We'd still like to get cleaned up, and maybe grab something to eat."

"Of course. Straight after we finish speaking." He placed his hands on his hips. "I won't lie to you, son, events are spinning away on us, and we're definitely on the back foot here."

"When we spoke a few weeks back you mentioned that the first stone had some dates that paralleled with the mass extinctions of our past. And it also contained an image of the bug things we are calling silicoids. We are of the firm belief now that these things may very well have been responsible for those extinctions." He looked grim. "Now it seems it's our turn."

Matt blinked. "It's getting that bad?"

"Yes, *that bad*, and then some. It's a global plague," Hammerson said. "But what you've already been able to discern so far leads me to believe that the people that made these stones have seen this before, and knew about the creatures. Perhaps even knew how to stop them. After all, if not, then there'd be no life on Earth other than these goddamn things, right?"

"That's what I think as well," Matt replied. "The Aztlanteans were sophisticated enough to chart the creature's historical and future arrival. But there must have been something that stopped the bugs."

Matt's brows drew together. "It's pretty clear that they have come before, and it looks like it was often. Perhaps there are sporadic outbreaks that flare and then die out. And then there are the massive waves that wipe out entire species."

"The mass extinctions." Hammerson nodded.

"Yes, and people have vanished in the past – hundreds of thousands of people, and all inexplicably." Matt counted off on his fingers. "There were the Mayans of around 900 BC. A thriving population, or what was left of them, fled their cities and vanished into the jungle. The Indus Valley, three thousand years ago, where the Happen civilization that comprised almost ten percent of the world's population – five million people spread over a region that encompassed parts of today's India, Pakistan, Iran and Afghanistan – all just disappeared. And so many more, all gone, gone, gone."

Hammerson grunted. "It's like something was doing test runs. Or perhaps just a small portion of whatever it is leaks out, before a major event occurs: the mass extinctions."

Matt shrugged. "And no graves, no remains. The only way populations of that size could totally vanish is if there was nothing left to be fossilized. No bones, no teeth, no nothing."

Hammerson gave them a flat smile. "Please tell me you can find out the *when*, and the *where*." He lifted his chin. "There's fresh clothing and food prepared for you right here. Unfortunately, you cannot leave the base now, as we are all in lockdown until we get some answers."

"C'mon, Jack, I'm a prisoner?" Matt scoffed.

"Of course not." Hammerson held his arms wide. "You're an official guest of the Commander in Chief." He smiled. "You know the drill, son. Find us some answers, and do it quick."

Matt walked slowly toward the two stones. "If the answers are here, I'll find them." He held up a finger. "But on one condition. I need to check whether my mom and annoying cousin are okay."

"We can reach out, but you can't be discussing anything that's classified. Which is basically everything you're working on," Hammerson replied.

"At a minimum, I want to check they're safe." Matt lowered his brow.

"No problem, where are they?" Hammerson smiled.

"Walnut Grove, Minnesota."

Hammerson worked to hold his smile. "Sure, Matt, leave it with me."

*

Following a scalding shower and a huge breakfast, Matt reentered the laboratory. First thing he saw was a long bench that held both stone tablets, and standing beside it were two people, a man and a woman he hadn't meet before. The man, tall and slim, walked toward Matt with his hand outstretched.

"Doctor Phillip Hartigan." He motioned to the intense but attractive-looking young woman standing beside him. "And my colleague, Doctor Lana Miles."

The woman was maybe early thirties, and perhaps of Sri Lankan heritage. She had the largest and darkest eyes Matt had ever seen.

"Matthew Kearns, professor of linguistics." Matt shook their outstretched hands.

"We know. We know all about you and have been looking forward to meeting you," Hartigan replied. "The colonel speaks very highly of you, so we're also looking forward to pooling ideas and working together."

"Sure." Matt beamed. "What are your specializations?"

"Entomology, evolutionary biology, chemistry, and with a specialization in disease vectors," Lana replied casually. "And surfing."

Matt's brows came together at that. "Uh, me too. In fact, I love it."

"Ever been to Bells Beach?" she asked.

"What?" He grinned. "Yes."

Hartigan poured Matt a coffee and handed it to him. "We think these creatures evolved at a time long before the first carbon-based life-forms appeared. Somehow their eggs get released to the surface from time to time, they hatch, and then seek out sustenance."

"Unfortunately that seems to be us," Matt added, and glanced at Lana who toasted him with her coffee.

"Actually, not just humans, but anything and everything that has a worthwhile level of silicon and calcium in its physiology. This in itself is revolting, sure, but we could probably deal with that," Hartigan said. "The problem is we think that perhaps something in the atmosphere or the sunlight is accelerating their evolutionary growth. Millions of years of evolution in mere months."

"It took mankind four million years to go from a three and half foot high hominid on the grassy plains of Africa to where we are today. These silicoids will be on the same evolutionary rung as us in a few more months' time." Lana shrugged. "In another month, beyond that."

"But something stopped them before," Matt added. "Like Jack Hammerson said, otherwise, we wouldn't be here to even talk about it." He stepped up closer to the stone tablets. There were downlights playing on their surface and the stones had been fitted together so their seams joined.

Matt traced a hand from one to the other, and then nodded. "Look here. This completes the date structures. It'll at least show us when the next quakes will occur and release the next swarm."

"But not where," Hartigan said.

"No, and the Earth is a damn big place." He ran his hand across the ancient language pictoglyphs. "It's August, now. The final event calculated is 21 November – the final swarm."

"Unless we stop it," Hartigan said. "So how did they do it before?"

Matt found the ancient quote again. "*They have come and they will come again. Each ending greater than the last. Only those from the center,* or maybe – *core, can stop them, when ...*" He traced across the split in the stone to the next one. "When ... *the gal-ka-tar blooms.*"

Matt frowned. "The language is a root language and shares overlaps with many ancient tongues. This word string here – *gal-ka-tar* – has a close comparison to the Sumerian word, ka-tar, or fungus. It's paired with the symbol gal for large or tall." He shrugged. "An ancient tall fungus, or tall mushroom?"

"How ancient?" Lana asked.

Matt shrugged. "Might have to be many millions of years old for all we know."

"Prototaxites," Lana said confidently.

"Great, what are they, and where are they?" Matt said.

Lana turned to Hartigan and they both laughed darkly. Hartigan lifted his hands. "We didn't even know what they were when they were first discovered."

"So, they're rare?" Matt asked.

"You might say that." Lana sighed. "Imagine you were in a time before any creatures had come up onto the land, and the only thing living on the planet was mosses, lichens, and some primitive ferns. Then in among this low-level boggy matting, rising up twenty feet like green telegraph poles were these massive fungi. They were the mighty redwoods of our very young primordial planet." She smiled. "That's what prototaxites were – a giant anomaly."

"Sounds amazing," Matt said. "Where are they now? And even better, how do we get one?"

"Got a time machine?" Hartigan gave him a crooked smile. "Unfortunately, they're all gone."

"Once they were all over the planet ... once." Lana nodded. "The prototaxites died out between three hundred and fifty and four hundred million years ago."

"That's not possible." Matt scowled. "The Aztlanteans knew about them, and my gut feel is they also used them somehow. Maybe like a pest control."

"You mean biocontrol." Lana smiled. "We do it right now, right here. It's a method of controlling pests such as insects, mites, weeds, and plant diseases using other organisms. It relies on predation, parasitism, herbivory, or other natural mechanisms. It's very effective, if done right."

"The red ladybug," Hartigan added.

"Correct, and a good example. *Rodolia cardinalis*, the red vedalia ladybug was imported from Australia to California in the nineteenth century, and was used to successfully control the scale bugs." She smiled and tilted her head. "A good example of it being used properly."

"The cane toad." Matt smiled with little humor. "Is an example of not using it wisely, and an example of the US sending a little something Australia's way that didn't work out." He went on. "In 1935, the Australians released some specially bred cane toads from Hawaii to control the cane beetle problem they were having. Well, it was later discovered that the toads could not jump very high and so were unable to eat the cane beetles that stayed on the upper stalks of the cane plants. So, instead the toads started feeding on everything else, even other toads, frogs, then lizards, and also small mammals.

"Unlike in Hawaii, in Australia they had no predators." Matt exhaled as he remembered his biology. "And they grew big, some the size of a dinner plate. Oh yeah, and they had poison sacs on their shoulders, so anything trying to eat them usually died."

"Doesn't work forever," Hartigan replied. "The local predators are now adapting. Some snakes are now immune to their poison."

"Takes generations," Matt replied.

"I know, and that we don't have." Hartigan sighed. "But it does work. And besides, we've kinda got our backs to the wall right now. So if using a fungus slows these bugs down or kills them, then we run a unit test on it, then a field test – and then we use it." He snorted softly. "So where is it? Where did these mystical people of yours find them?"

"I think they told us, and where, on a map," Matt said.

*

Matt went back to the first stone, and moved back and forth between the two. The map he'd found previously made more sense when the details were fleshed out with what anyone else would have thought were random dots and lines.

He let his hands trail over the greenish stones. "It's my firm belief that the *gal-ka-tar* they refer to was either secreted in some hidden place or came from this place." He sighed and he stared at the carved images. "I'm sure it's a map." Matt frowned as he read through the words that accompanied the simple picture. "It's not clear," he added softly.

"What can I do to help?" Lana asked.

"Be my sounding board," Matt replied. "Are these damn things supposed to be coordinates?" He sighed. "Okay, let's think a little more laterally – the Aztlanteans were the greatest seafaring race of their time, and the land and shorelines didn't look the same as they do now. Plus, they undoubtedly used an entirely different measurement system."

"Given the time frame, that makes sense." Lana opened her search engine. "Tell me what to look for."

"I need to get inside their heads. So far, I can read that the destination is …" He traced the ancient words. "*The tiny jungle covered*, something, something, *green jewel of the great warm ocean*," Matt translated. "That could be the Indian or the Pacific Ocean. Maybe referring to an island in one of those oceans."

Lana typed into her computer for a moment. "Well, there are a hundred and fifteen islands in the Indian ocean." She continued to type.

"Not too bad." Matt nodded. "And what about –"

"Oh boy." She laughed softly. "There's twenty-five thousand in the Pacific Ocean."

"Oh good grief." He sat back. "Twenty-five thousand?" His brows slid in defeat.

"The rim of fire," she said. "The Pacific Ocean islands are on the edge of a tectonic plate and are mostly formed from volcanic activity. Plus from coral sandbar accretion. More form up every single year." She sat back. "So, which one will we start with?"

"We have an image of the small landmass we are looking for. It even has marks on it where we are supposed to look." He sighed. "Look for that geography as a first pass."

Lana grabbed the image and scanned it; she came up empty. "The computer doesn't recognize it. And for all we know it's not an island at all. Maybe it's a state boundary, or a physical boundary. After twelve thousand years the land identified might be totally submerged or washed away."

Matt nodded, and then turned to point at her. "What you said."

"It's a state or physical boundary?" Lana asked.

"No, no – that it's all wiped out or washed away." He clicked his fingers. "Because of course."

She glided closer. "What have you found?"

"We're looking for an island shape based on today's geology, and sea level. But twelve thousand years ago, the sea level was hundreds of feet lower, so ..."

"So the island today will be smaller, and its shape different." Lana clapped. "Very well done."

Matt entered a subject date into the computer, and then ran a simulation of the global landscape as it would have looked about twelve thousand years ago. The computer gave him his answer back almost immediately.

"Now we'll see if this global model matches to our island shape."

He entered the new data and ran it again. The small circle turned on the screen as the processor searched for a match.

While it did its work, Matt snuck a glance at Lana. He knew he'd never met her before, but something about her was familiar.

Lana caught him looking and smiled back a little mischievously. "Have we met before?" she asked with a gleam in her eye.

Matt snorted softly. "I'd remember."

"Are you sure?" she asked, with one delicate eyebrow arched.

The computer pinged with a proximal hit on their search. Matt turned back to the screen and read. "Close enough, I guess." He folded his arms and turned to Lana. "What do you think?"

"Really?" She raised her eyebrows. "Easter Island?"

"Why not?" He hiked his shoulders. "Remote, Pacific Ocean, has been inhabited for about eight hundred years, and before that, it was a remote uninhabited jungle paradise – a green jewel."

"That's the place with the huge statues that are half buried, right?" she asked.

"That's the one. Now let's see what we have to deal with." He created a three-way comparison of the image from the stone with the extrapolated map of the island of how it would have looked twelve thousand years ago, against how it looked today.

Matt resized them so they were a physical match. The stone's image showed a mark on the lower western area of the map. The extrapolated version showed a green peninsula, and then Matt looked across to the current satellite version of the map.

"Somewhere around here." He pointed. "There's the southwestern end of the island, water, and then an even tinier island that's more like a rocky outcrop." He traced the map, following where the coordinates took him. "Damn."

Lana's eyelids drooped. "Well, who didn't see that coming?"

"It's underwater. It's between Easter Island and this small island." Matt shook his head. "Come on, guys, you couldn't have picked somewhere a little more inland?"

"Oh well, look at it this way: if there's anything to find, it'll be in some place that people haven't been tramping over for eight hundred years."

Matt got to his feet. "We'd better tell Hammerson he'll need some divers."

CHAPTER 31

The Schneider Compound, Treptow, Germany

Rudolph Schneider watched as his first team equipped with helmet cams entered the cave. He steepled his fingers as they approached the large slab of stone and eased it aside.

Without taking his eyes from the screen he lifted his hand to the microphone headset and repositioned the receiver bead in front of his mouth.

"Be careful, no trace now. Let's not show our hand."

"Roger that," came the reply. Then: "There's goddamn something in here with us … alive."

Schneider sat forward. "Stay quiet, go to infrared, and hurry up."

After another few moments of watching his team progress, Schneider smiled and sat back as he saw the inside of the receptacle revealed. "One step ahead, always one step ahead."

He chuckled and then turned to the bell jar and the flaking head within. "You were always one step ahead, mein Führer. If you weren't double-crossed, this world would be yours now."

He turned back to the screen.

"But we'll fix that aberration very soon."

Schneider waited until his first team secured their objective and were on their way out, and then turned his attention to the next element in his plan. He had organized for some samples of the creatures to be collected, and he had dispatched a second team of his best workers under the supervision of one of the top university biology professors he funded to facilitate the animal gathering.

Right now they were approaching one of the smaller swarms on the outskirts of Inzlingen, a small village in the district of Lörrach in Baden-Württemberg.

His team were equipped with cameras, and he only needed to press different keys on his keyboard to swap between images.

The university professor, Deiter, led them from a scientific perspective, but Heinrich, an ex paratrooper, was the point man on the ground. Two other men carried glass specimen tanks and three-foot long metal poles with a steel claw on the end for grasping the things.

All of the men wore thick neoprene tear-proof suits that he bet were stifling even in the mild heat down there. He smiled – better you than me, but that's what you're paid for.

From Heinrich's camera he saw Deiter point to the hill.

"I see the approaching swarm. We'll collect two live specimens and then withdraw."

"Proceed," Schneider said and pursed his lips, watching intently.

The swarm came at them like a wall – some flying, some crawling, but all of them bristling and shining like black ceramics in the sunshine. From the men's microphones he could hear the deep insectoid *zumm* and the beating of thousands of veined wings.

"*Gott im himmel,*" he heard one of the men whisper.

In a few seconds his team was engulfed and over the speaker he heard the scrabbling of thousands of tiny sharp feet. The creatures clung to the men, first a few, then dozens, and then many more. He watched from Heinrich's camera feed as the man grabbed one from his arm and held it up in one large hand. The eyes were amazing and horrible in that they seemed more mammalian than insect, and they swiveled to stare up at Heinrich with great interest.

Schneider narrowed his eyes as he watched; there was intelligence in the thing's gaze that unsettled him. He reached for his cup of coffee.

"*Ouch.*"

The single word spun Heinrich around to see Deiter trying to brush one of the things from his shoulder.

"They're puncturing the suits," Deiter wailed. "They're getting in."

"Impossible," Schneider countered.

Heinrich held up his hand, and Schneider leaned closer to the screen. The creature he held was the size of a small dog, all over black, had around eight legs, and bristled with spikes and thick insect hairs. It wriggled furiously in his hand, but then it stopped, leaned forward, and let its proboscis bloom open like a fleshy flower.

It used those tiny pulpy digits to attach itself to Heinrich's hand, and then something that looked like a needle shot out from their center, and went straight through his toughened glove and obviously into his hand.

Schneider was entranced and watched open-mouthed as Heinrich roared a curse, and flicked his hand. But the thing clung on, its legs also digging in. Heinrich used his other hand to grab it and wailed his anguish. In the background Schneider could see the other men battling the horde, with one of them down on the ground.

"Pull back," he said softly. The men continued to wrestle and fight with the things. Schneider licked his lips. "*I said, pull back, you fools.*"

Heinrich's hand suddenly sagged, and then the forearm. Other creatures joined in, clinging to him, from his feet to his face.

"It hurts." Heinrich's scream was extraordinarily high for such a big man, Schneider thought as the ex paratrooper flopped to the ground.

The man continued to scream, but oddly, his voice became mushy and the words indistinct as though his tongue was too big or he had cotton wool in his mouth.

There was a deep sob, a wet blubbering sound like a fart, and then silence. Schneider breathed out slowly through his nose, and reached forward to turn the screen off.

He slowly took his hands away from the monitor controls. *That ... did not go well.*

CHAPTER 32

Inbound, Easter Island, south-eastern Pacific Ocean

Roy Maddock half smiled. "You live an interesting life, Professor Kearns."

Matt nodded. "Yeah, and sometimes whether I like it or not." He sat back. "So, the sub, how long until it gets there?"

"It's already on its way," Vin said, grinning. "We have a navel base, Fort Aguayo, in Concón, ninety miles north-west of Santiago, Chile's capital. The rescue submersible we've been loaned will accommodate all of us."

"Who's going to pilot it?" Matt asked.

"Them. Chile doesn't trust us that much." Vin grinned. "But all HAWCs have submersible experience, so we're all good."

"I've been snorkeling, but diving to two hundred feet is beyond my capabilities." Matt turned to the scientists. "Have you dived that far down?"

Phillip Hartigan nodded. "I've deep dived before on wrecks in California Bay. I have my own kit, but I'm told I won't need that."

"Nope, not dived that deep. I can swim like a fish, snorkel, and surf, but that's it." Lana Miles smiled up at him.

"Where do you surf?" Matt smiled back.

"Everywhere." She wiggled her eyebrows.

Klara glared. "We'll only be in two hundred feet of water, not two thousand. Hull ruptures at two hundred you might burst your eardrums but can still survive. Most of you anyway." Klara laughed and nudged Matt.

"Thanks for the pep talk." Lana scowled at the female HAWC.

Klara lowered her face a little closer to the female scientist. "Don't forget your water wings."

"That's enough," Maddock ordered. He turned to Lana. "We'll be fine, and probably won't even need to leave the submersible."

Lana nodded and exhaled through circled lips. She turned away to face the small porthole window of the airplane.

Maddock turned to Phillip Hartigan. "Remind me again what we're looking for. Briefing notes says some sort of tall fungus that doesn't exist anymore."

The chief scientist nodded. "That's right. It's called a prototaxite, and died out around four hundred million years ago. Perhaps we have, or had, some sort of remnant species existing there, or at least some further answers." He smiled and turned to Matt. "We're all following Professor Kearns' trail of breadcrumbs on this one."

Matt shrugged. "Wish I felt more confident. Unfortunately, the place we're headed to might have been the perfect isolated laboratory for a remnant species. That was until people turned up around eight hundred years ago. And don't forget that where we're supposed to look sunk under two hundred feet of water," Matt added. "My limited understanding of fungus and fungal spores is that it has a physical aversion to salt water."

Lana turned from her window. "Obligate marine fungi grow exclusively in seawater. But they're a very different species. Most perish very quickly."

Klara snorted. "So could be a waste of time?"

"We know next to nothing about the ancient fungi – its preferential growth conditions, lifespan, composition – so it might not be a waste of time at all." Lana faced away again.

"No, it won't be." Maddock's voice had an edge. "Given what's occurring around the world right now, I don't think any search for answers is a waste of time."

Klara sat back. "Just saying we could have dropped a submersible drone. Done some advanced recon, and saved us a trip."

"The colonel disagrees with you. Feel free to take it up with him on your return, Second Lieutenant." Maddock eyeballed her. "We're already in motion, so let's do our job."

In another forty minutes, the chopper landed on the green grassy cliff top, and a few local Chilean military personnel were already there waiting for them. There were tents set up, which made Matt wonder just how long Hammerson expected they'd be there.

They had touched down on the western side of the main island alongside a long-dead volcano crater that had been worn down. Its rim only rose a few dozen feet and in its bowl was a shallow, marshy lake.

The chopper bounced and the group piled out. They dropped their gear and the HAWCs grabbed the last of the equipment and then waved the chopper off.

Maddock saluted the Chilean soldiers and talked to them by himself while Vin and Klara headed straight to the tents.

Matt, Hartigan and Lana stood on the grassy slope and turned slowly.

"It's just a green desert," Lana said. "Nothing growing above a few feet." She turned to Matt. "The Aztlanteans described this place as a jungle so green it was like a jewel."

Matt nodded. "Yeah, I had to do some research on Easter Island in my final year of studies. It was a sad tale, and a warning of using up scarce resources. Everything is gone; even the original culture and language has been lost."

The group gathered in closer to listen, and Matt cast his mind back to his notes and the pictures of the island's sad demise.

"At their peak, the Rapa Nuians, as they called themselves, numbered about three thousand. When a Dutch navigator by the name of Jacob Roggeveen first arrived in 1722, he described a place of robust natives, magnificent stone idols, and lush forests. It wasn't a happy visit as he was attacked, and it ended with the death of around twenty of the islanders.

"People steered clear for half a century, but then in 1774, the Englishman Captain James Cook arrived and also mentioned the idols, but sadly, he noted that many were knocked over, made no mention of forests left at all, and he found the natives in a terrible state."

Matt sighed. "It seems that something happened. Perhaps the last of the trees was felled to assist in the rolling of the giant idols into place. But their beautiful island and idyllic life were gone."

"That's terrible," Lana said.

"It was." Matt turned to them. "Everything was consumed or lost, even their ability to read and write their own language, the Rongorongo script. It's why I became involved because it was the only Polynesian script to have been found to date, and there was no one left who could decipher their lost language."

"Those poor people." Lana looked around the green desert island. "Did they ever recover?"

"No." Matt shook his head. "The visiting sailors also left the survivors with smallpox and then tuberculosis. By the mid-1800s there were only just on one hundred people left here."

"It's like they were cursed," Klara said evenly.

"Maybe they were. Maybe destroying the island's ecology, or not maintaining the upkeep of their moai statues, angered their primitive gods. But this once island paradise, the green jewel, was turned into a prison of disease and death."

"The island was cursed with people." Lana put a hand to her forehead to shield her eyes from the sun as she looked out over the sparkling ocean. "It must have been magnificent twelve thousand years ago, when the Aztlanteans first came. It's just a grassy lump in the middle of the ocean now."

Roy Maddock walked closer to the cliff edge. "Right now, what's happened above sea level is of no interest to us. Let's just hope whatever is waiting for us below is worth our time."

"What are we expecting?" Vin asked.

"Good question." Lana turned to Matt. "What exactly are we looking for?"

Matt snorted softly. "Answers." He shrugged. "Anything out of the normal."

"Seriously?" Klara's laugh was like a bark. "Define *normal*."

*

Matt joined Roy Maddock who stood on the cliff edge looking down at the dark blue stretch of water between the Easter Island landmass and the smaller rocky outcrop just on half a mile out.

Maddock acknowledged Matt and then nodded toward the outcrop. "I read that, as a rite of passage, the young Rapa Nuians had to swim out to that island and grab a bird's egg and then swim back. The only problem was the area was infested with sharks. Big ones." He turned to smile. "And I thought the HAWC entry testing was a tough gig."

Matt laughed. "So what do you think? Will we find anything?"

"Shouldn't I be asking you that?" Maddock shrugged. "This whole island, Easter Island, is basically three volcanic cones joined together. The thing about volcanic rock is it weathers in different stages." He turned to Matt. "And that means it leaves plenty of holes. So, if I had to guess, I'd say there is a cave down there. But I'm betting it was hidden, and at two hundred feet we start to lose the light, so …"

"So it might be there, and we might never find it," Matt said.

Maddock grinned. "If it's there, we'll find it. We didn't come all this way just for a sub ride, right?"

CHAPTER 33

Walnut Grove, Redwood county, Minnesota

Karen Kearns pulled up out front of her home, with Megan still grumbling in the seat beside her after she had driven into town to pick her up.

Her house was a well-kept American Foursquare dating from 1919. It had handcrafted woodwork, was the typical boxy design, two-and-one-half stories high, and a large front porch with wide stairs that she loved sitting out on in the late, warm spring evenings with her dog, Belle.

"C'mon, Meg, cheer up. We've got plenty of food, booze, and wood for the fire. Plus Matt promised to try and be here for Thanksgiving dinner." She grabbed one of the bags.

Megan grabbed two more bags. "Yeah, well, my bestest cousin Matt blew me off, the conference was boring, and Danny isn't talking to me. My life sucks right now. Thank god for booze."

"That's the spirit." Karen grinned as she headed up the steps. At the top she dropped the bag and squinted at a small card stuck in the doorframe.

"What is it?" Megan asked.

"Looks official." Karen turned it over. "Someone from the government was looking for me. Asking me to contact them." She checked her watch and then shrugged. "Too late now, I'll do it tomorrow maybe."

She tucked the card into the side pocket of her jacket. And forgot about it.

CHAPTER 34

Matt quickly typed in a message to Jack Hammerson asking about his family and sent it as the helicopter winched them down onto the deck of the Chilean dive command ship.

At the rear, tied to the huge platform, was their submersible, the machine was a brilliant yellow and shaped like a vitamin capsule. At its rounded front was a large domed window, and underneath were folded mechanical arms, like those of a praying mantis, which ended in what looked like long-nosed pliers and a cutting tool.

Matt checked his phone – no response from Hammerson. He cursed and looked back at what was going to be their home for the next few hours. Along the side were tiny portholes and he had already been told that the submersible was tested to a depth of twelve thousand feet, certainly not the deepest of dives by this type of craft, but considering they only needed to drop two hundred or so, it would be a walk in the park. He hoped.

"Load 'em up," Maddock yelled, and Vin and Klara climbed up the side and dropped in.

Damn, he thought. "Just a minute." He stared at his phone, willing it to answer. Hammerson was usually good at responding. Unless, that is, he didn't want to.

Hartigan went into the sub next, and Lana grabbed his arm. "Come on, or all the best seats will be gone."

"It's not a fun park ride, you know." Matt grinned as she slipped on a rung; he gave her ass a push up the ladder.

His phone buzzed and he stopped to read the message: *Haven't located them yet. Will keep at it. More soon. Out.*

"Come on, Mom, where are you?" he whispered, and then tucked his phone away and climbed in through the hatch.

The submersible was even more cramped than the helicopter. The three HAWCs, doctors Lana and Phillip Hartigan, and Matt, plus the single pilot of the submersible, Miguel, a small man with wild hair like dark wire, were jammed in tight.

Matt nudged Lana. "Remind me which of these seats were supposed to be the good ones."

"Stinks," she whispered into his ear.

Matt inhaled. "Yep."

She was right; they were sealed in with the smells of oil, cold steel, body odor and a hint of bad breath.

Each of them was close to a window, but most of them faced forward toward the larger domed window that acted as the main viewing portal. In minutes they were being lifted and then hoisted over the side.

It was a sun-filled day, and they were told they'd have good visibility for the first hundred feet, and then more of a deep blue twilight following that. Matt knew it would stay like that while they remained in the epipelagic zone that extended down for around six hundred feet. But below that, in the mesopelagic zone, everything suddenly turned to a lightless dark.

And that lightless dark wasn't far way; the entire island was a volcanic uplift and though they would be traveling along a shallow, submerged spit, its slopes fell away for thousands of feet. Matt blew air through pressed lips. He felt a little claustrophobic in the lemon yellow tin can.

The submarine reached the bottom and, even though there was faint light, the powerful lamps came on. The bottom was rocky with patches of weed and a few large blue gropers watching them from small caves, their thick lips hung open and fat fins kept them in a hovering position as they watched the submarine power past.

Beside him Lana crowded close to his porthole. "Try and imagine what it was like all those years ago. It was dry land and people were walking out there."

Matt nodded. "They might have walked along some sort of path with trees all around them as they headed toward what would have been a narrow peak many hundreds of feet high. That's now just a tiny rocky outcrop poking a few hundred feet above the waterline."

"Is that what we should be looking for, a stone pathway?" Lana asked.

"Unlikely. It might have been more like an animal track. I think at the time the island was as remote as you could get. So that was why it was chosen as a hiding place, or why the fungi survived here in some sort of last outpost. Whichever way, there'll be no telltale signs or structures. At least no external construction anyway," Matt replied.

"Whatever we find, it'll be flooded." Lana turned to him. "After twelve thousand years, there's no such thing as watertight."

"Certainly not if it was on a downward slope." Matt turned. "But if it was in an upward-sloping cavern, it'd be in a bubble, right?" He smiled. "Let's stay positive."

"Coming up on the island outcrop now," Miguel said.

The outcrop was only a few hundred feet in circumference above water, but down here it was nearly a thousand around, and looked to be a sheer wall rising up before them. There were a few pockmarks in its surface and some kelp waved lazily on its side.

Miguel moved the light beams slowly back and forth over the bottom, and then lifted them to the rock wall.

"Starting our circuit now." Miguel maneuvered the craft along the wall's face. "We'll corkscrew around it toward the surface," he said.

Maddock moved up to the front of the craft to take a seat beside Miguel. Vin crouched between them, as it was the largest window with the best view, while Klara, Hartigan, Lana, and Matt took up positions on the individual porthole windows and stared out into the twilight darkness.

After twenty minutes Matt felt the beginning of a small tension headache behind his eyes from concentrating so hard. He rubbed at his temples with thumb and forefinger for a moment and then stared again.

"All stop," Maddock said softly, and the pilot engaged a little reverse thrust to keep the craft hovering in the same spot.

Maddock turned. "Professor Kearns." He motioned Matt forward.

Matt clambered to the front and Vin stepped out of the way to make room.

"What have you got?" Matt asked.

Maddock pointed. "You were looking for an opening?" He turned and grinned. "I give you an opening – a damn big opening."

Matt grinned as he stared at the huge cave opening. "But twelve thousand years ago the island was heavily forested. The cave mouth might have been overgrown." He ducked forward to try and see inside the cave opening.

"Do you think we can fit inside?"

Miguel bobbed his head. "I think yes, just fit."

"Then take us in, sir," Maddock said.

The submarine inched forward as the pilot worked the small joystick like a gamer, and Maddock worked one of the spotlights, panning it around the cave mouth.

Proximity warnings flashed on the console.

"Going to be tight. Please take your seats and strap in," Miguel said as he gently pushed the stick forward.

The submarine eased inside and only scraped away a little of the weed walls from the cave mouth as Miguel threaded the needle.

"Big," Matt whispered.

Inside, it was larger than any of them expected. Once out from under the entrance lip they found themselves in a sunken cathedral-sized cavern.

"Going to do a circuit." Miguel switched on all the external lamps, and the cave wall glowed all around them.

A shape glided past that looked like a long gray, striped torpedo.

"Whoa, that is some shark," Maddock said. "Tiger, fifteen footer."

"Man-eater," Matt observed. "And also woman-eater." He turned and winked at Lana.

She wrinkled her nose at him in reply, as another shark followed the first. It was only slightly smaller.

"Chances of me swimming are now less than zero," Lana pronounced.

"Seems this is their home." Maddock snorted. "And the early Rapa Nuians had to swim to this island."

Matt nodded. "You can see now why many never made it back."

Miguel moved the submersible around the perimeter of the cave at about three knots, and everyone pressed themselves up against their respective windows, trying to see everywhere at once.

"I'm not seeing anything," Vin said. "Big old empty cave with a few fish wondering who the hell we are."

"We haven't gone all the way around yet. Everyone keep a lookout for anything that looks like it's not natural – like statues, broken fragments, columns, or maybe even writing. But even straight lines are an indication of past workmanship," Matt said.

They continued to maneuver around the outside, coming to the center of the cave.

Maddock suddenly sat forward. "What about steps?"

"What, where?" Matt unbuckled himself and crawled forward. "Where?"

Maddock pointed. "I'm pretty sure they're not natural, wouldn't you agree, Professor?"

"No, I mean, yes." Matt smiled and then spoke over his shoulder. "Lana, come see this."

The woman crawled forward to wedge herself in between the men. "That's definitely carved."

"Miguel, can you get us in a little closer?" Matt felt his excitement rising.

"I'll try and get in under this lip of stone." The pilot lowered the craft until they just heard the gentle scrape from below as their undercarriage kissed the bottom for a moment.

He eased in, and then slowed. "Can't get us any closer than this."

Matt looked at the steps and then along the cave walls. There were no other adornments or markings. He craned his neck to look up.

The steps seemed to disappear at the end of a flat, shimmering roof. "What's that?" he pointed upwards.

The pilot followed his gaze, and then nodded. "That is the surface. Seems there might be an air pocket in here."

"Could only be a few inches of clearance up there. Or ..." Maddock turned to Matt.

"Or a complete cave system, that's hopefully dry." Matt rubbed his hands together. "We gotta go see."

"Agreed." Maddock sat back. "Take us up, slowly, Miguel."

The pilot checked his console, and then blew a little ballast to gently ease them upwards. He kept his eyes on his instruments while Matt and everyone inside the submersible were glued to the windows watching for the breach of the surface level.

"Can't see a thing," Lana observed. "We might breach onto solid rock."

"Miguel knows what he's doing," Maddock said calmly.

Miguel simply watched his instruments. "Breaching in, three, two, one ..."

"Brace," Maddock said softly.

They continued to rise, and Miguel slowly lifted the craft's windows above the water level. Miguel shook his head as he read data from his instrument panel.

"Is amazing. We're still one hundred and sixty feet below sea level, but we're in a dry cavern. Big one."

Water poured down from the windows, but the team saw nothing but their own reflections.

"Switching on lamps." Miguel flicked switches along the top of his panel, and the cavern became illuminated.

"Wow." Matt saw that the steps continued to climb out of the water and onto flat ground. He scrambled forward and looked out of the very top of the large domed window.

Matt glanced down at the console and saw that the air temp was eighty-two degrees. "It's like a greenhouse out there." He turned to Lana. "That's good, right?"

She bobbed her head. "If it was fully sealed off from the outside world, then the conditions certainly could be favorable."

Matt turned to Maddock. "Can we go out?"

"It's why we're here." He got to his feet. "Vin, Klara, you're up. Everyone fix headlamps, it's gonna be dark."

The two HAWCs rose, did a quick weapons check and headed for the hatch. Maddock pointed to the steps. "Try and get us in close, Miguel. Don't want us getting in the water with all those striped bear traps swimming around out there."

Miguel nodded. "The water is calm, so we can bump right up against the platform edge. Lose a little paint, but okay."

"Good man." Maddock turned to watch as Vin climbed the metal ladder and unscrewed the hatch. He cracked it and immediately air rushed in, popping everyone's ears.

Vin inhaled deeply. "Smells like old wet socks out here."

Matt followed them up, but stayed just inside the hatch tower. Maddock crossed to Hartigan, and Lana. "Everyone should come, but if you want to stay, then feel free."

Lana had unbuckled, pulled the headband with flashlight onto her forehead, and then shot past him.

"Do you know how often we get a budget for field work?" Hartigan chuckled. "We're coming."

Matt perched on the small tower as he watched Klara and Vin leap down onto the rock platform. He turned about slowly, letting his pipe of light illuminate the shelf, and tried to take it all in. An odd breeze ruffled his hair as if a small gust had blown by.

He turned – the water surface was like a sheet of black glass so it was a little weird to feel wind, seeing how deadly calm it was in this void. *Must be a hole in the cave wall somewhere*, he thought. *No, impossible*. The water pressure would flood the place in minutes.

He climbed out and carefully leaped to the rock platform and then looked back to the submersible. The sub had seemed dull and dark when he was in there, but now, compared to the stygian darkness of the cavern, it seemed lit up like a Christmas tree.

He could see the top of Miguel's head showing in the huge glass-domed front window as he sat at his command chair.

Phillip Hartigan was the last to jump down, leaving the hatch lid open for their return. Everyone's lights moved one way then the other, creating a chaotic strobing effect.

Matt was about to turn away, when he noticed movement. Beyond the submarine, the calm water was now home to several v-shaped ripples as shark fins cut the flat water. He guessed that the activity, or maybe the electrical impulses of the submarine, had drawn them.

Some members of the group switched on extra flashlights, but it did little to dispel the deep shadows.

"It's a shell," Lana observed. "Halo-ooo," she yelled.

The inside of the tiny island was completely hollow, and hundreds of feet above them her echo bounced back. Matt knew that they were still below the sea level, so that meant the cave roof was sealed and this cavern under enormous pressure; otherwise the water level would be equal with that outside.

Behind him the rock wall disappeared directly into the water. He heard a splash and the submersible bobbed, grazing up against the rock platform with a metallic grinding. It was probably one of the sharks coming up to take a quick look, maybe at Miguel, or perhaps at the several soft two-legged creatures just out of reach, for now, up on the rock shelf.

Matt watched the fins sailing around in the inky water. Sharks had amazing vision, and could see above and below water, and with their special eye lenses saw perfectly well in darkness, making them excellent night or depth hunters.

Maddock walked back to the rock shelf edge to look back down into the water for a few seconds. As he did, something large, gray, and conical lumped up in front of him, making him step back as rows of serrated teeth worked in the air for a moment.

He looked over his shoulder at Matt. "Seems the locals aren't taking too kindly to us being here." He turned back to the dark water. "Sorry, buddy, but no one is going swimming, so not a chance."

The rock platform was only about one hundred feet across, and empty except for some fetid-looking rock pools and patches of dark mosses. At its end there was a rock face, but in one area, there was a small alcove.

Lana pointed. "That's not a natural formation."

"That's a tunnel," Maddock said. "Let's go." He walked them toward the opening in the wall. Arriving at the outer rim, they saw the carving and Maddock stood aside. He held up his flashlight at the markings. "Professor, your opinion please."

Matt pushed forward. "Yes, yes, this is it." He translated: "*Hiding* or *secret place of the gal-ka-tar* – the tall fungus." He looked over his shoulder at Lana and Hartigan. "Pro …?"

"Prototaxites," she said.

Vin looked around in the gloom. "Not much sun for them, if this is where they've been for millions of years."

"They don't need sunlight. The primordial Earth that they once inhabited was mostly still shrouded in volcanic vapors. They shouldn't be hard to miss as they grew to thirty feet tall," Lana replied.

"So, we're looking for a tree that grows in the dark." Matt turned back to the tunnel.

"Nope, more like a thirty foot stalk of asparagus, and shouldn't be hard to miss." Lana smiled. "Ouch, *hey*! What the hell?" She put a hand to her head, frowning.

Everyone turned to her, and she scowled as multiple light beams lit her face up.

"Something hit me." She brought her hand away and her mouth dropped open. She held her hand out. "Blood."

"Falling rock?" Klara asked.

"No, it felt … alive." Lana scowled in the light beams, and kept a hand on her head.

Maddock drew his weapon. "Eyes out, there's something in here with us."

Matt suddenly remembered the small gust he had felt before – it wasn't a breeze, but something taking a swoop at him.

"Could it be bats?" he asked.

"How?" Hartigan asked. "The cave is sealed … and underwater."

"Can't see anything," Vin said.

"Let's get into the tunnel, at least it's a smaller place to defend," Matt said.

"Agreed. Let's move it." Maddock waved them in.

The tunnel mouth was cramped and the small space turned out to be an alcove only about six feet deep. The group had their backs to the wall, facing outwards.

"What were they?" Matt asked, shining his light out.

Something flew past that was too fast for them to see in their light beams.

"Too quick to draw a bead on them." Maddock had his gun up.

"Whatever they are, they've been trapped in here for about twelve thousand years," Hartigan said. "They could be bats, some type of nocturnal bird, or even giant insects."

"More bugs, *huh*. That'd be fucking great." Klara shook her head.

"Whatever they were, who knows what they are now." Hartigan shone his light around. "Standard rule is it takes around one thousand generations before one species evolves into another species."

"What the hell have they been feeding on?" Lana asked while backing in closer to Matt.

"Given they're taking a run at us, I'd say they're meat eaters," Hartigan added.

"If we can see them, we can hit them," Klara said, holding up her gun. "I can light 'em up with a flare. Just say the word, boss."

"Save your ammunition for now," Maddock replied.

"We need to be away from them." Lana turned to face the wall and placed her hands against the damp stone. "This can't be all there is."

"No," Matt said. "Give us some more light here and also a little more room." Matt stood back but saw that the end of the tunnel was far too flat and straight for it to be natural. One thing he had learned: nature doesn't do straight lines.

He snorted softly. "Yep, this has got to be a wall, or maybe a door." He pushed against it, but there wasn't an ounce of give in it. He felt around the edge, looking for a button, lever, or some other ancient mechanism that was used on sealed crypts, or chambers.

He crouched and brought his light close to the floor – there was a line along the bottom of the wall – it wasn't attached. He ran his hands along the mossy ground, feeling some tiny grooves in the stone.

"Gotta be a pivot point." He stood. "Vin, we'll just push on one side, and see if we can budge it." Matt put his shoulder against the stone. "Count of one, two, three ... heave."

Nothing happened.

"Try the other side." Matt moved along the wall face.

The two men pushed hard and were rewarded with an inch of scraping.

"That's it," Matt said. "Again, on three, two, one ... now." The pair shoved even harder this time, and the huge seven by six foot slab made a grinding noise as it was pushed inwards on a central pivot. A gust of air was thrown back out at them.

Maddock stood aside. "Vin, Klara, check it out." The HAWC leader then got behind the group and faced out at the dark cavern, making himself a shield. He grabbed at Matt, who went to follow them. "Give 'em a minute, Professor."

"Okay." Matt looked into the new tunnel's darkness. There was nothing but blackness and silence coming from inside, and just the pipes of light from the soldier's flashlights swiping one way then the next.

He got on his toes and sniffed a couple of times. The new section smelt of seawater, and dark dank spaces like from under rocks, or in sunken wrecks washed up after a storm. Lana moved up right behind him.

"Clear," Vin shouted from the darkness.

Matt and Lana went in fast with Hartigan right on their heels. Though their curiosity was urging them on, they also wanted to be away from the large chamber where the mysterious flying things were darting around in the darkness.

Maddock backed in slowly, keeping his eyes on their rear position. Multiple lights now moved around in the total darkness. Matt saw huge shelves of stone, rock pools of fetid water, and dripping slime everywhere.

"Lana, tell us what we should be looking for," Matt asked.

"They should be impossible to miss." Lana turned about. "Like I said, a thirty-foot tall stalk of asparagus."

"From their fossil records, I suspect they'll be spongy but firm. As wide around as a light pole, I think," Hartigan added.

"I'm not seeing it. I'm not seeing anything like that." Matt grimaced. "Damn."

The chamber wasn't that huge, maybe two hundred to two hundred and fifty feet square. But the rocks were slick and black and the humidity in the air carried the scent of salt within it.

"You said they didn't need much light, right?" he asked.

"Yes, they can survive with little sunlight." Lana shook her head. "But I doubt they could thrive for long in total darkness. Plus there's too much seawater," Lana crouched and scooped her hands through the slime. "Anything that was sealed in here would have been turned to mush in a few years. If this place has been seawater-logged for twelve thousand years, then I'm afraid not even the tiniest spore would have survived." She stood and wiped her hand on her pants. "Or even its DNA."

"We just bounced around the world for an empty cave. Someone fucked up," Klara seethed.

"Feel free to get a second opinion." Matt glared. "If you can find one."

"Shit." Maddock shook his head. "This is not a call I want to be having with the colonel."

Me either, thought Matt. "Look, this place was sealed for a reason. They were here, right here, and they knew something about the plague. And they knew enough to seal the answer, or remedy, or cure, or whatever it was, away in this hidden place."

He flashed his light around. "Look at the walls, the floor, everywhere – they must have left some sort of mark or record. They *must* have."

Beams of light waved around as the group separated. Lana was at his side.

"Matt ..." she eased in closer to whisper. "Do you think we missed something?" she asked.

"No, no, impossible. This is the place. I know it is." He sighed. "More like we're just too late." He kicked at the slime on the floor and it stuck to his boot. "This crap might be all that's left of the prototaxites."

"We don't even know how we were supposed to use them – drink it, spray it, burn it ..." She waved her light across the cave floor.

"Here!" Vin leaped up onto a rock shelf.

The group followed him over. There seemed to be a slab of stone like a cap over an area. Its was roughly six feet long and three wide. Plus about three inches thick. The young HAWC grunted from the strain for a moment but then slid it aside, and shone his light down into the cavity.

"Something in here."

Matt leaped up to also shine his light into the hole. There was nothing but rocks, all sitting in a few inches of glistening slime.

Lana got down on her knees and reached in. "Same as the stuff on the floor; its all degraded to nothing," she said. "Maybe the rocks were holding down the plants somehow."

She got down even lower by the side of the cavity, and reached into her bag, pulling out a small sample jar and long probe. She spent a few minutes reaching and scooping some out, and dropping it into the glass vial. She held it up, shining her light in on it.

"The protein coat on fungal spores is incredibly strong, and can survive freezing, extreme heat, radiation and, in some cases, acidification. But immersion in seawater will eventually destroy it. We can test it when we get back, but my view is that it's all gone now." She reached back into the pit to rummage around a little more.

Hartigan sighed. "Fungal spores can definitely infect insects, and some fungal types disperse millions of spores from a single organism. They adhere to the carapace and can cause sterility, abnormal behaviors or can even short-circuit their nervous system." He shone his light around, and the beam was reflected back off the glistening walls. "There's nowhere in here that hasn't been soaked." He turned back to Lana. "Twelve thousand years ago, this cave was probably dust-dry and the spores would have remained in a state of dormant preservation for many millennia."

"But not now," Vin said.

"Well, the spores might have remained intact ... if where they were stored was sealed." Lana straightened. "And they probably were."

Matt turned to her, and saw her rubbing her fingers together. She sniffed them, and then held them out.

"Beeswax."

Matt and the rest of the group just stared for a moment, processing what she had told them.

"Look." She reached back into the pit, grabbing a few things and then placed them on her palm.

Matt craned closer. In among some small dark pebbles, there were brownish pieces of a broken circle, like a rim, and made from wax.

"I've seen something like this before," Lana said, pushing them with her fingertip. "From within the great tombs of Egypt where the pharaohs and high-ranking people were mummified. Their internal organs were removed and stored in canopic jars." She looked up. "And then sealed with beeswax."

"Where ..." Matt frowned. "Where are the jars then?"

"Ah, shit, boss." Vin shone his light down into the stone-lined hole. "I got a boot print here."

"What?" Maddock surged forward, and Matt noticed his eyes seemed to burn as he stared at what Vin had found. "*Goddamn!*" he roared. "Someone was here before us." He spun, his eyes near volcanic. "Who did you speak to?"

Klara pointed her flashlight into Matt and Lana's faces like a gun. "Dammit, Matt."

Matt held up his hands. "Whoa, no way, we told no one."

Lana also shook her head. "We only just deciphered it when we were with you guys, back at the USSTRATCOM labs. And we've been with you the entire time since. Spoke to no one. Why would we?"

"They're right," Hartigan said. "We've all been together."

"Damn civs, leak like –"

"Sieves?" Matt finished.

The female HAWC, normally so friendly to him, growled. He wondered what had made her change.

"Professor, we've come a long way. For nothing." Maddock's light shone in Matt's face, and for the first time his voice had a bite to it.

"My translations were good. I mean, just look around – the Aztlanteans were definitely here." Matt held his hands out. "This is the place ... or was." He hiked his shoulders. "And someone else thought so as well."

"So someone is dogging us. Somehow." Maddock lifted his eyes to the roof and groaned. After a moment he dropped his head. "So, we think there was one or more sealed jars in there. And someone came in and beat us to them." His jaws worked in his cheeks for a moment. "When?"

Lana got to her feet. "Could have been centuries ago for all we know."

"Or yesterday," Maddock added. "That's a boot print, not a damn Roman sandal."

"Yes, of course." Lana dropped the wax fragments into another sample bag. "Unfortunately, they even took the jars. We might have been able to gather some of the residue if they'd have at least left us a broken shard or two."

The group stood in solemn silence for a few more moments, before Maddock turned to Matt.

"Professor, could there be another site? Anywhere?"

Matt hiked his shoulders. "I don't know. Islands are perfect places of isolation, especially ones a long way from anywhere else. I'm guessing there could be. But it seems like, twelve thousand years ago, Easter Island was the last holdout for the prototaxites and the Aztlanteans collected some samples and stored them, knowing that they might disappear one day."

"There might be others, somewhere," Lana said. "Remember the Wollemi pine that was discovered in a hidden valley in Australia? It was supposed to have been extinct for two hundred million years."

"True," Matt said. "But we don't have time for an exploratory expedition." He turned to Hartigan. "Is there any way you can synthesize the compounds?"

Lana shook her head. "What compounds? From where? There's nothing for us to work with. There might have been something unique here to begin with. But right now, we have no way of knowing what that was."

Matt crouched again beside the pit, and carefully shone his light around the exterior, finding nothing, no markings, writing or pictoglyphs. He even had Vin and Klara turn the capstone over, but it too came up blank.

"Nothing." He stood.

Maddock took one last look around. "We're done here, let's pack it up."

"But ..." Lana held her hands up, but then murmured, "nothing."

Matt had that empty feeling of disappointment in his gut as they walked toward the entrance.

Lana grabbed his arm. "I still think we're missing something."

"Maybe. We can look at the stones again, but the reference to this place and our translation was pretty solid. Also this island cavern was sealed up because it held something important. And it existed at the right time."

"You were right, this *was* the place." She looked up at him, the whites around her deep brown pupils luminous in the darkness. "Someone else sure thought so as well."

He nodded. "But who? And what do they plan on doing with those samples?"

CHAPTER 35

The Schneider compound, Treptow, Germany

Rudolph Schneider held up the test tube, looking at the murky liquid inside. He jiggled it and then turned to his chief scientist.

"This is it?"

The man nodded. "It is the distillation of what you recovered. The properties are quite unique. But of course, whether they make a difference, remains to be seen."

Schneider smiled. "It will. This is what the ancient race at the bottom of the world used to control the plagues. I'm confident it will work. But as to what effect it will have, that is what we must ascertain in a test."

Schneider hoped for some sort of stupefying effect, or something that rendered the creatures docile enough to control. Adolf Hitler had expended many millions of marks, and countless hours in pursuit of the *aussterben steins*, which were to lead him to this very substance.

He looked one last time at the muddy fluid in the tube. It was fitting that Schneider should be the instrument for enacting the Führer's grand plan.

"So, you will be testing them on living specimens?" the scientist asked. "You secured living specimens?"

"Yes and no." He smiled. "They proved a little more dangerous than I expected or am able to deal with. So, I have developed a partnership with a Russian laboratory. They have facilities and several of the creatures ready and waiting for me."

"Good, good. I wish you luck, Herr Schneider." The man almost bowed.

Schneider could barely contain his pride. If the test were successful, then he would be at the dawn of the new Reich.

Rudolph Schneider smiled as his vision turned inwards. He would be there, standing at the shoulder of his master. And the world would once again tremble.

CHAPTER 36

The Kearns family home, Walnut Grove, Redwood county, Minnesota

Karen Kearns was woken by the shaking of her bed. She lay with eyes open, listening and waiting as the rumbling and movement finally settled down.

Belle rested her chin on the bed and whined. Karen laid her hand on the German shepherd's large head and rubbed it.

"That was a big one, wasn't it?" she whispered in the darkness.

Karen kept stroking the dog's fur, waiting to see if there were any aftershocks. She turned to the west wall of her room – there were no windows in the large main bedroom as it was situated in the middle of the house, but she stared as if seeing through it to the yard outside.

Belle whined again and Karen looked into the dog's large liquid eyes. "I know, I know, we should have evacuated when they told us to." She turned on her bedside light.

Her room was a treasure trove of memories, and she remembered why she didn't evacuate. "Because if we did, the looters would have emptied my house by now."

Karen wondered whether Megan had been woken by the tremor, and after a few more moments of quietude was about to lie back down when a distant shriek of hair-raising intensity pierced the air.

"Oh." She swung her legs over the side of the bed.

Megan knocked on her bedroom door and then opened it. Karen looked back at her niece. "I heard it."

"What was it?" Megan seemed unperturbed, and her suntanned arms were athletic-looking in her pajama top, which exposed her pi tattoo on her bicep.

"Probably just a deer." Karen gave her a fragile smile but didn't believe it either. "We can look in the morning."

Megan nodded, but there came another scream, this one definitely from a man, and this time the voice held bone-chilling fear. It finished with a strangled gargle of agony.

Belle whined and licked her lips, a sure sign the dog was nervous. Karen just stared, indecision freezing her.

Megan's eyes narrowed. "I'm going to take a look. Call the sheriff." She paused. "Do you still have Uncle Dan's gun downstairs?"

"You're not going outside, are you?" Karen jumped to her feet, her hands balled into fists in front of her chest.

"No, but ... just call the sheriff and see what he says we should do. I'm just going to have a quick look downstairs. The gun?"

"Yes, yes, in the cabinet locker." Karen sat down again.

Another scream came, followed by a dog barking madly that became a yowl of pain. Belle ran in circles for a moment before tilting her head back and howling her distress like a wolf.

"*Stop that*, Belle." Karen grabbed the dog and held it close to her leg, where it immediately quietened.

"Phone." Megan pointed.

Karen nodded, and then grabbed the phone to her ear, but crouched down beside the bedside table as though trying to make herself as small as possible. Belle sat rod straight in front of her as though acting as a wall of furred defense.

"You two just stay put, back in a few minutes." Megan closed the bedroom door.

*

Megan went down the steps on her toes and headed straight to the living-room gun cabinet. She remembered the keys were in the drawer below and, while there, she thought she heard someone outside the house. She hurried to unlock the cabinet and remove the shotgun, a Remington 870 that still smelt of gun oil.

She grabbed a box of shells, opened it one-handed and hurriedly loaded several shells into the port. She also dropped a few more into her pajama shirt pocket.

She stood silently for a few moments holding the gun two-handed at waist level as she continued to listen for noises. She felt the coolness of the polished floorboards beneath her feet, smelt the fruit in the bowl on the table, and even heard the soft ticking of her wristwatch; such was the heightened level of her senses.

Megan was just contemplating heading back upstairs when she heard someone trying the front door handle.

The hell you will, she thought.

"Don't even think about it. I'm armed, and I *will* shoot." She yelled at the door, lifting the gun.

Megan gripped the gun hard to stop her hands shaking. She knew how to use firearms, but had never fired one at another human being. Fact was, she never wanted to. She didn't want to hurt or kill anyone, but she'd damn well do what was necessary to protect her family, and so, she advanced.

"The sheriff *has been* called. Last warning, asshole." She shouldered the gun.

There came an enormous weight against the door and the frame creaked ominously. From above her she started to hear the roof tiles being torn up, and then a window smashed out back somewhere.

"Ah, Jesus," she whispered, feeling a tingle of fear run from her scalp to her ass. She racked the gun, more to use the noise as a signal of her real intent. "I am *fucking* warning you." She hated that her voice trembled now.

The front door began to slowly open, but that was only because the wooden doorframe was being crushed inwards, and splinters rained down to the linoleum floor. Whatever was opening it had enormous strength, and it made Megan swallow in a dry throat. At least the latch-chain was still on, she saw.

Around the door came a hand, shiny black, and looking like it was wearing gloves. The fingers were enormously long and ended in sharp points. Then another hand appeared above it, and then another below it. All only had three fingers. They combined to push against the door chain.

Jesus, Mary and Joseph, give me strength, Megan prayed, as she aimed.

More tiles were torn from the roof and then something dropped into the room above her. *Karen*, she thought, and heard Belle growling.

"Give me strength," she said through fear-gritted teeth and watering eyes.

Upstairs she heard the dog working herself into a snarling fury, just as the chain exploded into pieces and the front door burst open.

She fired.

Time seemed to slow down. In the split-second flash of the discharge Megan saw the things that had broken in. They stood about five feet tall, were in three segments and had multiple arms and legs. But the eyes were large, human-like and dispassionate, and they fixed on her with deadly interest.

The blast blew the first thing backwards, but then the ceiling caved in and more dropped into the room with the sound of armor plating landing on a hard surface. From upstairs she heard Karen's fear-filled scream.

"*What are you?*" She yelled and fired again, and again, until she was grabbed and stabbed by something in the neck. It was so agonizing she dropped the gun.

She raised her hands, but they went stiff as something freezing flooded her body. She fell to the floor, stunned and unable to move.

Megan felt herself lifted up, and from the corner of her eye she saw another of the horrifying beings dragging Karen by the hair down from her bedroom. Somewhere, a long way away, she heard a dog's mournful howl as she was dragged out into the cold night air.

*

Belle circled in the bedroom where she had been shut in. Den mother had gone out to investigate the bad smells, and then came the sound that had been a dagger to the dog's heart – her den mother's scream.

The hundred-pound German shepherd looked at the bar door handle, trembling now with rage and fear, and tried to calm herself as she remembered watching how it had been used. She lifted a paw to rake at it, again and again, until the handle lever was dragged down, and the door opened a crack – it was enough to get her nose in and then to shoulder it open.

Belle sprinted down the upstairs hallway and skidded to a stop at the top of the steps in time to see den mother being dragged. White-hot fury shot through the dog, and base impulses were all that remained: defend, attack, *kill*.

Massive teeth bared, she leaped.

*

Hammerson sat, still as stone, his eyes unblinking as one of the drone operators followed the huge silicoid bugs on the outskirts of Walnut Grove.

He was in awe of its size as the things were nearly as tall as a man now. He gripped the armrests of the chair so hard the leather popped as he watched one of the horrors drag a body, or stunned person, into the mouth of a disused mine shaft.

"How many are missing?" he asked evenly.

The young soldier checked the data, and then half turned. "Very few heeded the evacuation call, sir, so just over four hundred stayed behind. They're all missing."

Hammerson ground his teeth for a moment. "Follow it in."

The drone pilot dropped the near soundless, compact flying machine to ground level and entered the shaft. Inside, the walls and floor were coated in a thick resin mixture like solidified molasses. After another few minutes of tracking the strange creature they entered a larger juncture point in the mine.

"Found 'em," the soldier announced.

Hammerson sat forward – there were the missing people, hundreds of them, all stacked and piled around the shaft sides. The drone camera zoomed in on one of the bodies. Thankfully it still seemed to have bone mass within it and hadn't been sucked dry.

He suddenly had a thought. "Are they alive?"

The pilot pressed some buttons and then read the data. "Got heat signatures, but very low." He turned. "Like those people are in hibernation."

As the drone panned around in a slow 360-degree spin it picked out all of the bodies.

"Get in lower." Hammerson said.

The drone approached one and lowered to hover only a few feet above it. Hammerson craned forward, speaking softly through clenched teeth when he saw what had been done to them.

"You sons of bitches."

The body was covered with what looked like opalescent pearls the size of golf balls. It didn't take a genius to work out what they were – eggs.

They're eating us and also using us as freaking incubators. Hammerson bit back the gorge that rose in his throat.

This is what they're doing now, he thought, *taking the bodies and storing them in a hive.* This must be the newest form of their evolution, to rapidly increase their swarm population.

His first instinct was to incinerate it and turn it all to ash, if he even could. But with living people in there, he needed to try and get them out. He pressed a button on his speaker.

"We need to get a team –"

"Sir … they're hatching."

Hammerson stared back at the screen as the soft eggs bulged, blackened, then finally burst open with splash of muscousy fluid. The fist-sized creatures immediately swarmed over their immobile hosts, seeking out exposed skin.

One of the creatures stopped at a female arm, the bicep, near a tattoo. Hammerson squinted, it looked a little like the mathematical symbol for pi. As he stared the tiny horrors buried their heads into the flesh.

Hammerson watched the bodies soften and flatten as the bones and silicon were liquefied and then drawn out.

"I've seen enough." Hammerson got to his feet. "From now on evacuation orders will be militarily enforced."

The HAWC leader looked one last time at the screen as the drone withdrew. All the bodies were now covered in the feeding bug larvae, and there would be no survivors.

He lifted the phone and called through to General Chilton. It was time for the president to authorize a deep burn. Starting with this damn mine shaft.

CHAPTER 37

Matt felt a sense of gloominess as they headed for the large stone doorway. He'd never even thought about having a plan B, so this setback was beyond depressing. Added to the personal failure, he felt he had let everyone down: his team, Hammerson, and maybe the entire human race.

As they came to the huge slab of door, Maddock pushed past the group. "Hold." He pointed to Vin and Klara. "HAWCs, take us out, eyes open."

The pair lifted their guns, and went out spreading left and right. They waited for a second or two, and then Maddock nodded for Matt, Lana and Hartigan to follow.

"I don't know where we go from here," Matt said to Lana.

She gave him a crooked smile. "Well, my dad used to say that sometimes opportunity knocks, and if we don't answer, then it just goes and waits around the corner until we're ready."

He chuckled. "Wow, that dad of yours was the ultimate optimist."

"That he was." She grinned back. "The answers are still there for us to find them, you'll see."

He shrugged. "I'd feel better if someone else hadn't beat us to them. I just hope they use them for the same reason we were."

He looked at her in the beam of his flashlight, and saw her mouth turned down. "Yeah, I'm not confident," she said. "You said Hitler thought they were a weapon."

Matt nodded. "Whoever controls the solution will control the world."

"Let's go." Maddock herded the rest of the group out.

They came out onto the rock platform, and saw the submersible hard up against the shelf waiting for them. Miguel lifted his head above the waterline behind the domed glass front to give them a small salute.

Lana waved back, just as something swooped at her. She shrieked and ducked. "Damn things again."

"We got company." Klara had her gun up and swung about. "Too fast."

In the flashlight and headlamp beams the things darted by far too quick to see what they were.

Then Vin cursed, and they turned to see something hanging onto the side of his face. His reflexes were like lightning and he reached up to grab and tear it away before it did too much damage. His face still bled profusely and in the glare of their lights they saw him holding something about the size of a large bat that wriggled and thrashed in his gloved hand. A scaly tail whipped for a moment and then wrapped around his wrist.

He held it out. "A lizard," he said. "It's a flying fucking lizard."

The thing was about a foot long with a flat tail, wedge-shaped head and large round black eyes. It squealed and snapped vicious jaws lined with razor-sharp teeth like a piranha.

"Wow, evolution at work," Matt said. "There's a gecko native to Easter Island. I'm guessing this is what happens when they get trapped in a cave for twelve thousand years."

Suddenly, as if in response to the captured creature's squeals, the air was full of the creatures. Vin tossed the thing away hard, but more came at him. They also landed on Lana.

"They smell the blood, they're going into a frenzy," Vin shouted.

Lana covered her head and cried out, "Get them off me."

Matt leaped to her and threw his arms over her head as they crouched together.

"Everyone get down!" Maddock yelled.

Klara remained on her feet as one came at her. She shot a hand out to grab it from the air. The crunch of bones was audible as she crumpled the body in her grip. Another shot past, this one taking the tip from her ear.

"*Sonofabitch.*" Klara drew her gun, held it two-handed with the flashlight along the barrel, and started firing. Her aim was deadly, or there were just so many that she couldn't miss, but every shot exploded one of the things out of the air.

"Hold your fire, goddamnit," Maddock roared. "And get the hell down."

Klara screamed, teeth bared, blood running down her neck. She pointed her gun in the air as something much larger landed on her upper back. Large talons sunk into her shoulders.

In the glare of the wavering beams, it looked like a scaly chimpanzee with triangular mouth and slit eyes. On the top of its membranous wings were hooks that it used to fix itself to the female HAWC.

Vin swung to aim at it, but Klara fired upwards and it flapped away. But as soon as it was gone, another even larger reptilian creature slammed into her, and she staggered for a moment under its weight. Then, with a few beats of huge wings, it began to lift off taking Klara with it.

"*Shit.*" Maddock ran at his HAWC, but already she was ten feet in the air screaming curses, and firing wildly.

Blood rained down as more of the flying reptiles landed on her and assisted in taking their prize back to whatever loft they had waiting high in the cavern.

Klara fired and fired, with most shots missing their target, until high up in the darkness above them one must had struck a weak spot in the cave roof.

The high-energy projectile cracked the rock. Already under enormous pressure from the seawater, the thin skin of the dome was capping and holding down millions of tons of pressure from the compressed air in the cavern.

The small crack lengthened. Like spidery veins it branched out in all directions. And then a fist-sized section of the cave roof blew out.

A shaft of light was thrown down onto the cave floor like a spotlight and an unearthly scream filled the cavern. But it wasn't from any animal's scream of pain, instead it was the air rushing to be released from its many millennia-old prison.

The ancient environment was breached. The fist-sized hole blew out to a basketball-sized opening, and then manhole-sized. The air rushed around them like a tornado.

The reptiles panicked and fled. And then, from out of the air, Klara crashed to the ground. Amazingly, the torn and bloodied woman staggered to her feet, and tried to reload.

Maddock sprinted over and grabbed hold of her. He planted his legs wide to keep his balance and stared upwards, yelling something to her over the maelstrom and then pointing upwards.

Klara looked up, nodded, and then widened her own stance. Vin stood and did the same, but Matt, Lana and Hartigan crouched and hugged the rock. Everyone continued to watch until a louder noise dragged their heads around – the sound of steel scraping on rock.

"The submersible!" Vin yelled over the gale force winds.

They turned to see the water rising and lifting over the rock shelf. The submersible was also lifted, but being dragged onto its side. They could see Miguel working frantically on the controls, and the propeller kicked up water behind it as it began to tip over.

Oh shit, Matt thought, we left the hatch open. "*Miguel!*" he yelled and motioned to the top of the craft.

Miguel left his seat, maybe to attend to the hatch. But in a blink the submarine went from being upright to being sideways and flooding with water. The steel craft went from buoyancy to dead weight in a matter of seconds. If Miguel tried for the exit he never made it, as he would have been pushing against the torrent of water rushing in.

"The ocean is coming in, the cave's going to be flooded!" Maddock yelled.

Matt turned from the HAWC leader back to the water, but the submersible was already gone. And Miguel with it.

There was now only one option. "Climb!" Matt yelled.

They sprinted for the cave walls. Matt grabbed a handhold and then briefly turned. As the water started to rise higher, so too came the water's occupants.

"Ah, shit no."

The shark fins circled ever faster as if excited at the prospect of getting access to the warm and soft land-dwellers.

Matt had surfed all his life, and the one thing that scared the hell out of him when he was sitting far out behind the breakers was seeing a shadow in the water. He felt his scalp crawl from fear.

"Lana," he yelled.

"Get moving," she yelled back, already way ahead of him and a dozen feet up from the platform floor.

They scaled up the inside of the hollow seamount, Matt climbing beside Lana who was proving more capable than he was. Vin, Klara and Maddock also scaled the rock face like professional rock climbers, only Hartigan seemed to struggle.

Perhaps the scientist had chosen a poor place to climb or had never before scaled anything but he quickly fell behind, and in a few seconds, he was only just keeping ahead of the fast rising water.

From above, a large chunk of stone fell away. It struck like a bomb and showered them with seawater. It also threw down even more sunlight, further illuminating their prison.

Matt looked up to see the flying lizards being sucked through the hole, and he wondered whether they'd enjoy their freedom, or would soon perish in a world that had different rules, different predators.

"Look." Lana hugged the wall momentarily.

Matt gripped onto a stony protrusion and turned. Lana nodded with her head toward the wall just across from them.

"A message," he said and squinted. An area of the rock face had been smoothed, and there was writing, and images. Matt squinted as he tried to quickly read it.

It was from the Aztlanteans – their final message for the future.

Matt grimaced as he tried to get a little closer. The water was coming up fast, but he *had* to read it. It showed images of the sky, and what had to be things striking the ground with long, fiery tails.

He translated, yelling over the roar of the rising water. *"Here lie the last grains from the bloom of the sky flowers."*

Lana frowned. "Sky flowers?"

"Sky flowers blooming." He turned to her. "I've seen this type of reference before – *blooms in the sky* ... meteor explosions."

"So, what does that mean?" Lana looked over her shoulder to the water level. "Keep climbing."

Matt began to climb again. "I think it wasn't fungal spores they kept stored in that hole." He grunted as he levered himself up another few feet. "I think instead it may have been meteor fragments."

"That's what they stored away?" she asked. "That was what was precious to them?"

"Antarctica is home to more meteor drops than any place in the world. These days they sit on top of the snow and ice like choc drops ..." He groaned as he lifted himself. "... on a vanilla icing."

Lana lost her grip and slid down the rock wall a foot, and screamed. She managed to cling on, and Matt scaled across to put an arm under her shoulders and hold her tight for a moment. Looking back down, he saw the water was now only a few dozen feet behind them.

She caught her breath and then looked up at him. "Matt, we have to go back. We were looking for fungal residues, but there might have been meteor fragments inside those pits."

Matt looked down again at the rising water. "Not now, just climb."

Below them the water was surging, chasing them up the rock face. Matt felt a jolt of fear as the extra light meant he could clearly see the large torpedo shapes moving in the water below.

As the cavern roof above them crumbled, chunks of stone continued to fall and explode into the water like falling cannonballs. One the size of a walnut bounced off his head.

"Ouch." He cringed, and was thankful his long hair padded the impact.

But Phillip Hartigan wasn't as lucky – a chunk of stone as large as a bread loaf flew down to strike his shoulder. The crunching impact could be heard over the chaos as it crushed his clavicle bone. His arm and shoulder broken, he fell backwards from the wall.

"No-*ooo*," screamed Lana, who looked for a second like she was going to go after him.

Maddock leaned out, hung on with one hand, and pulled his blade. But as he was about to leap to the man's rescue, several huge gray shapes converged on the scientist and the water immediately turned into a boiling explosion of red foam.

The HAWC watched for a few seconds more, and then resheathed his blade. He stared at Lana. "*You!*" His voice boomed even over the maelstrom. "Climb. *Faster.*"

Matt stared down at the water for a moment more and swallowed down some bile; he just hoped the man was unconscious when he hit the water.

"Goodbye, Phillip," he whispered.

Larger pieces of the roof now started to fall away, some as large as dinner tables. With the huge holes opening up, the gale force wind died down, and the water started to ease its rapid upward surge.

Before they even reached the top, holes opened up in the cave wall, and first Vin and Klara squeezed out, and then the others through different sections.

Once out, Matt went to roll onto his back and suck in air, but Maddock yelled for them to keep moving away from the hollowing area. And just as well, because in another few moments the entire roof fell in.

Millions of tons of rock just collapsed inwards, leaving a huge water-filled crater that still swirled, bubbled and boiled like a giant's cauldron.

Matt turned to watch the water in the crater as it became level with the sea surrounding the tiny island. Although it was still a bubbling, muddy soup, it was quickly settling. He knew that everything below would have been buried in dozens of feet of broken stone – Miguel and his submersible, perhaps the sharks that attacked Phillip Hartigan, and possibly any meteorite fragments that might have held the answer they sought. All the hidden cave's secrets were now gone.

A few dozen feet away, a nightmarish creature crashed to the rocks and flapped awkwardly. It had triangular teeth around a wide mouth and looked like a type of reptilian simian crossed with a cathedral gargoyle. Its skin was almost translucent and there was steam rising from it, as the creature of eternal darkness was bathed in strong sunlight.

Klara leaped to her feet, and drew her weapon.

"That's the bastard."

She fired into its body three times and finished by stamping on its head with the heel of her boot.

"Payback delivered," Vin said.

"What a day." Matt sat then lay down on his back, letting the sunlight bathe his sweat-slicked face as the sea breeze dried it off. Lana did the same with the HAWCs gathering together to discuss strategy.

Lana turned to him. "This is your life?"

"Not all the time." He kept his eyes closed. "Only when I feel like trying to kill myself."

She scoffed. "Sure beats Bells Beach, I guess."

Matt opened one eye. "What did you say?"

"I mean, you're in your element here: blue water, sunshine. Isn't that right, Matthew267?" She giggled.

Matt sat up slowly, and turned. "Lana … *LanaPHD*. No way."

"Pleased to meet you?" she sat up and stuck a hand out. "Now we know what those 'distracting' jobs were that dragged us both away."

Matt chuckled and pushed long hair back off his face. He grabbed her hand. "This has got to be fate. Those jobs pulled us in different directions, only to throw us together."

"Kismet, we call it." She showed a line of perfect teeth as she smiled. "It was meant to happen."

He nodded as he stared at her. She was beautiful, courageous, smart, and funny. She was everything he hoped she'd be.

"I'm really glad we made it out alive."

She reached out to rub his arm. "Like I said, it was meant to happen." She dropped her hand and her expression darkened.

Matt saw there were tears on her cheeks and her mouth was turned down. *Hartigan*, he remembered.

"I'm so sorry, Lana."

She nodded and mouthed *thank you*, but kept her eyes closed and head down. "He was my friend and mentor."

"We need to ensure his death wasn't wasted. We need to gather our thoughts and fight back," he said.

She nodded once.

Matt looked around. They were on the eastward slope of the small rocky outcrop that they had entered from below. Just a quarter mile from them was the southernmost tip of Easter Island, and everywhere else seemed to be endless ocean.

He wiped his hands on his pants' legs. "Somehow the Aztlanteans knew about the meteorites – *sky flowers*."

"Meteorites." She lifted her head and turned to him.

"Yes." He half smiled. "I think they meant falling meteorites were somehow able to control or kill the silicoids. But the *gal-ka-tar* translation was clear – *fungus*." He clicked his fingers. "Maybe the meteorites contained the fungus."

She put her hands over her face and rubbed her eyes. "And it still means that the fungus is the thing we are looking for. The spores must be somehow detrimental to the silicon creatures. But now we have another element to consider: the meteorites." She raised her eyebrows. "So how do they fit?"

"Somehow the Aztlanteans observed them fall, and made use of what they retrieved from the 'sky flowers'. Then they tried to save the knowledge for posterity, but ..." Matt shrugged.

"But?" Lana sat forward.

"But, shit happens." Matt leaned back on his elbows. "And now they're gone."

Lana rummaged in her pocket and pulled out a sample jar that contained a small dark piece of rock. "Not all of it."

Matt sprang forward. "You, magnificent ..."

She handed it to him. "Don't get your hopes up. This rock has been soaked in brine humidity for over ten thousand years. Salt water would have destroyed any and everything terrestrial." She handed it to him.

Matt held it up, examining the tiny rock. It looked like an everyday pebble, but a little darker and rougher than usual. "What secrets do you hold inside you?"

Lana held out her hand. "I can test it when we get back. But bottom line is, I'm not hopeful." She looked out at the ocean. "We just needed one tiny fragment that had remained dry. Fungal spores can resist cold, dry, radiation, and even the vacuum of space – they are one of the universe's great time capsules. There's only one thing they can't stand ..." She tilted her head to Matt.

He nodded. "Yeah, damn salt water."

She sighed. "Yes, and after a length of time, even the hardest rocks become saturated."

"Close but no cigar." He looked up and out at the blue divide between their tiny island and the larger one just on half a mile away, and slowly shook his head. "I'll tell you something right now – I'm not swimming back."

CHAPTER 38

USA – USSTRATCOM Headquarters, sub-level 1 laboratories

"Any biological material is long gone," Lana said. "But the sample contains four peculiar minerals in high concentrations. They are plagioclase, feldspar, olivine, and ilmenite." Lana sat back, shaking her head. "That's unbelievable."

"So they're rare, huh?" Matt asked.

She turned and her eyes gleamed. "Only on Earth."

"What?" Matt grinned. "So where are they *not* rare?"

"The moon, of course." She returned his smile.

"Of course." Matt laughed.

Hammerson folded brawny arms. "Wait a minute, are you telling me that little thing is a piece of our moon?"

"I believe it once was," Lana replied.

"It's a damn moon rock." Matt threw his hands up.

"Look, there are no absolutes here, and I'm working on probabilities. But those four minerals account for ninety-nine percent of the crystalline material of the lunar crust. Whereas the most common minerals on the surface of the Earth are quartz, calcite, magnetite, hematite, micas and amphiboles.

These lunar minerals are almost non-existent. A chunk of pure, flawless diamond would be less rare." Lana opened her hands. "Of course, it could have come from somewhere else in the universe, but my money is on them being, yes, moon rocks."

"The meteorites," Matt said. "They're meteorite fragments, perhaps blasted from the moon's surface, thousands or millions of years ago. The Aztlanteans found them, most probably in the Antarctic, and they somehow witnessed their effect on the silicoids." Matt rubbed his jaw. "Then they saved them … for us."

"But they never expected their hiding place would be drowned," Lana said. "The meteorite must have had fungal spores on them that were somehow toxic to the creatures."

"Nothing grows on the moon, it's totally devoid of all life." Hammerson's brows knitted. "What am I missing here?"

"Let me try and explain." Lana got to her feet and began to pace. "This is a long shot, but it's all I've got. We all know that the moon was born of the Earth. About four and a half billion years ago during a time called the Hadean Period, something the size of Mars crashed into the Earth, or what was known as Gaia then. The impact, called the Theia Impact, would have been cataclysmic, and would have nearly shattered our planet. But the impacting mass, Theia, and Gaia joined into a final form that became what Earth is today." She pointed a finger upwards. "But not before a massive chunk of the primitive Earth was blown into space."

"But it was captured," Matt added. "Earth's gravity stopped it from being flung out into the cosmos, and held it in an orbit, a lunar orbit. It became our moon."

"Yes, and today it is a nearly fifteen-million square mile lump of geology just floating about one hundred and eighty thousand miles above us. Sometimes a lunar impact blasts a chunk off and it can fall to Earth. But they're unbelievably rare," Lana replied.

"So, we think they contained some sort of fungal spore from the Hadean period of Earth." Hammerson made a noise deep in his chest. "I assume you and Dr Hartig—" He cursed softly. "Sorry, I know he was a good man."

"It's okay," Lana said, but looked away.

Hammerson went on. "I assume you tested the creatures' vulnerability or resistance to other fungal samples."

"Yes, most of them, and even some ancient spores from archeological digs. There was no effect," Lana replied.

"Is there any way you can extract spores from that moon rock?" Hammerson asked.

"There's nothing there now." Lana sighed. "Unfortunately our piece wasn't sealed in a watertight container. And after immersion for so long, the rock is saturated with salt. Nothing remains."

Hammerson groaned, but then turned. "We are trying to track whoever it was that stole those samples from under our noses. But if we get them, can you test them on the silicoids?"

"No." Lana's lips compressed for a moment. "The creatures we had all degraded."

"Degraded?" Matt asked. "They died?"

"Yes, but then the samples all disintegrated into their base composite elements." She laughed softly but there was no humor in her expression. "They degraded into dust, silicon dust, that was nearly indistinguishable from common sand. They left us nothing to work with."

Matt nodded. "You know, that makes a lot of sense. It might be why there's never been any evidence of these things in the fossil record. For large incursions, the silicoids appear, wipe out most of the life on Earth, and then either they run out of food, reach the apex of their life cycle, or something stops them somehow." He scoffed. "Then they just turn to dust and vanish."

"Until the next incursion, or upwelling, or whatever we want to call it." Hammerson exhaled in exasperation.

"Upwelling." Lana tested the concept. "Yes, that sounds accurate, given the eggs were in underground bodies of liquid."

"They're here right now, and multiplying, and we've got nothing." He looked along their faces. "Give me some suggestions, people."

"Let's just get more rocks." Matt turned to Hammerson. "You guys mentioned that the Aztlanteans must have gathered the moon rocks from Antarctica, so why don't we go back and search for more?"

"Moon rocks are incredibly rare," Lana said. "Thousands of times more rare than normal meteorite fragments that fall to Earth. That's because most meteorite fragments have an iron base and can be detected. As I mentioned before, the composition of moon rocks means they're a lot softer and lighter, and they look indistinguishable from normal rocks."

"They're lighter, so that means they sit on top of the snow and ice, right?" Matt asked.

"That's true, but only about one in ten thousand would be a moon rock. We could spend years looking for a single one."

Hammerson began to chuckle.

Matt grinned back at the tough HAWC commander. "Okay, what, Jack?"

"I've seen moon rocks." He smiled. "Plenty of them."

"Huh, how could you?" But then Lana clapped her hands together. "Of course ... the Apollo missions."

"Exactly." He pointed at her.

Matt sat down at one of the computer consoles in the lab and started to furiously type.

He sat back. "Oh yeah." He turned the screen around. "The Apollo missions collected over two thousand samples weighing all up at about eight hundred and fifty pounds."

"Where are they now?" Lana asked.

"The majority of the Apollo moon rocks are at the Lunar Sample Laboratory Facility at the Lyndon B. Johnson Space

Center in Houston, Texas. There's also a smaller collection stored at White Sands Test Facility in Las Cruces, New Mexico."

Matt nodded as he stared at his computer screen. "And stored in nitrogen to keep them free of moisture." He turned to Lana. "That's good, right?"

"Sure is. Dry is very good."

"A-*aaaand*, they're considered priceless." Matt turned.

Hammerson snorted. "It's national, *global*, security at risk. And besides, it'll be a hellova lot more palatable than nuking your own countryside. I'll requisition them … *all* of them."

Hammerson made the call, then turned and gave Matt the thumbs-up. "On their way."

"Good," Matt said. He moved closer and held out his phone. "Jack, there's something else." He lowered his voice. "Ah, I've got some pictures of my mom and cousin, Megan, to forward to you. You know, for when you're looking."

Hammerson nodded, but his lips were drawn into a tight line. Matt showed him the pictures scrolling past each – his mother and then Megan. There was one showing the tattoo on her arm.

Hammerson craned forward. "Go back."

Matt swiped back to the tattoo shot.

"Stop." Hammerson looked at the image for a moment more and then nodded slowly, his expression glum. "Son, prepare yourself, but I've seen that tattoo before." Hammerson straightened.

"Where? When?" Matt's eyes were wide as he gripped the colonel's arms.

"I'm sorry, Matt, but I saw it on a body." Hammerson's gaze was dead level.

"What?" Matt released Hammerson, his mouth working for a moment. "She's dead? Are you sure?" He blinked several times. "Can I see …?"

"No, because the bodies were incinerated." Hammerson nodded. "Contamination."

Matt felt like he had been punched in the stomach. He staggered and held out an arm. Hammerson grabbed it and guided Matt to a chair.

Lana rushed over. "Is he okay?"

"He's just had some bad news. His cousin." Hammerson let Matt slide into the chair where he slumped.

Lana put an arm around his shoulders.

Matt suddenly reached out to grab Hammerson's shirt. "My mom, did you see her there too?"

Hammerson shook his head. "No, Matt, we're still looking. But if they were together ..."

Matt covered his face and broke down.

CHAPTER 39

Office of the Chief of the General Staff, Russian Ministry of Defense, Moscow

Colonel Nadi Borishenko stood at attention as he waited for the general to finish his call. His hands were sweating, and he felt he stood on the precipice of greatness ... or on the edge of an abyss.

General Yevgeni Ivanovich nodded as he listened for another moment, and then: "As you command, sir." He slowly hung up and then just as slowly turned to Borishenko.

His pale eyes stared for a moment as though X-raying his soul. "You can control this?"

Borishenko stood rod straight. "Yes, sir. The German, Schneider, is working with us to provide us, and us alone, with an insulating component. And antidote, if you will."

"Why?" The general sat back.

Borishenko permitted himself a small smile. "He believes he has unfinished business with America. He wants to make them pay." He met the general's eyes. "I can vouch for him, and his usefulness."

"Can you?" The general continued to stare, and Borishenko felt the tickle of perspiration run down under his arms.

"This meeting didn't happen, and there will be no record of your project." The general nodded. "Your mission is approved."

Borishenko felt his heart swell with pride and a little nervousness. It meant President Volkov himself had authorized his mission. He saluted, and was about to turn away.

"Colonel." The general's gaze was reptilian. "Remember, you vouched for him. You own this."

"Yes, sir." Borishenko saluted again and then turned and quick marched out the door. His plan had been simple. Following the successful test over Ukraine, they would undertake a larger and more ambitious attack.

This time, their rival was someone a lot bigger and had a lot more to lose. There was a fast freighter, the *Illiansk*, already loaded with twenty-four sealed drums of the silachnid eggs waiting in Severomorsk, and now ready to go. Its target was the port of New York and New Jersey, the third largest working port in the United States, with a surrounding population of over eight and a half million people.

The swarms would be released and infiltrate the entire American eastern seaboard. Millions would die and they would tie up resources for years. Perhaps forever.

If that happened and everything went as Borishenko hoped then recognition, promotion and greatness was his.

He felt nothing for his adversaries, as he too had unfinished business with America. And also with Colonel Jack Hammerson – he just wished the American colonel was on the front line.

Yes, I do own this, he thought. Borishenko beamed with pride as he marched down the long corridor, humming an old Russian song.

CHAPTER 40

USA – USSTRATCOM Headquarters, sub-level 1 laboratories

"Don't give up hope, Matt." Lana still had an arm over his shoulders as the pair sat together.

"It's been too long." Matt slumped forward, staring at the ground. "She's out there, somewhere, alone." He looked into Lana's face. "I can feel it."

Lana simply nodded.

"She's not safe." Matt rubbed both hands up his face, hard, trying to wipe away the mental images of his mom screaming for him. "Megan was with her," he said softly.

"I know, but ..." Lana didn't know what else to say. Frankly, she didn't hold out hope of seeing Matt's mom alive again, but would never say that out loud.

"I know her. I think she's hiding somewhere until these things are gone." Matt sat back. "And that's why we have to kill these bastards. Make them go away forever."

"Damn right." Lana stood, and held out a hand to Matt. "So help me do it."

Matt gave her a broken smile. "Yeah." He took her hand and she hauled him up. "Yeah, let's do it."

Lana led him in through the lab doors. She had been allocated an entire laboratory and twenty chemistry, biology, and geology specialists, plus an army of technical assistants to work with her.

Matt was an invited observer, and Hammerson, though an observer himself, watched like an impatient bird of prey as the teams worked.

Lana also had at her disposal an electron microscope and gene sequencer. She looked at the waiting samples – all she needed was a single viable spore.

She let her eyes travel along the wall where, stacked in layers, waited two dozen sealed metal cases containing the priceless moon rock samples.

Since their retrieval from the moon, all had been examined and tested, and then all had been pronounced inert to the point of being sterile. The presiding wisdom was the dryness, the vacuum of space, and also the prevailing exposure to solar radiation, had totally sterilized them over countless millions of years.

But Lana also knew that fungus was one of the most resilient living things in existence. And fungi were radiation resistant. Decades ago, they survived when an explosion blasted radioactive material throughout northern Ukraine. They had been found in reactor pools in Chernobyl, and had been grown in the orbiting space station.

Fungi were tough. Fungi could, and did, adapt. And something else ... fungi could hide.

Lana called for the first case to be opened. The moon rocks had been extensively examined, photographed and X-rayed. But most only externally. They were so valuable that only a handful were ever internally examined, and most times they were pulverized to examine their mineral composition only.

She drew in a deep breath, readying herself. She knew, if she had to, she would examine every one of the rocks internally, twice. And that meant breaking each and every one of the rarest things in the world open, and potentially destroying them.

One of her assistants brought her the first sample. It was roughly shaped like a large pockmarked peanut, and was colored a purple–gray. It had the texture of pumice.

She had a facemask on, and also a small electric rock saw. She brought a magnifying glass down in front of her face from an extendable arm.

"Making a preliminary cut, on sample ..." She checked the label on the slot in the case. "... 275x013."

The saw started with the high-pitched whine of an angry mosquito as she gently applied it to the stone. Dust was thrown to the sides and the saw cut easily through the soft rock. In seconds she had it in half and then opened the pieces out to see what secrets they held.

Inside there was solid matter, heat burnished from the saw. She turned it slowly under the magnifying glass, searching for her clues. After another moment she placed one piece in a small vice, and then let the computer take control so it could shave away a slice that was only a few microns across. After that, she dropped it in a sterilized solution.

Lana slid it under the microscope. She knew what she was looking for – the telltale spores of fungus were usually rounded shapes. But could also be spiky, rods, cones, or coiled threads.

But in this one, there was nothing like that at all.

"Logging sample 275x013 as having no visible presence of spores at two hundred times magnification. Sending to spectrometer and electron microscope for lower level analysis."

Though the technicians would review the sample at a chemical level and a much higher magnification, she knew that there would be nothing. But she still had high hopes as there were hundreds more samples to go.

She selected the next. "Sample 275x014."

She began the procedure again. And again. And again.

Lana performed the same process eighty-three more times, and even though she had taken several rest and coffee breaks, her wrists and fingertips ached from gripping the tiny saw, and she often needed to blink to clear her blurring vision. Plus she felt the beginning of a needle of pain deep in her skull – the telltale sign of a concentration headache started to form up like a storm front.

She was almost about to brush sample 275x098 aside, when her brain replayed the image again in her mind. She froze, and then pushed the slide back under the viewer.

There – a long thread of things that looked like bubbles all joined together.

"Hold it, hold it ..." Lana adjusted her magnification, and stared hard into the lens.

Matt, who had been chatting by a coffee urn, stopped his conversation and turned.

Hammerson fast walked toward her desk. "What have you got?" he demanded.

Lana began to grin as she continued to stare into the scope. "I think I have a globose spore shape that would translate nicely into realized community assemblages."

"And once again in English?" Hammerson asked.

She pulled back. "Putting it up on screen."

Lana switched on the projector and the images she was looking at were displayed on a huge monitor on the wall. The group watched and she sharpened the focus to reveal something that looked like a long and lumpy loaf of bread.

"Those spore globes are all fitted together nice and neatly." She started to smile. "I really think we might have something here."

"Well done," Matt said.

"Is it viable?" Hammerson asked.

"Only if we can manage to rehydrate it." Lana whistled softly as she increased the magnification again. "This is one tough little son of a bitch; it's surrounded by an outer rodlet layer of hydrophobic proteins and melanin – basically, it's super armor-plated."

"It would have to be to survive the Theia impact, solar radiation, and then a few billion years on the moon." Matt grinned back.

"Damn right." Lana used the microscope and precision tools to commence her work. "Okay, going to release it from the matrix, and then try and rehydrate just one of the spore globes."

Her teeth clamped together as she carefully worked at a near microscopic level. In a few minutes she moved to using a needle probe to extract a single tiny globe and place it on a dish. She then added a drop of liquid.

"First up, just sterile H_2O."

She went back to the scope, and everyone turned to the projected images on the screen.

Lana changed the magnification to five hundred times and the translucent globe hung in the solution. Lit from below it shone like a tiny full moon.

They watched, and waited, and the seconds turned into minutes. Lana squinted into her eyepiece.

Hammerson exhaled impatiently. "How long?"

Lana looked up, scowling. "Minutes, hours, days – we don't exactly have a rule book or any precedents to follow on this."

Hammerson's jaws worked behind his cheeks, as his glare seemed to intensify. "We haven't got days to wait for that thing to germinate, or whatever it's supposed to do. If it doesn't, I want you to try something else."

"But ..." Lana started, but then wilted under his gaze. "Okay."

"Time is one of our biggest enemies right now. Instead of waiting for a single test thread to complete, why don't you try the other tests at the same time." Hammerson lifted his chin a fraction. "Sound like a plan?"

Lana nodded, and then started to prepare some other test dishes. "Going to bathe another globe segment in a glucose solution, and another in –"

"Silicon," Matt said. "Try a silicon solution."

"Yep." She nodded. "Good idea."

Lana prepared the next sample segments and their solution baths, and within an hour she was carefully placing the tiny specks of the globe segments into each of them.

She changed the viewscreen into multiple sections so they could watch each one at the same time.

Again they waited, minutes passed. Hammerson paced, slowly, his boots squeaking on the linoleum floor. Lana exhaled and sat back in her seat, and tried to think of other tests.

"It might not be a viable specimen after all." She turned to the steel cases. "If it isn't, I'll have to keep searching."

"Look!" Matt's voice spun her back to the screens.

The sterile water and glucose sample remained inert, but the spore in the silicon solution had what looked like a single fine hair sticking from it.

"Is that contamination?" Matt asked.

As they watched the thread vibrated.

Lana beamed as she held up her hands in front of her mouth and clasped her fingers together. "A hyphae ... it's germinating."

"Into what?" Hammerson asked.

The wall of the spore bulged outwards as the thread thickened and was then enveloped by a wall of its own. The long shoot-like thread began to swell.

"It's absorbing the nutrients in the solution." Lana was transfixed. "Unlike plants, which use carbon dioxide and light as sources of energy, fungi meet these two food requirements by assimilating organic matter. Carbohydrates are usually the preferred source, but they can readily absorb and metabolize a variety of soluble carbohydrates, such as glucose, xylose, sucrose, and fructose …" She turned. "But when it comes to this tough little guy, it's silicon."

"Amazing," Matt said. "And it's getting bigger."

The long trunk-like tendril expanded at its end into small filaments that looked like claws. In a few more seconds, the growth and movement stopped.

"What happened?" Hammerson squinted. "Did it just die on us?"

"Unlikely," Lana said. "I think it's just absorbed all the available nutrients, so has gone inactive."

"There's only one thing I care about: will it destroy the silicoids? Will it do the job we want?" Hammerson demanded.

"I don't know. Most fungi are saprotrophic, meaning they obtain their food from dead organic material. What we want is for it to be a parasitic fungus that gets its nutrients by feeding on living organisms. In this case, on the silicoid bugs."

Lana's vision turned inward for a moment, as she thought it through. "We need to do a test." Lana swiveled her chair toward the HAWC colonel. "And for that, we'll need more live specimens."

CHAPTER 41

Hammerson watched from the war room with growing unease. They now knew that the silicoids seemed to feed until they hit a certain growth point. Then they'd burrow under the earth where some sort of rapid evolutionary metamorphosis took place as the next growth phase occurred. When they reemerged, they were bigger, stronger, smarter, and just damned different.

Plus they were now laying eggs in hives and the swarm populations were increasing in size. It all meant that the human race was under a grave threat and facing its very own extinction event.

The last reports he had indicated the silicoids were as big as a man now, and probably three times as strong. *How do you separate and capture a few specimens when they were in among an army of their own kind?* he wondered.

He thanked all the saints that at least they didn't fly anymore. Maybe it was the energy to weight ratio making it too costly for them. Or they had simply evolved beyond that. And their evolution continued.

"And then what comes next?" he muttered.

The satellite detected the heat bloom on the soil surface of the field outside of Cedar Rapids. The good-sized town had over a hundred thousand residents that had all been emergency evacuated. The silicoids were coming up, expecting to swarm into the town for a free meal on all those innocent people. Instead they'd find nothing but an inferno.

But that was the second part of their engagement plan. The first part was to grab a few of these monstrosities for Doctor Lana Miles and her labs to do their work on.

It was a simple process, and one that had been used for decades to trap birds or other fast-moving creatures: The bugs passed a certain point triggering ground-level canons to fire, dragging a hundred square feet of iron mesh over the desired patch of ground. When it dropped, its weight pinned down anything underneath it. He hoped the huge gauge steel mesh would be enough to hold a few of the bastards so his team had time to hog-tie them.

And that was the easy part. Before they rained hellfire and damnation down on those hellish things, they needed to grab the trapped silicoids and get them out. He knew the bugs would be fighting back, and the entire swarm would undoubtedly be trying to eat his team alive.

Hammerson laughed with little humor. When it came to missions like this, there was no one skilled enough, brave enough, or maybe mad enough, to do the job other than his HAWCs.

Hammerson looked up at the countdown clock on the satellite image of the site on screen before him. It was time.

"Come in, Bravo."

"Bravo in, boss." The deep voice of Roy Maddock came back, calm and cool.

Hammerson looked at the satellite image as it panned across from the heat blooms of the outer fields to the HAWC position.

His team had dug foxholes, and the three HAWCs were in deep, with shielded cover ready to be pulled over them for insulation.

Maddock was easily spotted as his six foot two inch frame was bulked up even more by the armored suit he wore. With him were Klara and Vin – each warrior was worth a dozen standard Spec Ops, and Hammerson trusted them to get the critical job done. Or die trying.

"Bugs are coming up. Get ready," Hammerson said.

"Confirm. We're locked and loaded and ready to rumble," Maddock replied.

Hammerson smiled grimly. *Locked and loaded, and tech'd up to the hilt*, he thought. He just hoped it was enough.

"Sir, we have emergence."

Hammerson turned to the technician. "Show me."

On his screen another satellite image drilled all the way down to ground level. It now showed manhole-sized eruptions in the earth as the things started to burrow upwards.

"Showtime, Bravo." Hammerson folded his arms, sucked in a huge breath and let it out real slow as he watched.

*

"Roger that, out." Maddock turned to his team. "Muscle up, people, we have incoming."

"*HUA.*"

Maddock did a weapons check one last time, which took a few extra seconds considering their armaments. Though the HAWCs had several forms of weapons and munitions, from modified flamethrowers to high-speed shotguns, and even concentrated emitted-light weaponry, lasers, they all knew that their objective wasn't to stand and fight, but one of retrieval – snatch and grab.

The HAWC kit was for defensive purposes. It was hoped that their armor would protect them when they went in, grabbed their targets, and then pulled back to shelter while the air force obliterated the things on the surface.

They wore battlefield combat armor plating that was a mix of titanium composite with some molded biological plating that was harder than steel. Theoretically, no standard small arms on this earth should have been able to puncture it.

Maddock rolled his shoulders; the suits were heavy, and would have been impossibly cumbersome, except they were hydraulically supported. Inside their helmets they had good vision, but also computer-assisted analytics – they were basically flesh and blood warriors driving human-shaped tanks.

The three HAWCs stood in fortified pits, with hatch tops thrown open. They knew what needed to be done, and which of their tasks were priority. It was boiled down to several key event steps: the swarm arrived, the net cannon fired, hopefully trapping one or more of the bugs underneath it. Then the HAWCs would emerge from their pits, with Vin and Klara going for the bugs, while Maddock gave them cover. Final step was to bring their captures back to the pit, seal themselves in, and let the air force thermo-blast the shit out of anything moving on the surface.

"Stand ready," Maddock said softly.

He saw the swarm approaching. This time they didn't come by wing, but like a boiling river of chitinous bodies that blackened the landscape. He could feel them through the soles of his boots – he'd been involved in heavy-combat traffic zones when they got charged by a thousand rebel fighters in Sudan, or a convoy of weaponized motorbikes in Syria, and each time the pounding on the ground felt like a herd of stampeding beasts coming at them.

But this time, he actually heard them over his suit's external mic. It wasn't their footfalls, but the clatter and crush of their bodies as their scales and chitinous armor brushed up against one another.

He didn't feel fear, just a burning desire to get the job done. The odds didn't matter. He knew he and his team made a difference, and bottom line was, anything that threatened him, his family, his home, or his country with deadly intent was to be taken down, and hard.

"Here they come." Maddock lowered himself down behind the lip of the pit, and Klara and Vin followed his lead. He counted down the seconds. And then ...

There came the triple boom of the three cannons firing at once and throwing the net over the front-runners of the approaching horde. As hoped, it flattened and captured several of them and the disturbance caused most of the others to change course as they scrabbled toward the now empty town in search of their prey.

"Go, go, go!" Maddock yelled, and went up and over the lip of his pit.

With a whine of the hydraulics in their suits the three HAWCs charged. Vin and Klara held titanium cable nets as they hurtled toward the first of the struggling creatures. Neither of the HAWCs looked at the other creatures, and relied on Maddock to throw a defensive shield over them.

The first thing Maddock noticed was the silicoids were as big as a large man, and unbelievably the creatures were lifting the heavy mesh netting and even starting to stretch holes in it.

Whether it was the movement, heat, or scent of the humans – something attracted the attention of some of the other creatures and they scuttled back toward them. When they were close they reared up, standing on their hind legs.

Maddock felt a chill run up his spine as the alien-looking creatures now stood eye to eye with them. Multiple arms opened wide and shiny black claw-like hands with lethally pointed claws opened wide.

"Get it done," Maddock yelled to Vin and Klara and then lowered his shoulder and charged, ramming into the nearest rearing creature. The impact was heavy and hard, attesting to the weight of the things. Thankfully the crunch of armor came from the bug and not from his defensive suit.

The huge HAWC then blasted, lasered, and even punched and kicked the silicoid bugs away from Vin and Klara. Many times they were wrestled to the ground, and the pointed proboscis tried to pierce their suits' shielding to get at the soft flesh and bones beneath. But the suit integrity remained intact.

Maddock pulled his shotgun, and blew one of the things backwards, where they skidded along the ground to simply right themselves up on multiple legs and charge again.

"Hurry up," he yelled and then chanced a glance over his shoulder at Vin and Klara. He saw they had bagged a single specimen that fought furiously within its confines, and were working on their next.

"Got number two," Vin finally yelled, as they moved to number three, the final specimen.

There came a sound like someone strumming a giant harp, and Maddock saw the metal strands of the net being pulled apart. In another second one of the silicoids emerged to leap on Vin's back and began scrabbling at his armor plating.

Maddock also saw that the bugs they had captured wrestled furiously, and a single sharp claw poked through one of the capture bags.

"Gonna lose 'em," Maddock yelled.

Maddock was crushed to the ground and covered by six of the things and brought down on one knee as they tried to burrow into him, using their long dexterous claws to pull on individual plates, and trying to work their hypodermic-like probes in between the joints. It was only a matter of time until they succeeded. And then once they found a weakness, they'd inject their salivary enzyme. After that he was finished.

Maddock rammed one bug aside, grabbed another, and then took hold of one of its arms and yanked and bent. He felt the satisfying snap as the limb broke off in his hands. He managed to fight back to his feet. He engaged his mic.

"Time's up, the rain's coming – get to the foxholes." He punched down hard with his mech-assisted fist and it smashed into a silicon carapace. "Get those things back to the holes, we got incoming."

Vin and Klara dragged, pushed, and drew the two cable-tied creatures back to the pits, threw them in, and jumped in after them. They pulled the heavy steel lids down on top and sealed themselves in.

Maddock sprinted to his pit. He went in and immediately turned to backhand a clinging bug and then used high-speed blasts from his shotgun to clear the field, as he pulled the lid down on top of himself.

There came hammering on the steel lid, and in the darkness Maddock touched his mic. "Sir, we got two, and we have vacated the field. Over to you."

"It'll have to do. Well done," Hammerson said. And then: "Brace."

The first impacts made the ground shake around them, and were followed by a continued pounding like the beating of a titan's drum. Then came the red wave, the rolling thunder as the thermo-blasts heated everything to over three thousand degrees.

The HAWCs were six feet down, covered by a sheet of half-inch steel plate. Plus their armored suits were heavily resistant to heat. But they would still feel it, and would have to endure for the total burn-time, as the Earth's surface above them became an inferno.

Maddock felt his back start to singe first, and then rivulets of water ran down his body. Above him, the steel plate glowed orange and cast a hellish light down upon him. He kept his head down and both fists on the ground as though praying, but he was simply waiting it out.

Maddock clamped his eyes shut, and then his mouth. Soft tissues were the first to be punished. Like all HAWCs, in the face of extreme pain or trauma, during torture or other battlefield-related hardship, he had been trained to take himself away, to transport himself from his body, and just let his mind take him to a place of calm and safety, perhaps a memory of a holiday, or home, but it was there he'd stay until the hardship was over. And if it were never over, then he'd simply stay in that place until heaven or hell called for him.

The thunderous noise above shut off as quickly as it started. Maddock waited for a few more seconds and then lifted his head. His back felt tight and raw, and he was sure it was blistered. Smoke rose from the shoulders of his suit. Above him the steel was cooling to darkness and shadows ruled once again.

He flexed his hands, feeling the blisters across their backs, and knew his body would be covered. But it was a small price to pay for a successful mission.

"It's over," he said into his mic, and looked up. "Gonna be damn hot. Get ready."

He raised himself up, and used a fist to punch the steel plate back. It opened and thumped down hard ... on ash. The big HAWC stood and then whistled.

Maddock turned his head, slowly taking it all in – there was nothing left. Everything that was, was no more: trees, houses, grass, and most of the roadways were all reduced to nothing. There were no small fires burning because everything combustible was already exhausted. If there were any dead bugs among it, he couldn't tell.

With a thump of steel plate, Vin and Klara rose from their foxholes. Maddock changed the vision spectrum in his helmet lenses to amplification and scanned the geography. "No sign of any bugs." He leaned on the pit edge. "Bravo team to base, come in."

"We see you guys. How you holding up?" Hammerson asked.

"Char-broiled and got a real good tan. But nothing a cold beer and an ice bath can't fix. Any sign of the silicoids? Field looks clear down here," he said.

"A few stragglers, but for the most part that swarm has been obliterated. How are the samples?" Hammerson asked.

Vin and Klara hauled one of the things upright and Maddock could see its arms still struggling against its binding.

"Hot and pissed off, but still alive." Maddock looked around. "We are good for extraction."

"Bird on its way, Bravo team. See you soon." Hammerson signed off.

CHAPTER 42

Central Scientific Research Institute, Ministry of Defense, Shchyolkovo, Moscow

Chief Science Officer Mikhail Verinko met Rudolph Schneider at the security checkpoint and signed him in. Schneider was issued with a pass and followed the small Russian man to the secure elevator.

Inside, Verinko pushed the button for the lower floor and then looked up at the imperious-looking German gentleman who carried himself with disdainful authority. He had an air of arrogance surrounding him like a cloud of expensive aftershave.

"We appreciate your funding, and your offer to assist in the conditioning tests of the silachnids." Verinko smiled innocently. "May I ask, what's in it for you?"

Schneider looked from the side of his eye at Verinko. "All I seek is a positive outcome to the tests. This is a global problem that requires a global solution, yes? And my understanding is you have extremely advanced facilities."

"Why did you not go to the Americans? After all, they are Germany's allies and also have excellent facilities." Verinko raised his eyebrows.

"They are *not* my allies." Schneider stopped and turned. "I despise the Americans." He lifted his chin. "But I can still go to them if you would prefer."

Verinko, momentarily surprised by the venom in the man's voice, shook his head. "No, I am happy and fortunate that you have chosen us." He tilted his head. "Are you confident your discovery will stop the silachnids?"

"Very. This substance I carry is based on an ancient formula derived from a race that successfully dealt with these creatures long ago." Schneider looked away again. "It will work."

"Will you be sharing it?" Verinko asked, his eyes narrowing as he tried to analyze the man. He could tell he was lying, but he didn't quite know about what yet.

"Yes and no." Schneider smiled imperiously. "You can analyze the substance all you like, but its ingredients are, how would you say, *out of this world.*" He laughed darkly.

"The substance is in that case?" Verinko looked down at the wooden case the German carried. It was a dark polished wood, antique and expensive looking. And squarer than a normal carrying case.

"This?" Schneider held it up. "No, this is just some of my personal effects. You might call it my good luck talisman."

The elevator doors opened near silently, and Verinko pointed down a blinding white corridor.

"We are all set up and waiting for you. You'll need to dress in a specially secured bio-suit. Once done, we can commence immediately."

"Of course." Schneider smiled beatifically. "Today will be a good day."

*

Rudolph Schneider followed the scientist, making a concentrated effort to avoid small talk.

Truth was, he probably had less respect and even more antipathy for Russians than he did for Americans. But he needed their laboratory facilities, and given what had happened to his own team, he needed them to assume the risks, especially the dangerous ones.

If the tests were successful, he didn't need to do anything more than walk out the door. The Russians would never be able to recreate the distilled moon rock solution, no matter how much they begged or threatened. And when he was ready, he'd have his army of obedient creatures march right into Red Square. And the White House – he suppressed his laugh – and perhaps even Buckingham Palace.

Schneider thought he felt the wooden case in his hand jiggle. He smiled and wished he could open it.

Someone was getting impatient, he thought. Soon. Soon they'd know if the world was to be theirs again. He could barely stop himself from laughing out loud.

CHAPTER 43

Lana's eyes were wide and the color had drained from her face as she stared at the two creatures in the separated hermetically sealed rooms. Hammerson had his arms folded tight across his chest.

With them was Klara Müller, who had stitches on her cheek and a mangled ear from the cave attack, plus iodine on multiple burns. There was also a blistered Roy Maddock, who was still acting as the lead agent on the overall mission.

Matt marveled at these human beings and their ability to endure pain, and keep getting up to fight on. *They are like a different species to the rest of us*, he thought.

He turned back to the specimens in their cells. No, *these* were the things that were the real different species. They were a ghastly remnant of a time long past in Earth's history; one that should have remained locked away in some liquid subterranean tomb. Perhaps they would have been the rulers of the world if things had been different all those countless millions or billions of years ago.

"So, just how smart are they now?" Matt turned.

"Right now?" Lana continued to stare, as if transfixed. "Smarter than a dog or a chimp. But not as smart as a person, we think."

"Can they talk?" Klara asked.

"Talk? No. But communicate? Most likely, just not as we know it." Lana turned to face the group. "They make buzzes and clicks and some other noises we can detect, so maybe they communicate with their own kind. But their ferocity and predator behavior doesn't exactly lend itself to dialogue. With us, anyway."

Hammerson turned to Matt. "You're the linguist. Do you think you could talk to them?"

Matt inhaled deeply and let it out slowly through his nose. "Unlikely. It'd be more like a computer code than a language. We could try signing, mathematics, symbols, and the usual first start tools we have. But I don't think we'd be able to. We're too different to communicate meaningfully."

"Who was it that said that it was madness for sheep to try and talk peace with a wolf?" Maddock stared in at the bound creatures.

Lana nodded. "But they're smart, I can feel it."

The others turned to watch the creatures through the glass. In the sealed but separated rooms, the two beings were tied to upright steel tables with their segmented torsos, multiple limbs and head strapped securely down.

Even with the binding, one of them managed to slowly turn its head to stare back out at the humans. Its gaze was mesmerizing.

"Look at the eyes," Klara whispered.

They were large, round and fist-sized, with pupils like those of a human. And those dark pupils seemed to bore into the group with a dispassionate interest.

"They're studying us, as we study them," Hammerson said.

"The difference is, we're about to try and kill them," Lana responded.

Hammerson turned slowly. "Damn right we are. Because that thing and all its buddies are consuming every man, woman, child, dog and pony they can get close to."

Klara bared her teeth for a moment. "Well, I just hope it's painful." She turned. "When do we start the test?"

"Now." Lana held up a hand to a group of lab technicians waiting close by. They were wearing full biohazard suits and began to gather their materials.

"We have two tests planned: the first is an on-contact test of the fungal spores planted directly onto the exoskeleton of the specimen TX001. The second test is an aerosol dispersal into the room of the specimen TX002."

Lana leaned forward to type a few commands into a computer on the desk before her and then straightened. "And so, we begin." She turned and nodded to the first two suited-up technicians. "Commencing first test ... *now*."

The technicians first entered an antechamber, and as the group watched, they moved to a back door that opened into the room of specimen TX001. One of the technicians held what looked like a cattle prod, and the other approached the creature with a small bottle with an eyedropper in the top.

The silicoid became aware of them, and started to struggle against its bonds. From its proboscis it looked like a fleshy flower bloomed, and then a long dart like tongue extended as through trying to spear one of the technicians as they got closer.

"That's how it feeds – it latches on and then using that spear-like tongue to inject its saliva. Then it simply sucks up the liquid remains," Lana said.

"We've seen the results – horrible," Matt replied.

"Administering solution of fungal spores suspended in solution," came a voice over the speaker. There was a slight quaver in the tone.

"Proceed," Lana replied.

The technician lifted the top from the bottle exposing the small eyedropper. She placed a single drop of the solution on the front of the creature's thorax.

It tried to swivel its head downwards, its tongue continuing to dart out, but the technicians took a step back. Lana noted the time, and then swiveled the cameras for a close-up.

"Solution administered at exactly eight hundred hours."

Lana zoomed in to amplify the spot and a single drop of clear fluid could be seen on the dark carapace.

The group watched and waited. And waited. But there was nothing.

Hammerson folded his arms, and after another moment spoke over his shoulder. "Not enough?"

"A single spore should be enough. Unfortunately we can't get a microscopic shot from out here," Lana said.

"How long?" Matt asked.

Lana shrugged. "Another minute, another hour, several hours? Impossible to say. We just need to be –"

"Look." Matt pointed to the close-up image on the monitor.

The tiny bubble of fluid on the front of the creature's thorax had turned milky.

"Is that a chemical reaction?" Matt asked.

"No, I think that is an explosion of new fungal spores, the stuff is germinating, and hopefully beginning to ingest the silicoid's armor." Lana grinned. "I think it's growing."

As they watched the small drop transformed to an almost solid blob. And then it began branching out. First one, then two, then more tendrils snaked out to adhere to the creature's silicon exoskeleton.

One of the branches thickened, and then began to form another blob, that in turn started to branch out as well.

In a few more seconds, the silicoid started to thrash as the infected area opened a hole in the thorax. The fungus had obviously now spread internally, and the creature vibrated as if in a fit or from extreme pain.

"Yeah, that's it, suffer, you sonofabitch." Klara seethed. "Burn, baby, burn."

The medical table jumped and bucked and then after another few moments the creature slumped and became immobile.

"Is it …?" Hammerson walked forward.

The silicoid sagged even more, and finally began to come apart.

"Holy shit," Matt said.

The head fell away and when it hit the floor it exploded open like an overripe pumpkin. Inside was nothing but cobwebby material that must have been the fungal threads. The remaining thorax, abdomen and limbs continued to degrade and also fall to the floor.

Lana checked a timer. "Total elapsed time from introduction of fungus to full degradation of morphology, was two minutes, three seconds." Lana looked up and nodded. "Not bad." She raised an eyebrow to Jack Hammerson. "And in answer to your question, yes, it is dead."

Hammerson nodded once. "I'd say that was a successful test."

"Indeed." Matt grinned. "What's next?"

Lana was busy furiously typing some notes into her project folder, and talked over her shoulder. "The good news is we now know that the fungus is viable and works against the silicoids."

In the containment room there looked to be smoke in the air. "There's millions of free-floating spores in there, so it'll spread within a community." She made some more notes. "But that leaves broader dispersal issue requirements. We need to determine a way to spread it to the horde quickly."

Lana lifted her face to the second room. The creature there stared back with a baleful gaze from eyes that conveyed a cunning intelligence. It became aware of them watching, and began to struggle even harder.

"By now there are possibly hundreds of thousands – maybe even millions – of these creatures moving in separate swarms all over the globe. They're like an army that is almost impossible to stop."

Hammerson grunted. "We need a fast takedown. If these things get into the big cities, we can't exactly vaporize them, or the citizens. And evacuating a major city means millions of people on the move."

"And on the move to where?" Matt asked. "Sooner or later, we'd all end up with our backs to the ocean."

"Exactly." Hammerson agreed.

"So, we need to do a wide-area test dispersal." Lana sighed. "I wish we had more specimens."

"Tough enough getting those two. Let's work with what we've got." Hammerson said. "Start the test."

Lana relayed her instructions to the next two lab technicians, and they prepared to enter the second specimen cell. This time one of them carried a silver canister with an aerosol nozzle at the top. Matt noticed that the other technician strapped a sidearm to his waist for either security or moral support.

As they entered, the creature wriggled again, and then began to thump back and forward against its strapping.

"Commence test," Lana said into her microphone.

The pair closed in on the thing, and paused while it wrestled against its confines for a moment more. The technician with the aerosol lifted it above the silicoid. The creature started to thrash.

"You sure that thing can't understand us?" Hammerson asked.

Matt shrugged. "It could be reacting to the death of its colony partner. Maybe it sensed the distress through the release of some sort of stress pheromones, or they can communicate at a frequency we can't pick up. The problem is they are so different to us, we have no idea how they communicate, or what information it is sending or receiving."

The creature bucked again, furiously, and this time, one of its limbs popped free. It exploded in a blur of fury and bucked and wriggled until another limb was extricated.

The technicians backed up against the rear wall. One of them drew the firearm, now looking pitiful against the six foot tall silicoid.

"Goddamn, secure that thing!" Hammerson yelled.

Before anyone could move, the thing used its razor-sharp claws to sever and tear away the strapping and burst from its confines. It hit the hardened glass like a battering ram, and the entire pane boomed like a gong.

"Get 'em out of there," Hammerson ordered.

Klara and Maddock took up firing positions in front of the group. But Hammerson pushed them aside.

"Exit, exit!" Lana screamed into the microphone.

The two technicians backed away, but the sound or movement attracted the silicoid's attention and it spun to them.

In the blink of an eye it was upon them. The technician with the gun fired, but for a creature of such significant size and bulk, the silicoid moved amazingly fast, and dodged the projectile. The bullet smacked into the hardened glass in front of the group leaving a star-shaped impact mark.

With one spiked arm the silicoid swept the shooter aside, and they could see the man's arm snap like kindling. Then it grabbed the other technician.

They couldn't hear the man's scream, but knew it was probably reverberating within the small room. As they watched, spellbound, the thing's proboscis bloomed open, displaying a frill of fleshy tentacles and then from its center a spike shot out, smashed through the man's perspex face shield, and into his face.

Like some sort of ghastly balloon fast losing gas, the technician's body physically deflated before their eyes. The head dropped to the side, but inside the hazmat suit, the skull was softening like an emptying sack. The limbs went floppy and the entire frame sagged, and was only being held in place by the glistening black limbs of the silicoid.

"Oh god, no." Matt backed up.

The technician's mask fell free showing the face, and the man's eyes rolled pitifully toward them in the flattening skull.

Matt grimaced, because the facial muscles were still trying to work and in the man's expression was a plea for help. The tongue lolled out and fluttered, maybe in a final attempt at forming words before the entire mass was dropped at the silicoid's multiple feet.

The silicoid backed up again, and then it surged toward them. This time circular impact cracks appeared in the glass around the spot weakened by the bullet impact.

"It'll come through next time," Matt said, feeling a shiver of fear up his spine.

From behind, the technician who had been knocked down dragged himself with one arm to the dropped aerosol canister. He snatched it up and pointed it – a fine mist began to fill the room.

The silicoid spun as the room filled with the fungal mist. It launched itself at the prone man, and spiked limbs shot out, stabbing and tearing his body to pieces.

"Take it down!" Hammerson yelled, and Maddock and Klara went to enter the sealed room.

"Wait." Lana stood in front of them, holding up a hand. "Look."

The silicoid slowed and then suddenly hunched over. The glossy black shine of its silicon carapace started to become covered in a fine spidery mesh. The monstrous creature froze, stiffened, and its body turned the color of clay.

Then it just disintegrated into fine sand. There was silence for several seconds as everyone continued to stare.

"Those poor bastards," Hammerson said and walked toward the cracked glass.

"And, as we thought, that's probably why there is nothing in the fossil record of these things." Lana got to her feet and slowly approached the glass. "They degrade back to the chemical components; in this case, pure silica."

"Get those bodies out of there." Hammerson turned from the glass. "How long until we have enough of the fungi for a field test?"

Lana raised her eyebrows. "The good thing about fungi is it exponentially germinates – one becomes two, two to four, four to eight, and so on. We already have good stocks, but give me twelve hours, and you'll have enough to cover several hundred square miles."

"That's good," Hammerson said. "But we need enough to cover the planet." He headed for the door. "I'm going to speak to General Chilton, and prepare for a dispersal field test." He paused at the door. "It's also time we gave a few other countries some good news."

Lana nodded.

"Well done, doctor." Hammerson's eyes were deadpan. "But you only have eight hours."

CHAPTER 44

The Atlantic Ocean, five miles east of New York Bay

Captain Yakovlev held the field glasses to his eyes. The sea mist still cloaked much of the land in the distance, but he could just make out the tops of the huge rising edifices of the New York towers.

Yakovlev didn't know exactly what he was transporting, but his voyage was shrouded in mystery and he knew the shipping manifest claiming they had farm machinery was false.

The captain thought himself a good man, and patriotic, and was happy to take risks if Mother Russia called on him to do so. But still, given the focus on the spreading plague in the world right now, he didn't think he was bringing anything that was going to please the American authorities.

He had five miles of open water still to cross and then he'd be in the high traffic zone. The New York Harbor was at the mouth of the Hudson River where it emptied into New York Bay, and its wide welcoming smile drew him onwards. He could already smell the change in the air and he now detected car exhaust, oil and garbage.

This harbor was one of the largest oil-importing ports in the nation. It was modern and mighty, but it was also vulnerable.

The radio buzzed and the first mate answered it, spoke in muted tones, and then disconnected. He turned.

"They're coming," he said.

Yakovlev nodded.

Exactly to plan, there was a boat coming to pick them up and take him and the rest of the crew off. His ship, the *Illiansk*, would then sail on into the harbor on autopilot. Perhaps the port authorities would board it in time and slow its approach before it collided with another vessel, or perhaps they wouldn't, and then it would run aground somewhere on one of the shorelines he still couldn't see in the far distance.

He hoped his cargo wasn't a bomb, but his gut told him it was nothing good. He pushed the thoughts down, as his task was to point the *Illiansk* and then leave everything else to fate.

He had been instructed not to go into the hold and examine the cargo. His role was coming to an end, and whatever was onboard was primed to do the rest itself.

CHAPTER 45

Schneider stared, his eyes wide as he struggled to keep the elation he felt growing in his stomach from bursting out in dance or song.

They had aerosolized the formula and administered it to the specimens. The creatures had immediately slowed, become confused, and then stopped moving altogether. No amount of stimuli could then rouse them.

He turned to Verinko. "And so, we have complete control."

"It is amazing." Verinko breathed.

"I believe that any more of the substance will kill them, and any less will slow them down to a form of somnambulistic state. But this amount puts them into a full hibernation state."

Schneider bent to lift his wooden case. "Now we go in to examine them."

Verinko felt a moment of panic. "I think I will wait outside to monitor the test. But you can enter with the technical team."

"Fine." Schneider didn't need the dolt anymore anyway. A few last checks, and then he'd be gone. The Russians could play around with the formula residue, but they'd never be able to recreate it.

He waited impatiently as the team prepared to enter, and then followed them. According to his translations from the stones the creatures were now open to being controlled and he wanted to ensure they were imprinted by his image and scent.

Once inside their chamber, he placed his case on a tabletop, and unclipped it, opening it a fraction. Inside he saw the half-lidded eyes on the magnificent face and he was sure the mouth was curved up in a smile.

Schneider turned and clapped his hands together. He left the case open so his Führer could watch as his secret weapon and his success finally germinated.

*

Colonel Nadi Borishenko took the call as he sat before the satellite images of New York. He had arranged for the Kondor satellite system to be moved to a complementary horizon so he could watch the *Illiansk* as it steamed into the Hudson River mouth to deliver the silachnid swarm.

"Hello?"

"Colonel, we have an urgent problem." Doctor Mikhail Verinko's voice was high with agitation.

"Calm down, be clear, and be quick." Borishenko was in no mood for any frivolous interruptions right now.

"They've grown again. They're big now ... very big." Verinko made a noise that could have been a sob. "They tricked us."

Borishenko frowned and turned away from his satellite screen. "Are you drunk? What do you mean *they tricked you?*"

"Yes, no, not drunk. But yes, they fooled us all. Schneider's formula, we thought it rendered them placid or inert. But they were only pretending to be asleep when the German and the technicians entered the chamber." Verinko gulped air. "Please, sir, can you come to the laboratory?"

"No." Borishenko knew that the research labs for special weapons were several levels below his building, but he had no interest now that his own project was nearing a crucial phase. "I'm very busy."

"Please, this is ... *vital*!" Verinko yelled. And then softer: "Your project may fail."

"*Volloch*!" Borishenko bared his teeth, and glared at the receiver for a moment. He put it back to his ear. "I'm coming, but if you waste my time, it'll be your head." He slammed the phone down.

He headed for the secure elevator, and pressed his thumb to the small pad. He had been happy to take that stupid German's money, and his offer of some sort of process to keep the silachnids under control, but if he had caused them a problem, he'd find himself in a gulag by day's end.

In a few seconds the steel door opened and he selected "Sub-basement 4". The silent elevator took him down in seconds, and the door shushed opened. He was met by a highly disturbed and ashen-faced scientist.

Overhead, red lights turned slowly in a silent blaring alarm. Borishenko had never seen a man look so physically ill as Verinko did now.

The little man grabbed Borishenko's elbow and physically dragged him down the corridor toward the containment tanks. Overhead, the red lights continued to turn, like police cars, and he thought he could smell something strangely metallic.

Verinko tried to increase his speed and tugged harder.

"Release me, fool." Borishenko ripped his arm out of the scientist's grip, but Verinko's fingers picked at his sleeve and then he turned to wave him on.

"Just here, just here ... please, Colonel." He walked backwards his hands pressed together as though praying.

"Ach." Borishenko quickly glanced at his watch and then followed.

In another few seconds they stood before the containment testing facility. Borishenko knew that, due to the growth of the creatures, they had separated a lot of the swarms, plus many had been sent on the *Illiansk* mission. So each secured chamber now held only half-a-dozen of the monstrosities.

Borishenko halted, looking in at them now. Their eyes were far too knowing, and human. And the way they moved was not like a normal creature's movement – not insectoid or mammalian, but more sinuous and cunning. He felt revulsion for them. They were alien, grotesque, and made all the more terrifying by their size.

"My team went in with the German, Schneider. Five of them: Schneider, two technicians, and two guards. The creatures seemed to have been made dormant by Schneider's aerosolized solution. That's what we thought, and that's what the German told us, that his formula would render them docile." Verinko turned to him. "Until they were all inside and the door shut."

Borishenko stared in through the glass. He'd already seen what the things could do but the scene inside was an image straight from hell. Three of the people who had gone in had been consumed, and their bodies lay like empty suits on the ground. The creatures stood over them, like warriors, staring back at Borishenko through the glass. In their human-like gaze, there was a hint of triumph and perhaps even amusement. The two surviving human beings were obscured but Borishenko could see they had their helmets removed – either they had taken them off, or the creatures had.

Some sort of communication passed between the creatures as, all at once, they moved aside to show the two remaining captives.

One was the senior biologist, cowering in the corner with her hands held over her face. Beside her was an ashen-faced Rudolph Schneider, but his eyes weren't on the creatures or even on Borishenko. Instead they were on a wooden case open just a crack on a tabletop. His lips seemed to be moving as if he spoke to it.

"What is the German doing?" Borishenko asked.

"What?" Verinko turned. "I don't know. We need to get them out."

"How?" Borishenko shrugged.

"They'll kill them." Verinko's face screwed with panic.

"So what?" Borishenko looked at the diminutive scientist for a moment. "You said you had this under control. This is all your fault."

"But, they got smarter. They only pretended to become docile." Verinko grimaced. "They deceiv—"

"No, you just got sloppy." Borishenko looked back through the glass. "They're as good as dead. No one is to go in there."

One of the things reached out one long shiny black claw-like hand to gently lift the card key that was on a lanyard around the senior biologist's neck.

"Oh no," Verinko whispered.

"That can't be possible." Borishenko's eyes bulged. "Are they *that* smart?"

Verinko's mouth trembled. "I can't tell anymore."

In the chamber, Schneider turned to the creatures and began to yell. He then shot to his feet and marched stiff-legged to the table that held the case. He opened it wider and then pointed from it back to the silachnids.

"What the hell is he doing?" Borishenko frowned.

Verinko turned on the sound.

"*Im Namen von Adolphus Hitler, Führer und Reichskanzler of the Nationalsozialistische Deutsche Arbeiterpartei, befehle ich Ihnen, sich seiner Regel zu unterwerfen!*"

The man's face was so apoplectically red he seemed on the verge of a heart attack. He kept repeating the sentence and walked forward toward the lead creature.

"What's he saying?" Borishenko asked.

Verinko's brows knitted. "He's saying: 'In the name of Adolph Hitler, leader and Chancellor of the National Socialist German Workers' Party, I order you to submit to his rule.'" Verinko turned. "In the name of Hitler?" He shook his head. "He's gone mad."

"You think?" Borishenko scoffed. "Look in the fucking case."

Verinko turned back, and craned forward.

Just showing in the half-open case was a human head. The skin was dry and flaking, under the nose was a graying toothbrush mustache, and half-lidded eyes seemed to stare into the distance.

As they watched, Schneider approached the creature, and looked up at the thing's grotesque face, which now loomed a foot above him. He pointed from the case to the creature, all the time continue to scream his order.

Almost lovingly, the creature reached out a single insectoid arm, bristling with spikes and thick hairs, and grabbed the front of Schneider's tough suit. It pulled him closer.

"I think we can agree his solution is a failure, yes?" Borishenko said softly and couldn't tear his eyes away from the chamber.

Schneider was pulled closer and the thing lowered its huge head. Its mouthparts bloomed open like a fleshy flower, and it used them to cover the entire lower half of the German's face. His words were immediately muffled as his eyes widened.

Undoubtedly the proboscis was engaged, as Schneider shuddered as though receiving an electric shock, and his eyes were wide and rolling in both fear and pain. Soon his body shriveled within the suit, and then hung bonelessly limp. The silachnid then dropped Schneider, who flopped and folded onto the ground in a pile.

The creature stepped over him, and also past the still cowering female biologist. It held up the card key, and it, and all the other creatures began to move together. Toward the exit.

"I don't think so." Borishenko reached out a hand to the console in front of the glass.

Verinko, seeing what he was planning, lunged. "No!"

Borishenko held him off easily and changed hands. The creature had the card key held out and moved toward the exit panel. The Russian colonel flipped up a clear cover, and jammed a thumb down on the red button underneath.

The entire room was flooded with flame. Even though the glass was heat resistant, they both felt the warmth through the pane. There was a high-pitched scream, but it ended quickly.

Was that the woman? Borishenko wondered. It didn't matter – the deaths were all Verinko's fault.

The flame shut off and the windows were stained with carbonized material. The boiling smoke filled the room, and Verinko hit the extractor fans to clear it.

After a moment, the smoke was sucked out enough for them to see. The furniture, technical equipment, and human bodies were all reduced to charred lumps. But standing in the center of the room, with smoke still curling from their shining black bodies were the insectoid creatures. Unharmed.

"They are now impervious to even these temperatures," Borishenko observed. "But they are trapped now."

The card key had been destroyed. In response, one of the creatures threw itself at the glass so fast and forcefully, it made Verinko fall backwards, and Borishenko stepped away from the console.

The colonel retained his balance and watched as the thing threw its armor-plated body at the window again, and again. Though the glass was shatterproof and heat resistant, the heat had weakened it, and after another charge an impact star appeared in the heat-darkened glass.

"*Shit,*" Borishenko whispered.

He took another step back and then turned to Verinko. "Hit the flame again. Make sure they don't get out – that is an order."

The small man stared at him open-mouthed for a moment, but jammed a hand down on the button again, flooding the room with boiling, blood-red flames.

Borishenko headed for the elevator, and quickly sealed himself in. As he headed upwards, he lifted the internal phone to speak softly to the building's engineers.

"Seal off sub-basement four immediately. No elevator access, no door access, all phone lines and internet connections to be cut, nothing in or out. The entire floor has suffered a contamination outbreak and is under quarantine until further notice. Is that clear?"

After getting agreement, Borishenko disconnected and stood silently as the elevator took him high above the lower-level facilities.

He drew in a deep breath and let it out slowly. *Would the creatures get out?* he wondered.

They were getting smarter, Verinko had told him. He believed the man.

The elevator doors opened and he headed for his office at a rapid pace. Maybe it was time he took a little vacation at his chalet at the Dead Sea. Things could look after themselves here for a while.

CHAPTER 46

Lanesboro, Fillmore County, south-eastern Minnesota

"You are *GO* for MASS dispersal. Good luck and God's speed," Hammerson said.

"Roger that, sir. Out," the steady voice replied.

The fleet of aircraft had been ready to roll and the pilots all had experience in aerial dispersal. Just recently they had deployed a Modular Aerial Spray System, or MASS, from the rear cargo deck of a C-130H Hercules aircraft.

Until a day ago, Hammerson's options had been to carpet-bomb the plague areas with the new thermobaric warheads. They grabbed the oxygen from the surrounding air to generate a high-temperature explosion, and the blast produced was significantly hotter, and of a longer duration, than anything delivered by conventional ordnance.

The bombs could be used against an individual building, block, or an area of a half-square mile. But given the prevalence of high-grade concrete structures in the target zone, plus subways, service tunnels, and basements, then the results were expected to be imprecise, and not one hundred percent fatal.

So that's where Doctor Lana Miles' fungal solution came in.

In ordinary times, no government body, or even military command, would authorize the use of weapons carrying a biological substance that hadn't been tested for long-term adverse effects on the human population. But taking risks was why Jack "The Hammer" Hammerson had the job he did.

Hammerson had no doubt that a lot was riding on the success of the mission. Lana had told him the fungal broth would spread like a virus, being passed from an infected bug to the uninfected. Given they were swarm-based creatures, none in a group should be spared.

If it was successful, then they had a weapon they could use. If not, and they failed to stop the spread of the swarm, then perhaps the human race might end up as nothing more than a sedimentary line showing as just another mass extinction.

"Freighter entering Hudson Bay, sir," the war room technician said mechanically.

"Roger that." *It never rained, but it poured*, Hammerson lamented. He had another issue to address. A Ukrainian flagged freighter, the *Illiansk*, was coming into the mouth of the Hudson Bay.

His split screen on the wall showed a satellite image of the nondescript battered freighter. When they had first spotted the non-responsive craft, communication efforts had proved fruitless and a scan of the boat had shown that there seemed no crew onboard.

Alarm bells had rung, and reviewing historical stored satellite images had shown the crew disembarking and boarding a high-speed boat. The crew had been quickly picked up as they attempted to board another ship up near Fire Island. Unfortunately, the Russian captain had chosen to commit suicide. But after intense and aggressive questioning of the crew, it was shown they had no idea what it was they carried, but they all knew it was important, and they had to be a long way away when it arrived at its destination – New York.

General Chilton had growled like an angry grizzly, and told Hammerson he was to totally obliterate the freighter.

Hammerson watched as the nose camera showed the Lockheed Martin F-35 Lightning II bearing down on the ship.

"In range, on scope," the pilot said.

"Permission to engage." Hammerson didn't blink as he watched with a dispassionate gaze.

"One away, two away." The pilot then turned the Lightning away as two streaks hurtled toward the freighter.

The bombs were Hellfire AGM-114N metal augmented charge missiles. They were twin bolts of pure death and, when detonating, burned hotter than the sun.

The Lightning came back around in time to see the missiles hit – the ship turned into a glowing ball with the same radiance as a supernova. In seconds there was nothing left but molten steel heading straight to the bottom.

The ship and its cargo were gone, but there was one last loose end – the architect of the mission. Hammerson's teams would see to that one personally, to send a conclusive message.

Hammerson checked his watch. Matt Kearns should be approaching his own mission profile now. If the MASS dispersals were successful, they'd know pretty quickly if they'd won and dodged an extinction event. Or was there more to come? They also still needed to know when these events were likely to happen again. And that was where Kearns came in.

Hammerson watched as the seawater boiled and the last scraps of the molten freighter sank, leaving nothing but a few wisps of black smoke. He switched off that portion of screen and concentrated on the dispersal bomber's approach to the Minnesota front line.

"Dropping to one thousand feet and commencing dispersal," the pilot said.

Hammerson's jaw set and his large hands curled into fists as he willed them success.

"You can do it," he said through clenched teeth.

CHAPTER 47

Macquarie Island, South Pacific, Australian Administered Zone

The enormous military helicopter set down and Roy Maddock, Matt Kearns and Lana Miles immediately leaped out onto the bare rock of the Macquarie Island shoreline. Maddock leaned back in to pull out two huge bags of kit and threw them to the ground.

The wind blasted them and Matt groaned and closed his eyes to slits. Macquarie Island was only just over twenty miles long and three wide and was home to seals, penguins, and tough lichens, all sitting on a remote, wind-blasted rock halfway between New Zealand and Antarctica.

"Freezing," Lana said in muffled voice.

Maddock yelled for them to move, and the trio ran from under the chopper blades.

Matt tugged his fur-lined windbreaker hood tighter around his face, and Lana bumped into his side and yelled up at him. "I can't feel my lips."

Which sounded like "I arn eel I ips" to him.

Matt smiled and regretted it – the wind stung his front teeth. He settled for nodding in return, and then slowly looked at the landscape. Many of the island's raw and exposed rocks were a greenish color and exactly why they were here.

Macquarie Island was the only place in the Pacific Ocean where there was an uncovered ophiolite layer, which was a section of the Earth's deep oceanic crust, and the mantle that has been uplifted and exposed above sea level.

The green-tinged rocks were the first clue the geologists picked up following their analysis of the stone tablets. And given that the German submarine had been returning from somewhere in the Southern Pacific Ocean meant that odds were high that this is where the stones had come from.

They'd learned a lot but there were still so many gaps in their knowledge about any future upwelling it demanded they seek out the source of the stones. Now they had that chance.

Maddock moved them to a huge rocky outcrop and hunkered down in its lee. Matt quickly looked about and then grimaced.

"We're looking for a cliff face, a cave, or somewhere that they may have lain undisturbed for a long time."

"Well, I've got good news and bad news – there's been researchers here on and off for decades, and no one has ever reported seeing anything like that." Maddock grinned. "Above sea level that is."

"I knew you were gonna say that." Matt looked out at the choppy, iron-gray water. "Crap."

"How cold is it?" Lana grimaced.

"Damn cold," Maddock replied. "This time of year, the seawater is about forty degrees. But the wind here is always blowing at about fifty miles per hour, and some gusts up to two hundred. That wind chill means the water actually feels like the warmest place to be." He winked. "Least that's what they tell me."

She groaned.

"I'm thinking that cliff face, cave, or undisturbed area must lay offshore." He turned to point at an uplifted fold of craggy rock rising a hundred feet and touching the dark and foreboding water about half a mile along the shoreline. "There's deeper water there, and a good place to start."

Matt nodded. "Looks promising."

"Well then ..." Maddock straightened. "This is why we're here."

The trio set to changing from their thick woolen clothing to cold-water dry suits. These ones had full-face masks with speakers built in so they could communicate. The dry suits didn't fit snugly like normal wetsuits – they worked on the basis of keeping water out, and keeping a layer of warm air around the body.

Lana slid the waterproof computer onto her forearm. "So, I get to be the mobile calculator, because you can't do math."

Matt shrugged and grinned. "I can't be good at everything, can I?"

When done, Lana stood with her swim fins under her arms. "Okay, I'm hot now."

"Good, keep that frame of mind." Maddock grinned.

Matt noticed that the baggy suit still looked good on the tall HAWC captain's physique, but he and Lana just looked like those dog breeds with excess skin folds.

"Ready when you are," Matt said.

"I'm ready now," Maddock replied. "Comm test." He pulled his facemask down, it fitted from his forehead to his chin. Matt and Lana did the same.

"Check, one, two," Maddock said.

"Three, four ..." Matt's eyes were on Lana.

"And open the door." Lana grinned.

Maddock pushed up his visor. "Okay, we are good to go."

Lana groaned theatrically and Matt knew exactly how she felt. It was bitterly cold in the wind, the water would be like stinging needles if it touched any exposed skin.

Maddock led the way over the bleak and stony ground toward the shoreline. With their full-face masks pulled up, the wind pricked their cheeks and tips of their noses, and Matt felt the cold radiating up from the stones and through the insulating rubber to his feet.

They maneuvered around a few lazy seals, laying like bloated barrels on the shoreline. The seals turned dark liquid eyes on them to stare disinterestedly for a moment before then rolling back over in post fish-meal torpor.

After a few more minutes, they came to the towering rock face that ended their shoreline. Maddock checked his equipment one last time, and then waded out into the freezing water. Matt and Lana checked each other's breathing lines, tank pressure, and then pulled their masks down. She looked up at him, eyes wide, and blew air between her puffed cheeks.

"Yeah, me too," he said and stepped into the water, still carrying his fins. After a few more steps, with the water at his knees, he could feel the biting cold right through the suit's skin. Underneath they wore thermal underwear, but the cold still pressed in on them.

They waded out some more, and when the water got to their waists, they pulled on their fins. Matt sucked in a breath, dived forward, and began to swim. Even though the insulation helped, he couldn't help catching his breath from the shock of the freezing water.

Matt liked diving, snorkeling, surfing, and swimming, but the water here confirmed he only really liked doing those things in warm places. Here there were dark kelps and other weeds. The sea urchins, conches, and starfish grew huge in the clean, plankton-rich waters, and things with all manner of spikes and knobs crowded the algae-rich rocks.

As the water deepened, they passed bright orange crabs the size of dinner plates hugging the rocks, and he could make out a few crayfish feelers sticking out from crevices and tiny caves.

Large-lipped cod gaped as they swum by, but without sunlight everything was in shadows or seemed to be muted greens, browns and deeper reds, broken only by the flaring orange of the crabs.

The bottom quickly fell away to about twenty feet and huge boulders littered the bottom where they had obviously broken from the cliff face hundreds, thousands, or maybe even millions of years ago.

"There." Maddock swum ahead and then dived deeper.

Matt saw he flicked on his flashlight and the strong beam cut through the shadowy water.

"Down we go," Matt said and also dived. On his wrist hung his flashlight and he grabbed it and flicked it on. Lana did the same.

There was a cave mouth; weeds billowing softly like ragged teeth in the wave action against the cliff face.

"This is it." He looked to Lana who swam closer and added her light.

"Let's see if anyone's home." Maddock entered the cave.

Matt looked to Lana. "Please don't let there be little flying lizards in there." He laughed softly.

"Or anything at all with teeth," Lana added.

Matt cautiously entered. He was curious as hell, but truth was he wasn't looking forward to entering the dark hole. Inside it was inky black, and their three beams moved over the interior of the small sunken cavern.

Huge flat streamers of kelp rose from the bottom, masking much of the cave, and Matt floated at the center of the void, arms out. He turned slowly with a few soft flicks of his fins.

"They were here," he said softly.

Lana screamed, and Matt spun in the water.

The kelp had parted and looming over Lana was an enormous creature. Maddock was already beside her, and had her by the waist. But with their collective light beams, they could see it was a statue, twelve feet high and rearing up in an attack pose.

"It's just an idol," Maddock said with relief.

"It's no idol, it was their enemy," Matt replied.

The likeness was of a giant beetle-like creature, eight arms, enormously powerful-looking, and flanked by two human warriors holding spears as they did battle. Its style could have could have been Roman or Greek, but where those two great civilizations depicted their champions fighting bears or tigers, this race had real monsters to deal with.

"They grew huge," Lana said. "This is what will happen now, unless we can stop them."

"The Aztlanteans must have won," Maddock said. "Or we wouldn't be here." He pointed at the stone monstrosity. "They would."

"Let's keep looking," Matt said. He swiveled in the dark water and saw there were columns set into the wall, and smaller alcoves that might have held urns, or burning torches.

"It must have been like a chapel, or place of worship to their gods," Lana said.

"Or a place of learning," Matt replied. "Where they brought young scholars to be educated about the monstrous things that boiled up from the center of the Earth."

"Professor." Maddock was along the far wall, holding clumps of tough brown weed aside. "This look familiar?" He let himself float backwards out of the way.

Matt and Lana glided closer. Matt lifted his light. There, on a large flat wall, were marks of a size that would fit the two missing tablets of stone. One was cleanly excavated, and the other broken away.

"The age difference of the exposed stone, one more raw than the other; it all fits." Matt said. "Hitler was rumored to have obtained his stone from an 18th century whaling captain's descendents. Perhaps the stone broke off washed out after a storm and ended up on the beach where the whalers found it. When Hitler got it he tracked the source back to here and sent his submarine crew to obtain the other."

Lana swam forward to pull more weeds out of the way. "This was the tablets' original home." She paddled back a few feet to take it all in. "Amazing. Their grasp of science was astounding. And all of this without computers."

Matt swum closer and used a hand to wipe away the weed and mosses and then traced some of the glyphic inscriptions with his fingers as he tried to read. He wished Megan was here now as the majority of the information seemed to be more coded in mathematics, and he felt a pang of misery in his belly at the thought of her.

"This was how they determined when the events would take place," he said. "When the silicoids would emerge – the minor events and the major ones."

"Take your time," Maddock said. "This is important."

Lana hung in the dark water beside him, and Maddock began to take pictures along the wall.

"It's the rings and ellipses again. They signify our planet and its rotation around the sun. Many cultures use the sun and stars for everything from navigation to measuring time. But the Aztlanteans used it for much more than that – they used the past to predict the future." Matt looked along the submerged story.

"I think I see what they discovered," Lana said through her mic. "Matt, come take a look."

She punched in some numbers on her gauntlet computer, moved to another set of figures, circles, and marks carved into the stone, and entered more data. Then she laid a hand on a set of rings. "They determined that once every five hundred and twelve years, the planets all lined up with the sun."

"The lining up is quite rare, right?" he asked.

"It sure is," she replied. "But that's not all. They also worked out that once every 1.6 million years, the planets all lined up on just *one* side of the sun."

"The gravitational effect must be enormous," Maddock said. "It'd create significant effects on our tides."

"It does more than that. There is strong evidence now that the moon affects everything from Earth's tides and geological forces to animal fertility," Lana said.

"Then the lining up could be what causes the quakes, and the silicoids to be released to the surface," Maddock said.

"That's what I think," Lana said. "And the bigger the magnetic effect, the bigger the release. Maybe whatever place these things were lying dormant in – an underground sunken cavern, embedded in some sort of matrix, whatever, was pulled open by the gravitational effects of the planets, and it allowed the silicoid eggs to spill out and bubble up to the surface."

Matt grabbed her arm as he translated. "There's more: when all the planets line up, and on the same side of the sun, *as well* as their orbiting moons, then it would create the biggest effect of all. How often is that?"

Lana worked the figures for a few seconds, and then looked up. "It happens once every sixty-five million years, and just for a few days."

"That's all they need. Once they're on the surface, they're self-sustaining. And I bet that timeline matches the mass extinction events from Earth's history," Matt replied.

The trio hung in the silent dark water for several moments, with only the sound of the respirators in their ears.

"The Aztlanteans must have observed a minor upwelling of the creatures, and stumbled onto the meteorite fungus by accident. They then worked out where the creatures came from and why," Matt said, and floated closer to another of the walls.

"And they also worked out how to halt them. Then this brilliant race tried to leave a message for the future, to warn us." Lana turned to him. "I wonder what happened to them."

Lana frowned as a tree of seaweed wafted aside revealing another enormous image.

"Events overtook them." Matt stared at the new image.

Lana came closer. "This doesn't seem related to the other images. What the hell is it?"

Matt couldn't form words for a moment. The image looked to be of a single eye in the center of a mass of coiling ropes.

Matt already knew what had happened to the Aztlanteans. Ten years ago, he'd been beneath the dark ice of the Antarctic and seen the remains of their civilization.

A creature had evolved in the stygian darkness. Perhaps once it was a sort of prehistoric cephalopod, but it had grown into something monstrous, powerful, and intelligent. Matt had encountered it himself.

"What is it? It's a deity of their underworld," he said softly.

Matt knew that when the great city had been submerged between the snow and ice, trapping the last survivors, the creature had hunted them in the dark, picking them off one by one. It was a terrible way for such a brilliant and noble race to end.

"Pretty freaky legend," Lana observed.

"Yeah, a legend." Matt felt a tingle on the back of his neck and slowly swiveled in the dark water. He held up his light, throwing the beam out to the dark corners of the cavern. Suddenly he felt exposed and vulnerable in the black, cold water.

Matt turned back to the wall where the stones had been removed and noticed a small piece still lodged in the corner that had broken off. He quickly swam closer and brought his light up.

"What is it?" Lana joined him.

He rubbed it clear of seaweed as his brows came together. "It's a missing piece, the Aztlantean symbol for a month – *December*."

"What does that mean?" she asked. "It's November now."

Matt tried to put it in context from what he remembered from the stones, but couldn't. "I just, don't know."

He hung in the dark water, a knot growing in his belly.

"I think we've got all we can for now, people. The rest is up to Colonel Hammerson," Maddock said. "Time to head back."

Lana lowered her light. "Will we be getting back to a functioning world? Or something very different?"

Maddock snorted. "Always trust the Hammer."

CHAPTER 48

The MASS dispersals had continued around the clock. As fast as Lana Miles and her teams could incubate and grow more stock, it was immediately aerosolized, loaded, and dispersed.

Colonel Jack "The Hammer" Hammerson stood with arms folded in his large office as he watched the satellite feed display the next dispersal run over a large swarm. The converted bombers blanketed the approaching horde of bugs, which were now taller than men. Some even carried tools that they used to pry open safe-rooms or basements to get at the people inside.

Hammerson ground his teeth as some of the monstrosities turned to look upwards at the plane as it passed over them.

The mist settled among their ranks, and they immediately shuddered, became chaotic in movement, and then, in mere seconds, their bodies became covered in spidery white webs. The next moment, they fell to dust.

"Back to Hell, you sons of bitches," Hammerson seethed.

Maybe in the future some geologist will comment on the layer of silicon in the environment, and it'll be a mystery to them. Unless, like the Aztlanteans, they left some sort of message to the world's future inhabitants.

Hammerson snorted softly. *And that only just worked out by luck rather than design*, he thought. If Matt Kearns hadn't been watching television then the planet would have new rulers by now.

Hammerson continued to stare at the video feeds as the minutes turned to hours. In a few more hours all the major swarms had been destroyed, and it was now a mop-up operation. The missions had been so successful, with a hundred percent takedown rate, that the fungal spores would be dispatched around the globe to every affected country.

Hammerson checked his watch. There were just a few loose ends, and he had a meeting to tie those up.

*

"*Ten-hut.*" Five-star General Marcus Chilton snapped to attention, and beside him Colonel Jack Hammerson did the same.

The Commander in Chief, President Dan Redner, strode into the room, filling it with his six foot five inch presence. At each shoulder came his most trusted political lieutenants. The first was Michael Penalto, Secretary of State, and also Mark Jasper, the Secretary of Defense. None of the men were smiling.

"Gentlemen, at ease." Redner took his seat at the table, and everyone else did the same. "Take me through it."

General Chilton nodded. "It was a Russian operation, and our people on the inside tell us it was authorized from the very top."

"That sonofabitch Volkov," Penalto growled.

"Yes, sir," Chilton replied. "But though we believe Volkov wanted to poke his finger in our eye as payback over Ukraine, we don't believe he knew the operational details. Those intricacies were engineered by one Colonel Nadi Borishenko, in their Biological Warfare Unit. He was the one that tried to take down New York."

"Over eight and a half million people in New York." Redner clasped his large fingers together. "That's how many people could have died, just because some guy wants to poke his finger in our eye." He sat forward. "This is an act of war. We should take out one of their cities – let them know that this sort of action has severe blowback."

"There'd be retaliation," Chilton replied evenly.

Jasper scoffed. "The Russian economy is the same size as Texas's, and their military is out of shape. Our war games determine they wouldn't last four days against us."

"That's a given, but we don't need to do that," Hammerson said. "We know the swarms are ravaging the Russian countryside and moving into the major cities. Soon, Volkov will be begging for the fungal spores. We can also leak to the Russian press that their military is responsible for their release. Then their own people would ensure that heads would roll and necks would stretch. The Russians do revolutions very well."

Redner folded his arms. "Not enough."

"I agree," Hammerson added. "But why punish your average Russian because a few assholes got a rush of blood? Begging your pardon, sir."

"Go on," Redner said.

Hammerson leaned forward. "So let's just punish the assholes."

Redner stared at Hammerson for a full twenty seconds, before he slowly began to smile. "Give Volkov a black eye, send him a message." His eyes became flint hard. "But the other guy ..."

Hammerson smiled back with zero humor. "Yes, sir. My team will deal with that personally."

CHAPTER 49

Volkov's residence at Cape Idokopas was also known as Volkov's Castle, and was a large Italianate complex with eighty rooms, two ballrooms, three swimming pools – indoor and out, a gymnasium, sauna, lavish gardens, and elaborate security measures. And all located on the Black Sea coast near the village of Praskoveevka in Gelendzhik, Krasnodar Krai. It was both his fortress and palace.

Jack Hammerson lifted the phone as the VELA satellite came up over the horizon and into a complementary orbit. His two teams were ready.

"Team one, go for Special Delivery."

"Roger that," came the deep and calm response.

Hammerson was like a block of stone as he watched the feed from the helmet cam that showed him everything his soldier saw. They had already deployed a communication net, blinding the compound from the outside world, and also anyone watching from inside.

The team went over the grounds like wraiths, their camouflage suits blending into the different environmental shades, dappling from green, to black, to mottled as they passed over patches of snow and grass.

Hammerson had used his deep, embedded agents in the Volkov household to orchestrate a shift change on the inside security – their mission window was open, but small.

They came to the external cellar door, and the team leader turned to his team, counting down on his fingers. Hammerson saw the huge pack slung over one of their backs – the special delivery for Volkov.

They got to zero and went in fast, moving like an elemental force along the corridor on the way to the master bedroom.

Hammerson smiled as they came to the huge bedroom; inside there was very little other than a four-poster bed looking big enough for half-a-dozen people, and all draped with plush red velvet. The HAWC leader made hand signals and the team worked quickly. In seconds it was over, and the team withdrew.

Hammerson smiled cruelly. "May the eyes of the dead be on you."

In just minutes more team one were already on their way home.

He lifted the phone again. "Team two, go for excision."

Hammerson ended the link, folded his arms, and watched the screen. This mission was a little more detailed. And final.

This time the helmet-cam wearer was speeding through the back streets of the wealthy resort area of Bulgaria. The waterfront was only one or two streets away but the villa that they sought was on a slight hill affording a magnificent view of the bay.

A gloved hand appeared in front of the camera and made several gestures to the three-man team. Hammerson recognized the instruction to spread out.

They had come to a rear wall, nine feet high and with razor wire coiled along its top. The gate would undoubtedly be locked and alarmed.

The camera-wearer was hoisted up, and he set to using a small laser cutter on the wire. It instantly melted through the hardened steel and the section was dragged away.

The small group went over the top, and landed softly. The camera moved fast again as the trio raced to the back door.

The satellite feed using thermal imaging had shown there were two people in the villa, both in the upstairs bedroom and both asleep – there was the 48-year-old Borishenko, and a sixteen-year-old female companion: a local escort.

Once again the glass door was alarmed, but the trigger was on the lock, and so they cut the glass pane out, attached a suction cap and lifted the glass away. They were in.

Like ghosts, the trio moved through the house to the stairs and then up to the bedroom door. It was an old-style door with an ornate bronze knob handle. Hammerson watched as the gloved hand held up a small flat device that scanned the inner workings of the locking mechanism. It showed no alarms and also that the door wasn't locked.

Next the gloved hand slowly opened the door and the darkness was illuminated a phosphorescent green. A long-barreled weapon was poked in, the target was the young woman, and with the sound of a soft sigh the dart hit her neck – she'd be out for another eight hours at least.

The gun was reloaded, aimed, and fired. The dart unerringly hit Borishenko's neck. But this dose was low, and would only take him out for ten minutes.

The men rushed in, removed the darts and then began to prepare for the next phase of their mission.

In his office, Hammerson hummed as he went to a cabinet and took out a half bottle of Jack Daniels and a single tumbler glass. He poured himself a good double shot, and then took the glass to the window and stared out over the training field.

Things would get back to normal soon. The people of the planet would survive and move on, perhaps a little wiser for the brush with the plagues. After all, nothing focuses the vision like potential extinction.

He smiled and sipped again, feeling the heat travel down his throat to bloom like fire in his belly. He felt good. And there was one thing that made him feel even better – a satisfying evening-up of the balance sheet.

*

Borishenko slowly felt his senses returning. He'd been having a wonderful dream and then it became filled with shadows and coldness.

He opened his eyes and smacked dry lips. He went to scratch his nose, but found he couldn't, and realized his arms were tied behind his back.

"What?"

He came fully awake then, and felt the chill of the night air on him. He was still in his silk pajamas, but was balanced on the balcony edge. And there was something rough around his neck.

"What's happening?"

Borishenko saw three huge men in all-over dark outfits, and full face-covering masks with night-vision goggles. They looked robotic, pitiless, and utterly terrifying.

He sucked in his stomach and thrust out his chest. "I am Nadi Borishenko, Colonel in Russian Military Defense. Who the hell are you and what do you want?"

The men said nothing, but one was holding a computer tablet, and he stepped up on a stool and held it up to Borishenko's face.

There was the image of a man there, brutal-looking, mid-fifties, with an iron-gray crew cut. His bearing was military and his eyes bored into Borishenko's. It took a few seconds, but then Borishenko recognized him – Colonel Jack Hammerson.

Hammerson began to speak. "By now, you are standing on a ledge and there is a rope around your neck. You planned an attack on American soil that was to result in major American causalities."

"That wasn't me," Borishenko spluttered.

Hammerson sipped from a tumbler and stared back at him like he was nothing.

"When I find you –" Borishenko began.

"For your crimes ..." Hammerson smiled just a fraction. "... the sentence is death."

Borishenko's first thought was to yell and bluster, but he saw there was not a single ounce of give in the man's rock-like expression.

"I was under orders," he quaked.

"It was your idea," the man replied.

Borishenko's mind spun seeking options. "Ten million dollars ... no, euros," he yelled.

"My one regret is that I don't have more time to inflict the pain on you that you had planned for our people. But this will have to do." Hammerson's eyes were pitiless.

Another of the men stepped forward and held up a note. In his other hand a surgical stapler and he pressed the paper to Borishenko's chest and fired off a staple into both flabby pectorals, pinning the note there.

The Russian howled with pain.

The man holding the computer stepped back, and before he shut it, Borishenko heard the American utter one last word.

"Goodbye."

He was then pushed. The second floor wasn't high, but it was enough to gain the drop speed required so the sudden stop of a man weighing around two hundred pounds would end with enough force to separate neck vertebrae. Which is exactly what happened.

In under a single minute, the three agents had removed all trace of their being there, and like ghosts vanished back into the night.

Borishenko's body swung, already beginning to drip escaping body fluids to the ground below. Stapled to his chest the note contained a simple message in Russian, a warning or a threat, visible to anyone, but aimed squarely at the President of Russia. It read: *If you come at the king, you'd better not miss.*

*

Volkov sat bolt upright as the scream shattered the morning air. His maid bringing his coffee had dropped the tray and its thousand fragments of fine bone china plus dark rich coffee now covered his marble floor tiles.

She had a hand up over her mouth, and he scowled, about to reprimand her, when he smelt it, something over the normal odors of his room, and the fresh coffee. It was an animal scent, and something else he knew well, the coppery tang of fresh blood.

Volkov followed her gaze and saw it: his beloved bear, Ursa, or at least a part of her – her severed head was jammed on a coat rack and staring mad-eyed and mouth agape at him in his bed.

There was a sign hanging around its neck in Russian. It contained just three words: *I see you.*

Volkov jumped up, yelling commands, but then after a few moments he sat down slowly. Because he knew then – they could have killed him. But didn't. This was a show of strength and skill and also a warning. Next time it'd be his head on the pike.

He closed his eyes. In a sea of predators, he was one of the biggest. But there were always bigger ones.

CHAPTER 50

The mop-up continued for days after the fungal dispersal but there was no further sign of the massive insect-like creatures from the inner Earth.

The search for survivors in areas that had been totally overrun also went on, but in most counties there was nothing left but empty countryside with curtains of mist moving across the landscape like the ghosts of a thousand battlefields of days gone by.

We can rebuild, we always do, Hammerson thought as he watched one of the drone feeds from ground zero in Minnesota. He was about to turn away, when he heard a shout.

"Hallelujah, we've got a survivor." The soldier grinned from ear to ear. "Make that two – there's a dog with her."

"Zoom in." Hammerson walked toward the screen as the camera on the drone enlarged the woman's dirt- and tear-streaked face. He exhaled and then looked skywards for a second. *Thank you*, he breathed.

"Get 'em out, ASAP." Hammerson pulled his phone out and began to dial.

*

Matt hugged his mother tight and wept onto her shoulder. Belle, the huge German shepherd, tried to worm her way between them, perhaps not ready yet to stop her guardian work over the small woman.

Lana watched and smiled with eyes swimming with tears. Matt blinked away his own tears. Karen had just learned of Megan's fate but she already knew the young woman was lost from that fateful night.

Matt hated himself for being away and not with them when he was needed. What was the value in helping save the human race when he wasn't even able to save the ones he loved?

"I couldn't do anything to stop them," Karen said in a trembling voice.

"Don't," Matt whispered. "You survived, that's all that matters now." He kissed her cheek again, hard, and put an arm around her shoulders.

He looked down at the dog. "And Belle, you have my permission to sleep on Mom's bed anytime you want." The dog grinned up at him.

He looked to Lana. "Ready?"

She nodded. "It's all over, let's go home."

Please be true, he prayed.

EPILOGUE

Drill site 2, Force Energy Corp, West Erregulla, Australia

10 years later – 21 December

Bill Frankston read off the details coming back from the drill sensors, and liked what he saw – they'd intercepted and started drilling through the high cliff sandstone at a depth of 15,280 feet, and they were now the deepest onshore drill site in Australia.

"Ladies and gentlemen, we are now number one." He grinned and held a finger in the air.

Frankston read more of the data: cuttings from these sections so far included clean coarse-grained quartzose sandstone, which had good gas-bearing prospects due to a protective clay coating. Once they punched through the shale, if they didn't find gas pockets, he'd eat his hat.

The equipment screamed as the drill fought against the harder shale. He might need to change the toothed bit if it began to slow its rate of cut.

An hour later, they finally broke through, and the sensor lights blinked, signaling their success.

"*Whoa*, cap it," he yelled.

But there seemed nothing to cap. Jerry Havers swung in his chair in the control room. "We got pressure, but no gas. I'm thinking its just liquid, boss."

"Oil?" Frankston frowned.

Jerry shook his head slowly. "I don't think so."

Frankston swore softly, and then sighed. "Okay, grab me a sample and let's see what we just spent ten million bucks drilling into."

It took an hour for the core rod to be withdrawn from the thousands of feet below the earth, and brought into the outer analysis rooms. The rod was slid out of the sampler and laid on the long steel bench as the geologists crowded around.

Frankston pushed them aside. "What the hell?" His brow furrowed. "Would someone like to tell me what the hell I'm looking at here?"

The group stared down at the six-inch thick, ten-foot long pipe of multicolored rock, soil, and other striated material, all laying in a spreading pool of viscous-looking liquid.

"I've no idea what this is." Jerry lifted a magnifying glass. "Some sort of fossil, or fossil residue, maybe."

Frankston leaned forward on his knuckles. "What did we just hit?"

The golf ball sized globes filled the core sample, and as Frankston watched, some of them began to blacken in the air.

AUTHOR'S NOTES

Many readers ask me about the background of my novels – is the science real or imagined? Where do I get the situations, equipment, characters and their expertise from, and just how much of it has a basis in fact?

In regards to *Extinction Plague*, there have been hundreds of large-scale extinctions in Earth's history. In addition there have been five mass extinctions where nearly *all life* was almost completely wiped out.

We understand why most of those events happened, except for one that occurred two hundred million years ago at the end of the Triassic period. At that time, something killed off eighty percent of all creatures on Earth, and we have no idea how or what was the cause. *Extinction Plague* poses my "what if" question.

Silicon-based Life-forms

Silicon-based life has been a TV trope for as long as I can remember. From *Star Trek* to *The Outer Limits*, we have seen rock monsters, lava people, and crystal demons.

But there is a good reason this element is used as the basis for "strange" and different life-forms. All known life on

Earth is based on the element carbon. It is the fourth most abundant element in the universe, but silicon is the second most abundant element in the Earth's crust after oxygen. Like carbon, it can form bonds with four other atoms at once, form long-chain polymers, and bind to oxygen, all of which is essential as the building blocks of life.

Carbon chemistry is perfect for life under the benign conditions on Earth. However, silicon-based life-forms might be possible under different conditions, as silicon bonds are more stable than carbon at high temperatures. Therefore, silicon-based life could arise on a planet that is too hot for carbon-based life.

Or they might not even be found on a planet's surface at all. The hot, hydrogen-rich but oxygen-poor conditions deep inside our planet, which are lethal to carbon-based life, might be perfect for the complex silicon chemistry. It was this theory that drove my design of the silicoids.

Global Mass Extinctions

The slate of life has nearly been wiped clean on the planet several times. Species go extinct all the time, and scientists estimate that at least 99.9 percent of all species of plants and animals that ever lived are now extinct.

Most extinctions happen gradually over millions of years, and some vanish in the blink of an eye. In mass extinctions, wide ranges of animals and plants have died out, from tiny marine organisms to some of the largest creatures to ever live on our planet. Climate change, volcanic events, and meteor strikes are usually to blame. But some are just mysteries.

There have been many significant extinctions. But a "mass" extinction is when over fifty percent of all life on Earth dies out. To date there has been five. A summary is as follows:

Ordovician–Silurian Extinction: 444 million years ago, 86% of species lost

Life on Earth was still young and confined to the oceans. At that time the abundant sea creatures were filter-feeding animals and were wiped out by a short ice age and change in the environmental gases. Paleo-geologists believe that the mighty Appalachians being uplifted (they once rivalled the Himalayas in size) exposed silicate rock that sucked the carbon dioxide from the atmosphere, radically chilling the planet.

Late Devonian: 375 million years ago, 75% of species lost

The seas were now filled with primitive life-forms long before the land was colonized by anything other than primitive plants. Trilobites were the dominant animals and their simple design of tough, spiky armor, multifaceted eyes, and omnivorous diet, meant they were ultimate survivors. But they were nearly wiped out in the second mass extinction. The prevailing theory was the newly evolved land plants that now covered the land fertilized the soils, creating nutrient runoff during rains that fed into the warm shallow seas. This triggered global algal blooms that sucked oxygen out of the water, suffocating the bottom dwellers.

End Permian Extinction: 251 million years ago, 96% of species lost

A collision of natural catastrophes created what is known as "the great dying", the worst extinction event the planet has ever seen. It nearly ended *all* life on Earth.

A mega-volcano eruption near Siberia blasted gases into the atmosphere. Methanogenic bacteria responded by belching out methane, a potent greenhouse gas. Global temperatures surged while oceans acidified, stagnated, and began expelling poisonous hydrogen sulfide. It took Earth 300 million years to recover.

Triassic–Jurassic Extinction: 200 million years ago, 80% of species lost

Of all the great extinctions, the one that ended the Triassic is the most baffling as no clear cause has been found.

Eighty percent of all animals vanished, including the large amphibians plus the therapsids (the primitive mammal-like reptiles), and other major predators. This vacating of terrestrial ecological niches had one benefit for our history books (and for fiction writers) in that it allowed for the rise of the dinosaurs in the Jurassic period.

End Cretaceous Extinction: 65 million years ago, 76% of all species lost

Sixty-five million years ago a massive asteroid impact blanketed the world in a cloud of dust and smoke, triggered a global cooling that lasted decades and caused the last mass extinction that wiped out some seventy-six percent of plants and animals and, sadly, ended the dinosaur's reign. In the oceans, the immense sea reptiles vanished, as well as the once abundant ammonites.

The Theia Impact

The giant-impact hypothesis, called the Theia Impact, suggests that the moon formed out of the debris left over from a collision between Earth and an astral body the size of Mars.

Around 4.5 billion years ago, in the Hadean period of our planet (so named after the Greek underworld to describe the hellish conditions of our world at that time), a massive colliding body called Theia (from the name of the mythical Greek Titan who was the mother of Selene, the goddess of the moon) struck our planet, then know as Gaia.

Following the collision, the enormous amount of debris thrown up into the atmosphere was captured, and in turn coalesced into the moon. Gaia was also reformed, and became what we know today as Planet Earth.

The Magical Necklace of Harmonia

I came across the magical necklace, referred to simply as the Necklace of Harmonia, when I was researching for my book *The Immortality Curse,* and knew one day I would get to use it!

In legend, the Necklace of Harmonia allowed any woman wearing it to remain eternally young and beautiful. It thus became a much-coveted object among women of the House of Thebes in Greek myths. It was described in ancient Greek passages as being of beautifully wrought gold, in the shape of two serpents whose open mouths formed a clasp, and inlaid with various jewels.

Hephaestus, blacksmith of the Olympian gods, discovered his wife, Aphrodite, goddess of love, having a sexual affair with Ares, the god of war. He became enraged and vowed to avenge himself for Aphrodite's infidelity by cursing, not only her, but her children and all her children's children resulting from the affair.

The curse of the Necklace of Harmonia seemed to be selective in its rewards and punishments as, along with bestowing eternal youth on the wearer, it could also bring them great misfortune; such as those of the ill-fated House of Thebes.

Was it real? Well, it left its mark on history, as the tyrant Phayllus, one of the Phocian leaders in the Third Sacred War (356 BC – 346 BC), stole the necklace and gave it to his mistress. After she had worn it for years her timeless beauty was said to be second to none. But soon her son became seized with a strange madness and set fire to their house, where she perished in the flames along with all her worldly treasures. She got her beauty, but also her misfortune.

Billion-Year-Old Fungi

Scientists recently found one-billion-year-old fungi in Canada, changing the way we view evolution and the timing of plants and animals here on Earth.

The fossilized specimen was collected in Canada's Arctic by an international team and later identified to be the oldest fungi ever found, sitting somewhere between 900 million and 1.1 billion years old.

The fossilized fungi were analyzed and researchers found the presence of chitin, a unique substance that is found on the cell walls of fungi (and also arthropods!).

Finding fungi that lived 1.1 billion years ago shows us that the planet's first life might not be how we imagined it at all (so much material for us fiction writers!).

CPSIA information can be obtained
at www.ICGtesting.com
Printed in the USA
BVHW071337230121
598529BV00002B/23